A PARAGON FOR THE VISCOUNT

LORDS OF VOLUPTAS - BOOK THREE

KATHY LEIGH

Published by Blushing Books
An Imprint of
ABCD Graphics and Design, Inc.
A Virginia Corporation
977 Seminole Trail #233
Charlottesville, VA 22901

Kathy Leigh
A Paragon for the Viscount

eBook ISBN: 978-1-64563-943-5
Print ISBN: 978-1-64563-944-2
v2

INTRODUCTION

*Voluptas: a Latin word meaning pleasure, delight,
satisfaction, enjoyment, gratification*

CHAPTER 1

*V*iscount Anthony Roland Alexander Donnington smiled, thrilled with the perfection of Mozart's *The Shepherd King.* The last notes of act one faded into the hubbub of voices as members of the *haut ton* began to meander from box to box, renewing acquaintances and sharing the latest *on-dits.* His close friends, the Earl of Sherbonne and Baron Adam Loxley, had joined the crowds, but Lord Anthony was quite content to remain in the duke's box, watching the parade of luxurious velvets, brilliant satins and colorful silks that heralded the new London season. Not even the prospect of flirting with the latest debutantes appealed to him as much as simply observing the splendor of the red and gold opera house and the endless variety of faces and figures.

Almost without thinking, he whipped out his sketchbook and his pencil began to flash across the pages, recording the vibrancy and vividness of the parade. He was just beginning to draw Lady

Sylvia's curvaceous figure, beautifully displayed in a low-cut gown of deep sapphire blue, when Lord Theo, the fourth member of the quartet who had been friends since their first day at Eton, leaned over Anthony's shoulder, peering at his quick sketches. The marquess chuckled. "Those are some very pretty pictures you're making."

Anthony merely shrugged and snapped the book closed. Theo slapped him on his shoulder. "One day you'll let us into the secrets of your art. Were you able to finish the painting Loxley asked for?"

Anthony fingered the pencil in his pocket. "Adam's painting was shipped to him a few days ago."

The dullness of his voice brought a frown to Theo's face and his next words lost the light, bantering tone. There was real concern as he said, "You mentioned in your last letter that things in are not quite perfect in your life right now."

The viscount gazed unseeingly out over the audience. "The doctors are concerned about my father's heart, and my step-mother is not particularly sympathetic to his plight. She makes rather pointed comments about having married a gentleman so much older than she is, and she insisted on coming to London even though Papa would have preferred to stay at the Abbey."

Theo gave Donnington's shoulder a sympathetic squeeze but commented lightly, "Your father has the same eye for beauty that you have and he could not resist the very beautiful Lady Lucretia. It is a pity that her character does not match her appearance."

Donnington laughed but did not answer and Theo left him to go and pour a glass of wine for his cousin. The viscount, left alone with his thoughts, was soon engrossed by the constant activity in the audience. He opened his sketch book to a blank page and, before long, had put aside all worrying thoughts as he wondered which colors in his paint box would best capture the rich auburn shade of Lady Whittemore's hair and the emeralds that gleamed at her creamy breast. He glanced up to ensure that he had captured her vitality perfectly and was distracted by a commotion in the box next to hers.

The box had been empty during the first act, but now a small party, consisting of a portly middle-aged gentleman, a complacent flat-faced lady who must be his wife, and an older, angular lady were settling down.

They seated themselves and the fourth member of their party came into view. All thoughts of Lady Whittemore vanished. Donnington raised his quizzing glass and gazed unabashedly at the vision of perfect beauty who was reading the programme as if it contained the secret to eternal life.

She was dressed in a simple white muslin dress that clung softly to the perfect proportions of her lithe figure and shapely roundness of her breasts. Like at least a dozen other young gentlemen, Donnington gazed at her, enraptured by her loveliness, but she was completely oblivious to the attention she had generated. Her serenity set her apart from the swirl and strutting of the rest of the audience.

The viscount flipped to a new page in his book and began to capture that beauty with his pencil. Her hair was soft and silky, the color of the first leaves in autumn, and her figure was as graceful as the boughs of a young willow tree. Donnington was riveted. This vision of perfection had wandered out of his dreams and into the Royal Opera House. Her soft pink lips begged for kisses and her rosy cheeks gave color to the cream of her cheeks. Although he could not be sure from that distance, he decided that her eyes must be the blue of summer skies.

Before the end of the intermission, the viscount had heard her name: Miss Clarissa Blakeney. Whispers rippled across the audience conveying the news that she was a debutante, newly arrived in London. Before the end of the evening, she was being hailed by most of the gentlemen as the epitome of beauty, the perfect embodiment of an English rose. Although most of the unmarried and a large number of the married gentlemen had tried to attract her attention, she ignored their efforts. She was so oblivious to the stir she had made that Donnington wondered if she was even aware that she had become the hottest topic of discussion. Where other young ladies simpered and flirted with arch looks over fans and curls tossed coquettishly, Miss Blakeney had not once even so much as glanced at any of her admirers.

Act two of the opera began, but Donnington no longer paid any attention to the soaring notes of the music. He spent the rest of the evening admiring Miss Clarissa Blakeney. His little sketchbook was quickly filled with images of her every graceful gesture, every gentle tilt of her head, every sweet smile.

Miss Blakeney's emotions were vivid and entrancing. She leaned forward and clutched the edge of the box when Elise plaintively sang of her woes in being forced to marry a man she did not love. And when the lovers vowed their constant love for each other, her face shone with delight. She showed none of the bored nonchalance affected by so many of the other audience members. And Donnington recorded each moment.

His heart was touched by little acts of kindness she did for the others in her party. When the gentleman dropped his programme, she retrieved it. Later, when the performance ended, she arranged a shawl over the elderly lady's shoulders with such gentle grace that Donnington was smitten. Her character promised to be even more charming than her appearance.

As the audience swarmed out of the theatre, the paragon of beauty vanished, but Donnington still stood staring at the place where she had been. He almost didn't hear Sherbonne declare, "The night is yet young. I believe a few games of faro at White's and a bottle of brandy will end the day well. We might even have time to visit Briar House."

Adam and Theo agreed enthusiastically, but Donnington shook his head. "I think I'm going to head straight home."

Loxley chuckled. "Ah, the muse has bitten. I look forward to seeing what great works of art the incomparable beauty of Miss Clarissa Blakeney will inspire."

Anthony was startled by the flash of jealous possessiveness that surged through him at Adam's words. He wanted to paint the lovely Clarissa, but he had no desire to let other men gaze at her beauty. He wanted her for himself.

As soon as Lord Anthony arrived at Donnington House, he headed for his studio. Putting aside the painting he had been working on, he placed a new canvas on his easel. He stared at the white space, and then began to fill it with rapid strokes of color.

ON THURSDAY EVENING, Clarissa stood sedately at her aunt's side, trying to hide her disappointment at the very plain rooms that housed Almack's assembly. The somewhat bare rooms and simple refreshments did not match her dreams of elegant splendor or the grandeur of the Opera House she had been to the night before. She frowned as some of the most elite members of the *haut ton* thronged the rooms, bowing sedately to one another and taking careful note of who was, and who was not, present.

Although the ladies were dressed in the most fashionable gowns and the gentlemen's cravats were tied in the most elaborate styles, she could not help feeling disappointed. The snippets of conversation she overheard were commonplace and superficial, and everyone was stiff and formal. No one smiled. Even the music was staid and ponderous, as if the musicians were aware of the seriousness of assemblies in this most sacred of society's temples. Clarissa glanced nervously at her dance card. It was empty, although some gentlemen gazed at her through their quizzing glasses.

Aunt Agatha, however, looked very satisfied. Under cover of the sedate music that accompanied the opening minuet, she whispered to Clarissa, "See, look over there. That is Countess Lieven herself. It was she who agreed to let you have vouchers, so we must be especially polite to her. Oh, and the gentleman in the bright blue coat is Sir Trenwith, from an ancient and respected family in Dorset."

Clarissa was not particularly impressed with the gentleman, no matter what position he held in society. Her sense of disappointment deepened. She had thought that at least some of the gentlemen would be as daring and dashing as the heroes of her dreams. Her eyes widened as she watched a portly gentleman with balding hair, whose shirt buttons strained against his corpulent waist, addressing the Master of Ceremonies and pointing at her. He had an air of smug complacency that Clarissa found amusing. "Who is that?" she asked her aunt.

Aunt Agatha surreptitiously consulted a little notebook in which she had made notes about eligible bachelors. She nodded. "That is Mr. Hemsby and although he does not have a title, he is dignified, respectable and not given to the wild exploits of so many young gentlemen."

Mr. Hemsby and the Master of Ceremonies came to Aunt Agatha and bowed gravely. For one wild moment, Clarissa thought Mr. Hemsby was going to ask her aunt to dance, but his eyes skimmed over her. She felt like an insect pinned to a board on display to curious eyes.

The Master of Ceremonies, Mr. Allston, cleared his throat. "Miss Blakeney, allow me to present Mr. Hemsby, a very reputable gentleman who would like to request a dance with your niece."

Clarissa almost giggled at the absurdity of the ceremony, but a glimpse of her aunt's face kept her in check. She eyed Mr.

Hemsby. He sounded and looked dull, but he was the first person to approach her for a dance and she could not refuse his invitation without causing a minor scandal.

Reluctantly, but with a polite smile, Clarissa followed Mr. Hemsby onto the dance floor. With great concentration, Mr. Hemsby lumbered through the first steps, and Clarissa almost tripped as he trod heavily on the end of her dress train.

After a few moments, Mr. Hemsby remarked, "It is gratifying to see so many couples dancing."

Clarissa glanced around at the twenty or so couples that made up the set, unsure of the correct response to such a commonplace observation. She smiled again and said, "It is indeed."

Mr. Hemsby nodded as if she had revealed the secret to eternal youth. He then commented on how pleasant the weather had been that day. Again, she agreed. The quarter hour of the dance dragged on in that fashion until Clarissa was ready to scream and her cheeks were aching with the need to keep a smile fixed on her face.

She was relieved when her dance partner returned her to her aunt's side and she no longer had to think of appropriate answers to his dull comments. The music changed to a cotillion and Clarissa began to sway to the livelier rhythm, a smile lighting up her face. Aunt Agatha placed her hand on her niece's arm. "Calm down, dear. You do not want to be considered hoydenish. The very best of society come to these assemblies, and while your good looks are sure to attract much interest, you must be careful not to give anyone the impression that you are not perfectly well-mannered."

Clarissa smoothed the soft muslin of her new white ball dress. It was the prettiest dress she had ever owned, and catching a glimpse of herself in a large gilt-framed mirror on the opposite wall, she smiled. She liked the way the dress swirled when she swayed in time to the music, but her aunt's hand on her arm reminded her that she was expected to be sedate. She schooled her face into the same kind of bored and impassive expression she noted on the faces of those around her and that she had been practicing in front of her mirror ever since her aunt had pointed out to her that respectable ladies were not supposed to show too much enthusiasm.

She stilled her hands at her sides and tried to recall the myriad rules of etiquette her aunt had been drilling into her. She was not to make any untoward gestures, she needed to speak very softly and only answer questions that were put to her, not ever beginning a conversation, and she should never dance more than once with the same gentleman in an evening. Any *faux pas* she committed would brand her forever as wayward and she would become a pariah, never able to attract the right kind of marriage proposition.

It was not long before her demure conduct and pretty face attracted the interest of a variety of gentlemen and she soon found herself pacing out the steps of the dances she had so painstakingly learned with the dancing teacher her aunt had hired. But all the time, she longed for something a little different, a little more exciting than the bland conversation and pompous posturing of the people she was introduced to.

She had just completed a quadrille with Sir Trenwith when a commotion at the door caught her attention. A tall, good-looking gentleman, with broad shoulders that filled his elegant blue jacket, and auburn hair that gleamed like burnished copper in the candlelight, entered the assembly rooms just as the porter was closing the door for the night. No one was allowed in after eleven.

Clarissa caught her breath. She had never seen anyone as handsome, as confident, as alluring as the tardy gentleman. He gazed around the room with something of a propriety air and a confidence that set him apart from the men she had been dancing with. His eyes came to rest on her, and she felt her cheeks turn pink as his gaze swept over her from the crown of her head to the soft folds of her muslin dress. She found it difficult to breath, especially when he ignored the other guests and came directly to her. He did not bother with the formality of introductions.

Lord Anthony bowed, his greeting taking in both her and Aunt Agatha. "Miss Blakeney, I am pleased to make your acquaintance. May I have the honor of the next dance?"

Clarissa smiled broadly, her blue eyes sparkling with delight and animating her expression. "Yes, please."

Aunt Agatha snorted softly but offered no demur.

Clarissa felt like a princess accompanied by Prince Charming during the magical half an hour that Lord Anthony led her through the dance.

As soon as the dance began, he said, "I saw you at the opera last night. What did you think of the performance?"

With vivid animation, Clarissa conveyed her delight. Before long, she was arguing her point that the story was delightful and although somewhat fanciful, the ending proved that real love was possible and desirable.

Lord Anthony laughed and continued to encourage her to express her ideas fervently. The conversation turned to music in general and then to the latest poetry. Every moment of the dance was filled with scintillating and lively discussion. And every time Clarissa placed her hand in his, a tingling sensation pulsed through her. Heat suffused her that had more to do with his touch than the exertion of dancing. Her breasts were heavy and tight, but she floated through the steps of the cotillion. Never, had she met anyone with such charming manners and such lively intelligence. He was, without a doubt, the most handsome man she had ever seen. Her eyes were starry with dreams and the previously dull evening now sparkled with promise.

When the dance was over, the viscount returned her to her aunt and brought her a glass of lemonade, and then he left her with the assurance that he looked forward to leading her in many more dances.

Clarissa had no partner for the first of the country dances, but her heart was light and it was only her aunt's stern look that kept her from letting laughter bubble up. Dreams of the charming viscount were all the company she needed. She took a sedate sip of her lemonade and tried not to make it too obvious that she was watching him as he conversed with a group of gentlemen on the other side of the ballroom.

Clarissa's elation lasted for the length of time it took the first couple to make it back to the top of the line for the Boulangère. Someone near her mentioned the viscount's name and she strained to hear what was being said, even though she knew it was wrong to eavesdrop.

"Anthony appears to have found a pretty new skirt to pursue. I hear he ogled her all through the opera last night and although he never comes to Almack's, it appears her charms have drawn him here tonight."

Clarissa tried to get a better view of the gentleman who had spoken. He was hidden behind the large fronds of a potted palm tree, but she could see his companion. The lady, who was quite a bit younger than her husband, was dressed in the finest display of sartorial elegance that Clarissa had ever seen. Her dress was of the finest pale yellow silk and had clearly been created by one of the best *modistes* in London. Diamonds glittered in her tiara, bearing testimony to her elevated rank. The lady turned slightly as she answered and Clarissa caught sight of her face. She had raised the look of ennui favored by the leaders of fashionable society to a level that suggested she had experienced all that life could offer and she dared anyone to actually offer her innovative amusement.

Her voice dripped with disdain. "I must applaud your son's taste; she is quite the prettiest little thing to enter London society in a while, although she shows a tendency to liveliness that is a little vulgar. She smiles too much."

Clarissa wasn't sure how to separate the compliment from the criticism in this stranger's words. She knew she should walk away, but she was riveted to the spot. The lady glanced in her direction, her eyes sweeping past her, as if she had not seen Clarissa, and yet Clarissa had the odd impression that the lady knew she could hear every word. It was almost as if she wanted Clarissa to hear her comments.

The gentleman's voice was drily ironic as he replied, "Anthony is still young and enjoys the hunt more than the capture, I think. He appreciates beauty wherever it is found, and this new little lady is very pretty indeed. She will keep him entertained for a while."

The lady's expression darkened. Her lips drew together in a straight line. The languidness of her reply covered her obvious irritation. "Anthony is like a child, chasing after the prettiest baubles, always wanting the newest shiny toy to play with. He has not yet learned to appreciate true quality."

The gentleman looked thoughtfully at his companion but picked up the earlier thread of conversation. "I would like to know a little more about this newest flirtation of his. It does help to be prepared when the mamas of his conquests come to me demanding my intervention."

The lady gave an elegant snort. "It is remarkable how quick young ladies are to hear the peal of wedding bells if Anthony so much as dances with them. If young ladies are foolish enough to misunderstand his intentions, then they have only themselves to blame. He has set up at least three flirtations already this season. The attraction lasts only until a new pretty face catches his eye. He has, I am told, left a trail of broken hearts and shattered expectations in his wake."

The couple fell silent for a few moments, and Clarissa, recalling her manners, was just about to move out of hearing distance when the lady spoke again. She laughed lightly. "I do not think this latest flirtation of his will cause any problems. After Anthony spent half the night ogling her at the opera, I did a little investigating. Clarissa Blakeney is the cousin of an obscure country squire who has pretentions to the aristocracy. Not much is known about her parents, but there are whispers of some scandal. Her aunt is convinced that her face is her fortune and that exposing her to the foremost ranks of society will gain her a titled husband. That is, however, unlikely. She has neither the polish nor the finesse of a real lady, and her dowry is not sufficiently large to cover any lapses in her conduct. She had best return to the countryside and marry a farmer."

Indignation choked Clarissa. There was a vitriol in the lady's words that puzzled her, but the general meaning was clear. Clarissa shifted her attention to the dance floor where Lord Anthony was now dancing with Lady Augusta. Her shoulders stiffened. She tried not to think of how wonderful it had been to be the focus of those intense green eyes. For a brief, happy half hour she had indulged a dream of being swept up into those strong arms and kissed passionately.

Her shoulders straightened and her back stiffened. Never again, would any person have a reason to criticize her behavior. She would be the perfect young lady, obeying every rule of etiquette demanded by society. Fierce determination seized her. Clarissa would not be duped by flattery, no matter how beguiling her dance partner was. She would crush her foolish attraction to Lord Anthony and never again be silly enough to fall for a gentleman's charm.

Just as she schooled her expression into a mask of impassivity and turned to greet her partner for the next dance, she heard the gentleman say, "He will bore of her as quickly as he does all the others. He has more sense than to marry a little nobody, no matter how pretty she is. He has been raised to be conscious of his rank and breeding and will honor the family name."

The lady smiled complacently. "He will marry someone like me."

The gentleman looked at her for a few silent moments and then agreed drily, "Yes, I expect he will marry someone like you."

CHAPTER 2

TWO YEARS LATER

*L*ord Anthony Roland Alexander Donnington moved slowly around the pure, marble statue of the young Grecian woman, entranced by her perfect beauty. The artist had caught her poised on the verge of fleeing. Her right foot was slightly raised, her body leaned forward, and yet she looked over her shoulder. The viscount was intrigued. Was she fleeing from danger or enticing her pursuer to catch her? Would she ultimately experience the thrill of yielding to her newly emerging desires or would she remain forever cast in stone, cold and unreachable, hovering between passion and propriety?

Viscount Donnington, a connoisseur of beauty and an artist in his own right, was, for a moment, able to forget the grief he still felt at his father's passing a few months back. Art always had the ability to console him.

He was fascinated by the artistry of the sculptor who had so perfectly captured the grace and trepidation of a girl on the verge of being a woman. He smiled as his pencil moved swiftly over the page in his small sketchbook. He paused and then made some adjustments, adding details of his own that would later tell the girl's story in a painting by the acclaimed artist, R. Alexander, whose works hung in some of the most prestigious houses in London.

He glanced at the statue again and then used his finger to rub out a line of his drawing. His pencil flew over the page, giving the girl wide-open eyes, slightly parted lips and hands half-open, like the petals of a flower just beginning to bloom. Her breasts were firm, round peaches, ripe for the eating. Later, the rich colors of his oil paints would add depth and definition to her dilemma. Every stroke of his brush would convey her desire to embrace her newly awoken sensuality and her trepidation at leaving behind the innocence of childhood to become a woman. He already knew what the painting would be called: Pursuit of Pleasure.

He paused and studied the statue again, his pencil pressed against the cleft in his chin. In his mind, the cold marble statue transformed into the very real, very living, image of an angelic face, silky blonde hair and a sylphlike figure with soft, enticing curves. His cock swelled and thrummed as he dreamed, not for the first time, of ravaging Clarissa Blakeney, of reawakening the passion and vivacity he had seen in her that first time he had danced with her at Almack's. In his imagination, her wide blue eyes softened with wary vulnerability and whimsical trepidation, glazing with the pleasure of surrendering herself to him.

With a shake of his head and a quick glance to ensure he was alone in the room, he ran his hand down the turgid length and gave a hard squeeze. Clarissa Blakeney was now in her third season. The eager gentlemen who flocked to her beauty called her the Paragon, but none had succeeded in winning her heart. She remained aloof, distant, as elusive as a butterfly, as ethereal as a fairy. She never danced more than once with any gentleman at any ball, and her conversation was always politely correct, firmly discouraging any hint of intimacy.

After that first delightful dance at Almack's, Clarissa had become distant, unapproachable. Anthony had been frustrated in his attempts to become better acquainted with her and his only consolation was that she was equally cool towards all her suitors.

Lord Donnington continued to worship Clarissa Blakeney from afar, only occasionally asking her to partner him in a quadrille or minuet, meeting her rebuffs at his subtle attempts to engage her more intimately with humor. His infatuation had not abated. In fact, in spite of the ribbing of his friends and the aloofness of Miss Blakeney, his obsession with her continued to grow. He had found little pleasure in the company of other women, and many nights he lay alone in bed, picturing Clarissa's loveliness while stroking his cock, imagining what she would look like laid out naked and exposed for him to admire and pleasure.

He glanced again at the drawing that was taking shape in his sketchbook, but this time a frown crossed his usually smooth brow. He brushed a lock of dark auburn hair back from his forehead and pondered his work.

"That scowl does not bode well for those who are eagerly anticipating the next of R. Alexander's paintings!" the droll voice of Baron Adam Loxley interrupted his thoughts. The baron was one of the few people who knew the real identity of the mysterious painter of sought-after works, which often depicted tantalizingly erotic scenes.

Anthony smiled wryly at Adam. "Loxley, I didn't see you come in. I thought you were planning to spend the morning boxing at Gentleman Jack's studio." As Lord Anthony greeted his friend, he snapped his sketchbook closed and quickly tried to slide it into his coat pocket, but the baron snatched it from him in a maneuver that reminded him that Adam had been particularly adept at snagging the last biscuit when they were schoolboys at Eton.

"I left Theo and Laurence sparring with each other," Adam explained, as he began to flip through the pages of Donnington's sketchbook. "Besides, you were in a bit of a gloomy mood last night, and I thought my company would cheer you up this morning."

The viscount shrugged, trying to make light of the complications arising from the settling of his father's estates. "Your ugly face is enough to send me deeper into the slough of despond."

Loxley chuckled but looked at his friend with sympathy and understanding. "Is Lady Lucretia still causing havoc?"

Lord Anthony sighed. "She is. I suppose when my father was smitten by her youth and ravishing beauty, and she so eagerly accepted his proposal of marriage, she did not anticipate becoming a widow before her thirty-fifth birthday." He paused and then explained, "She declares that the life of a widow does not suit her and so wants to sell the house Papa left her in Bath. She wants to come to London even though she has not observed the proper time for mourning."

Loxley gave a sympathetic chuckle. "I'm not sure that I blame her. Bath is full of octogenarians trying to regain their youth through the magic waters, and she certainly has no need of their restorative properties. She is a remarkably attractive woman and she has missed being at the center of society since your father's poor health kept them in Dorset."

Donnington was not amused. He shook his head. "In the meantime, she remains ensconced at Donnington Abbey, but she is frustrated. She is trying to find a way to increase the annuity left to her in my father's will, although it is very generous." He paused, gazing unseeingly at the statue for a moment. "She has some odd notions about how she can retain her position in society."

Loxley made a suitably sympathetic noise. "I suppose she still makes eyes at you whenever she can?"

Donnington shrugged impatiently but said nothing. Loxley, knowing that nothing could come of prolonging a conversation about Lady Lucretia, continued paging through the sketchbook he had snatched from Donnington. "These are some very... inspiring drawings."

Lord Anthony tried to rescue his book, claiming, "There's not much to see there, just vague ideas. Those Greeks depicted the human body so well that the statues are good models for my work." The viscount realized that he was beginning to babble and so he stopped talking, shrugging in resignation when Loxley began to examine the picture based on the young Greek girl.

Adam did not look up from the page he was perusing, but his lips curled up in a smile. "Mmm," he murmured. "It appears that young ladies of Ancient Greece bore a remarkable resemblance to a certain debutante of London society in 1807." He held the book at an angle and studied the drawing, comparing it to the statue. He nodded ponderously, emulating a professor of history they had studied under at Oxford. "The height is right, the figure is perhaps a little less robust in certain... uhm... delicate areas, but the face in the image, while as fresh and pure as the statue's, does not bear a strong likeness to the original."

Donnington could not help chuckling at the accurate mimicry of their old professor, but he tried again to reclaim his property. "Loxley, do give it back." Then he waved his hand towards the statue, offering an explanation, "There is a remarkable likeness between the statue and Miss Blakeney. I am sure even you can see that they both have an air of innocence that is very appealing, and when I began to draw, my pencil took over and the face transformed into hers."

All signs of teasing vanished from Loxley's face as he returned the sketchbook to Anthony. His voice conveyed genuine concern. "My dear chap, what are we going to do about you? This obsession, this infatuation you have with the paragon is becoming a tad ridiculous."

Donnington shook his head and shrugged as he turned his attention back to the statue. "I'd rather be thought a fool for admiring Miss Blakeney than attempt to woo any other young lady. She is the image of perfection and everyone else fades into insignificance before her."

Loxley made a light scoffing noise. "There is no denying that she is as lovely as any work of art, but she never gives anyone any reason to suspect that her heart might be touched. Bedding her would be as exciting as sleeping next to one of these statues. A cold and passionless experience."

Donnington bit back his irritation yet when he answered, Loxley could hear a tremor of vulnerability underlying his words. The viscount ran his hand down the shapely leg of the cold marble statue. The perfect loveliness touched some deep part of his soul. "I have reason to believe that Clarissa Blakeney is a woman of deep sensibility and warm passions that for some reason she keeps hidden from the world. When she finally surrenders to her passions, to someone whom she trusts, she will be exquisite, a true paragon of all that is womanly."

Loxley looked at the drawing again and then closed Anthony's sketchbook. "Life is not a Greek fable, where artists create the perfect woman of their dreams and statues transform into passionate living flesh because Venus intervenes on their behalf."

"Perhaps not, but with the right man, she will learn to live."

Loxley laughed. "And you are going to be her Prince Charming, the one who wakens Sleeping Beauty with a kiss?"

Donnington chuckled. "There is much truth in fairy tales although change happens more slowly in real life. Recently, she has regained some of the animation, some of the enthusiasm I found so appealing when I first met her." He slipped his sketchbook into his pocket. "Adam, I can't forget her. Thoughts and images of her obtrude into every moment of my day and night. I must have her or die unsatisfied!"

Loxley raised an eyebrow. "No need to be so melodramatic, old chap. You're beginning to sound like a schoolboy who's just discovered the effect pretty girls have on his dick."

A clatter of footsteps and a babble of voices interrupted the friends. They looked up to see an invasion of fashionably dressed ladies arriving to view the collection of antiquities that had drawn much interest in London society. They stopped first in front of a statue of a woman carrying a pitcher and bowl and draped in a loose garment that did not quite cover her breasts. Their comments carried clearly across the room.

"Why, those ancient heathens were quite shameless! Did they not have access to decent clothes?" exclaimed one stout matron. Loxley recognized the strident tones of Lady Carson, a lady well-known as a stickler for propriety whose daughters had never been heard to laugh.

"Indeed, it is quite scandalous, most shocking, Lady Carson," agreed her companion, a reedy looking woman with a sharp nose, peering aghast at a statue of a naked athlete, his private parts proudly on display. "I will not permit my daughters to come near this exhibition. I will not have their innocent minds corrupted by such indecent sights," she averred primly, even though she was peering very closely at the statue.

Loxley and Donnington exchanged amused glances at this evaluation of the art of Ancient Greece. Fighting back laughter, Loxley muttered *sotto voce* to Donnington, "What will her dear daughters think if ever they are confronted by a real cock?" He glanced meaningfully at his friend's breeches and obliquely gestured towards his own bulge. "Especially one of above average size, like those you depict in your paintings!"

Donnington shook his head with a soft laugh. "Girls like that marry husbands who will have... marital relations quickly with them in the dark, under sheets. They don't take off their clothes in the marriage bed, poor things, so none of them ever experience real pleasure. They are taught to believe that sex is an onerous duty to be endured and then wonder why their husbands keep mistresses or seek out prostitutes."

Loxley set his hand on his friend's shoulder as they started moving towards the gallery exit. All signs of humor vanished as he returned to his previous concerns. "Has it ever crossed your mind that a paragon of perfect behavior such as Miss Blakeney has been brought up with the same notions of strict propriety, that she too believes that passion and physical pleasure are vulgar and indecent? If she ever does marry, she will choose an eminently respectable man who will ensure she never knows any pleasure." He nodded towards the statue of a kneeling Aphrodite that Donnington had stopped to admire. "Miss Blakeney would be scandalized by such displays of nudity, even in a statue, and she would never accept our philosophy that pleasure is the greatest good."

Donnington gazed at the statue, and his hand reached into his pocket for his sketchbook. The perfectly rounded buttocks of the goddess of love inspired him and he wanted to replicate that beauty in a painting, but Lady Carson and her crony walked past them at that moment, nodding a brief greeting. With a sigh of irritation, he left his sketchpad where it was. There were too many people milling around for him to use his drawing to distract himself from Adam's questions.

He politely returned Lady Carson's greeting while trying to memorize the voluptuous curves and sensuous lines of Aphrodite. But even as he did so, his thoughts were churning over the dilemma of Clarissa Blakeney. She was one of the loveliest women he had ever seen, and Lord Anthony had always been drawn to beauty. Even as a boy, he had carried a sketchpad everywhere with him, and his friends often teased him about how he filled the pages with odd drawings. As he grew to manhood, that passion to record the loveliness that touched his soul had become paradoxically both more private and more public as people began to buy his paintings, although few knew he was the artist. Gentlemen of the aristocracy were not supposed to indulge in what was considered a professional trade.

Donnington ran his hand along the smooth marble of Aphrodite's arm. "I am sure that you are mistaken in suggesting that Miss Blakeney is immune to true pleasure. You have not danced with her and seen how her eyes light up when she talks of something that touches her heart. And I do not think she is as indifferent to me as she tries to appear. Often, when she does not realize I notice, I find her watching me. I am not a fool, and I know when a woman is attracted to me. I believe she is scared of her own feelings." He studied the marble goddess of love before him, fingering the pencil in his pocket, but his earlier creative mood had dissipated. Suddenly the rows and rows of clean, pure, white marble statues felt stifling. He needed to go somewhere like Covent Garden, filling his senses with the sounds and colors and movement of life.

He turned towards the exit, but his progress was halted abruptly by the sudden and unexpected appearance of Miss Clarissa Blakeney in the doorway of the long gallery.

The brightness of summer filled the room as she moved eagerly towards a statue of Apollo. Her fine lawn dress, the vivid blue of cornflowers, swirled enticingly around her legs, and Lord Anthony's cock jerked as the soft material draped her body, emphasizing the roundness of her buttocks and her slim waist. A stylish straw bonnet, trimmed with ribbons just a shade darker than her dress, framed her pretty face, and even from across the room, the viscount noticed how her eyes sparkled with enthusiasm. As she led her aunt past the ladies who were hovering around a statue of a very muscular Hercules, she gave a swift but graceful curtsey. The flurry of raised eyebrows and questioning glances did not deter her from gazing with avid interest at a statue of the god, nakedly displaying his manhood.

The viscount watched in silence, half-hidden behind Aphrodite. He murmured a soft prayer to the goddess of love and bit back a groan as blood rushed to his groin. Just being in the same room as Clarissa, made his cock as hard as the marble statues. Now, as she peered closely at the god's rather small prick, Donnington's dick throbbed. The ache in his groin worsened when Clarissa leaned towards her aunt, her eyes still focused on the statue, and whispered something. Her aunt's rather prim lips flattened even more and her eyebrows shot up almost to her stiffly arranged hair.

Donnington tore his eyes away from the vision before him long enough to slap Adam's shoulder. "What do you say now, Lox? Miss Blakeney appears to be almost crassly interested in what the god has to offer. She isn't fainting in dismay or running from the room in horror." He quirked an eyebrow, and a smile lit up his face.

Baron Loxley gave a wry chuckle. "She is definitely not responding like a prissy young miss."

The viscount made a rude sign with his fingers that only Loxley could see and stalked off, leaving his friend chuckling as he pursued his muse.

CHAPTER 3

*C*larissa Blakeney moved slowly around the white marble Apollo. She was puzzled. He had a cloak draped around his shoulders and was setting an arrow into his bow, but most of his body was naked. She studied his manhood, nestled between his thighs and resting on a tuft of curls. A small smile teased her mouth as she bent to whisper to her aunt, "Do all men look like that?"

Miss Agatha Blakeney, her father's youngest sister and her companion since her parents had died when she was just thirteen, scowled. "Never having been married, I am not familiar with male anatomy," she snapped.

Clarissa giggled. "It doesn't seem as big as I thought it would be."

"Really, Clarissa, that is hardly decent conversation for a young lady. If anyone were to hear you, they would think I had failed in my duty to raise you properly."

Clarissa's face fell and she took her aunt's hand in hers as they moved towards the statue of a young Greek girl. "Oh, Aunt Agatha, I do try to be all that is proper and respectable but sometimes it is so difficult. My mind wanders into unruly places and the strangest thoughts crowd my head. But I would never do anything to bring shame on you. You have been the best of aunts."

Somewhat mollified, Agatha Blakeney patted her niece's hand and then opened the brochure the gallery had provided. "This will give us the information we need to appreciate the statues as works of art and as examples of antiquities." She glanced across the room to where Lady Carson was leading her coterie to another group of statues. "You will be able to make the proper observations if anyone should ask you your opinion on the exhibition."

Clarissa huffed impatiently. "My opinion does not often concur with the bland descriptions provided in the brochures. I wish a proper young lady was allowed to have her own ideas about things and that people actually cared to listen to them."

This time, Aunt Agatha reprimanded Clarissa so sharply that she retreated behind her mask of polite formality. She had spent the last few years so carefully cultivating the perfect image of a young lady, that mothers and governesses often pointed her out as a paragon of correct behavior. But inwardly, she railed against society's expectations. Lady Carson's voice carried across the room, informing her listeners that the most one could say of the display was that it was a good presentation of the works of antiquity. Clarissa shuddered.

As she gazed at the statue of a young Greek girl, she blocked out the voices both in the room and in her head. It was a trick she had perfected over the years, and it had stood her in good stead when her aunt was on the rampage, so now, she was only vaguely aware when Agatha hissed under her breath, "I cannot believe his effrontery! He is headed this way and we will have to speak to him."

Clarissa was startled to hear the rich, deep baritone of Viscount Donnington greeting them with a polite, "Good day,

Miss Blakeney, Miss Clarissa. Are you enjoying this exhibition of works from ancient Greece?"

Suddenly the room felt too hot, and for a moment, Clarissa thought someone had removed all the air from the room. A flush of heat swept over her body, as it always did whenever the viscount was near, and yet she tried to treat him with the cool indifference required of a perfect young lady. Ever since that first time she had danced with him at Almack's, a constant war raged in Clarissa's heart between her genuine admiration for him and the memory of the cruelly casual way in which she had been dismissed as not worthy of a connection with the Donnington family. Over the years, she had spent many hours watching Lord Anthony closely and her dreams were filled with visions of his deep green eyes, his broad shoulders and his strong hands. She knew that he was not a callous flirt casually collecting broken hearts all around London, as his stepmother had insinuated that evening so many years ago, but gossip did suggest that he was a confirmed bachelor, not likely to marry for at least the next ten years.

Clarissa clenched her hands tightly but schooled her face to its usual impassivity, attempting to keep back the flush of pleasure that swept over her. She bowed stiffly, saying, "My aunt and I had heard much about this celebrated exhibition and believe it is enlightening and educative." Even to her own ears, she sounded stilted and knew she was being rude to the viscount, who had shown himself to be kind and intelligent in every conversation she had had with him.

Lord Donnington studied her intensely for a moment but turned his attention to Agatha Blakeney who was speaking, her tone dismissive and her eyes challenging. "Well, Lord Anthony, it is interesting to see you here. I had thought you would prefer to be placing bets at Tattersall's or lounging in your club rather than spending time at an exhibition concerned with art and history."

~

DONNINGTON'S EYEBROWS shot up at such an outright disparagement of his character. It took all his innate amiability and good breeding to refrain from snapping a retort. Although this was not the first time someone had colored him with the wrong brush, he was annoyed by Agatha Blakeney's uncalled for and uninformed censure. He squared his shoulders. The opinion of a middle-aged spinster whose chief ambition in life was to rid the world of pleasure would not deter him from the pleasure of Clarissa's company.

When he noticed the object of his fantasies looking at him through downcast eyelashes, the wave of rage that had swamped him subsided and he answered Agatha Blakeney politely. "As a *gentleman*," he placed subtle emphasis on the word, "I cultivate a wide range of interests. I do enjoy horses, and a good game of cards at White's can be stimulating, but I also find history intriguing and have a very personal interest in art." He did not mention that he had attained a first in Classics at Oxford and was considered an expert in the history and culture of ancient Greece. Agatha Blakeney snorted softly but took a step back.

The viscount, with a smile that made him look like a prince in a fairy tale, turned to address the living embodiment of perfect beauty who was still silently gazing at the statue. "Miss Clarissa, I see that you are intrigued by the same statue I was admiring a few minutes ago. What do you think of her?"

Aunt Agatha rustled the brochure that the museum had provided, reminding Clarissa that young ladies were not expected to have independent opinions. Clarissa bit back a sigh, straightened her shoulders, and grateful that she had skimmed through the brochure when her aunt had purchased their entrance tickets, gave the correct answer to the viscount's question. "This is a fine example of the Classic period of Greek art, sculpted from a good piece of marble and was probably owned privately by a wealthy family," she repeated dutifully.

The viscount did not respond immediately, merely looked expectantly at Clarissa as if he was waiting for her to add something to her stilted answer. Clarissa flushed under his steady perusal, unsettled by the way his lips quirked up as if he was laughing at some private joke. She dropped her gaze and forced herself not to fidget.

Aunt Agatha beamed her approval, but Clarissa continued to feel awkward until Lord Anthony, taking pity on her, broke the silence, his voice both soothing and compelling. "The brochure does provide interesting facts, however, to me, it lacks insight into the creativity of the artist. I am always fascinated to hear what emotions a work of art invokes in the viewer, and I like to imagine what inspired the artist, what story might lurk behind what we see here."

Aunt Agatha huffed derisively at this deviation from the expected course of polite conversation, but the viscount ignored the spinster, focusing on Clarissa. "For instance, I do not see only a good piece of marble, skillfully turned into an ornament for a noble family's house."

Clarissa's eyes flashed in fury at the implied criticism of her perfect answer. She hated being reprimanded, especially when her behavior was a perfect portrayal of exactly what was expected from a young lady.

Lord Anthony smiled at Clarissa; his voice was softer, gentler, as sympathy replaced the wry amusement of his previous comments. "When I look at her, I wonder what it is that she finds both so frightening and so intriguing." Lord Anthony was looking at Clarissa, not the statue as he spoke, and Clarissa had the oddest sense that Lord Anthony was no longer talking about the statue. Heat engulfed her. She tried not to squirm as he asked more pointedly, "What do you think she finds both frightening and alluring?"

The viscount's gentle coaxing loosened something inside her and she responded eagerly, no longer using the prim cadences of a schoolgirl providing well-rehearsed answers to a draconian governess. "Oh, there is someone very powerful whom she finds both alluring and alarming. She wants to stay, but is anxious about what might happen if she leaves the safety of what she knows." She did not realize just how much of her own predicament she conveyed to Lord Anthony as she added wistfully, "She longs for the courage to follow her dreams, her desires, her passions."

The viscount tilted his head and scrutinized Clarissa's face, examining every feature so carefully that she felt a tremble shiver through her body. Her hand flew up to cover her mouth as if by doing so, she could push the words back. She held her breath, nervous, wondering if she had said too much, if it had revealed too much of her soul. Would the viscount reject her as a maverick, a young lady who longed for things no proper young lady ever dreamed of? Anxiety flooded her eyes as she caught her lip between her teeth.

∼

LORD ANTHONY HELD Clarissa's bright blue eyes with his steady gaze. Slowly, his lips curved up into a smile. "I believe she would find happiness if she allowed herself to indulge in the pleasures that life offers her." In his earnest desire to convince Clarissa of the truth of his words, he stepped closer to her, placing his hand on her arm. "Life is, after all, far more complex and vital than a work of art."

Clarissa took a step backwards, trying to free herself from the disconcerting heat that emanated from the viscount's closeness. "No, don't flee, little one," he coaxed. "I will not hurt you, only help you to discover the beauty in life. There is no shame in being true to oneself, to being honest about the emotions that you feel."

Clarissa paused, her conflicting emotions clear on her face. The viscount leaned even closer, drawn by her vulnerability, her suppressed passion and her perfect beauty. It took all his common sense and control not to take her into his arms right there in the middle of the gallery and kiss her soft, trembling lips. With an effort, he kept his hand on her arm rather than pressing the little place on her lips where her teeth had left a tiny dent.

A derisive sniff from Aunt Agatha recalled Lord Anthony, and with a reluctant smile, he let go of Clarissa's arm. He gave a polite bow and stepped back, saying softly so that only Clarissa could hear, "There is much pleasure to be found in following your heart, and I will help you find the strength and courage to explore the splendor of the world if you will let me."

CHAPTER 4

*C*larissa sat at the small round table in her aunt's drawing room, embroidering a dainty butterfly on a tiny baby dress. Her exquisite stitching raised it from a simply utilitarian garment to a work of art. The silence of the room was disturbed when Mrs. Bedford, the housekeeper, entered, carrying the morning's post. She handed two letters to Aunt Agatha.

Clarissa sighed. They were probably more invitations to more soirees and balls, where she would be expected to smile politely and behave perfectly. She had begun to grow weary of the endless round of activities in London, the endless sameness of conversation that simply exchanged superficial comments that everyone already knew. The only bright moments were those she spent with Lord Anthony, but they unsettled her more than stimulated her. Talking to him reminded her of how her own thoughts and feelings were kept deeply buried under layers of social gloss.

Aunt Agatha opened the first letter. As she read, her shoulders stiffened and Clarissa was alarmed when her aunt's lips tightened. "What is it, Aunty? Is there something wrong?"

Aunt Agatha drew in her breath sharply. She dropped the

letter into her lap and attempted to smile reassuringly at her niece. "I was just thinking of how much I will miss you when you marry."

Clarissa dropped her sewing at this unexpected response to her question and swiftly crossed the room. She knelt next to where her aunt was sitting on the settee. With a shrug, she observed lightly, "That is not likely to happen any time soon, even if that letter contains yet another request from some gentleman requesting permission to court me. I have no desire to surrender myself to a husband, to bow and scrape to his every whim, ensuring that he is comfortable while I smile and nod my head, agreeing with him on every point."

Aunt Agatha pursed her lips. "Dear, that is not a very ladylike opinion. It is the duty of every well-bred lady to marry well and to honor her family by obeying her husband, making his home comfortable so that he can pursue greater matters outside the home."

Clarissa sank back onto her heels, a frown crossing her pretty face. There was a hitch in her voice as she said, "That sounds so dull and quite dreadful. I do wish I didn't have to grow up and be a perfect young lady and, worse still, a respectable and proper wife." With a defiant toss of her head, she declared, "I believe that I will be like you and remain a spinster and then I will never have to suffer the encumbrance of a husband."

Aunt Agatha shook her head. "That is not as easy an option as you might believe it to be. You do not have an independent fortune, and neither do I. I am paid an annuity to be your guardian, but it is not sufficient to support you as well." She poked at the letter in her lap. "This is from your cousin. Sir Bradley expresses his concern that you are in your third season and have not yet managed to, as he says, *procure a husband to take over paying for the expense of your upkeep*." She shook her head. "Sir Bradley has written to remind me, and you, that your dowry is dependent on your being married. You were given three seasons to establish yourself as an eligible wife. At the end of this season, your dowry will revert to your cousin's estate, and you will be dependent on him." She looked at Clarissa with sympathy. "Sir Bradley mentions that he would be prepared to take you into his house to help with his children if you are not able to find a husband." Aunt Agatha patted her niece's hand, which had turned ice cold during this explanation. "It would be far better to marry than to live as a burden to Sir Bradley all your life, to be constantly at his beck and call and an unpaid nursemaid to his children."

Clarissa rose to her feet and began to pace up and down the small sitting room. "It would not be very pleasant to live under Sir Bradley's jurisdiction," she agreed as she made her third turn about the room. She stopped in front of the table where she had been sewing earlier and scowled at the baby dress. "I suppose it might not be all that dreadful to marry. It might be bearable to be attached to a respectable gentleman, if he allowed me a little freedom to think my own thoughts."

Aunt Agatha heaved a sigh of relief at this much acquiescence from Clarissa. She had begun to think that her recalcitrant niece would never accept the inevitability of marriage. Relief seasoned her tongue with asperity. "I do not understand this strange desire of yours to be independent and have freedom. It makes you sound like one of those dreadfully radical French people." She was on firmer ground now, resorting to the kind of lecture that she had perfected over the years of trying to guide Clarissa into a semblance of acceptable behavior. "Young ladies do not have the sense to make decisions for themselves and are far better off accepting the security of their families."

She put Sir Bradley's letter aside and picked up her own sewing. "Although I have never been married, I have observed that gentlemen tend to give their wives some independence when it comes to managing the household and raising the children. They have their own interests to pursue and do not interfere very much with their wives, as long as the home is comfortable and meals are regular."

Clarissa stared at her aunt in consternation. She said nothing as her aunt brought her lecture to what she considered a triumphant conclusion. "So, my dear, when you marry you will not need to see your husband very much. You will live amicably side-by-side and as long as you ensure his comfort, you will have a semblance of the independence you so desire."

Clarissa shivered. Cold dismay gripped her heart. She could choose between marrying a man she did not love or living out her days as a drudge in her cousin's home. There was no place in the grim reality of her bleak future for the dreams she indulged in at night before she fell asleep. She would never know what it felt like to be swept up in Lord Anthony's strong arms and crushed against his hard chest. No matter how attentive Lord Donnington was to her, how many times he danced with her, or how pleasurable it was to talk to him, he would eventually choose a wife with a large dowry, impeccable breeding and good family connections.

Clarissa sat down at the table where she had been sewing earlier and picked up the baby garment, but her fingers fumbled with the dainty stitches of the tiny butterfly. She tried to obliterate the memory of how the viscount's deep green eyes had focused so intently on her at the museum, but as always, thoughts of him did strange things to her body. Her skin felt too tight, her breasts were heavy and her nipples hardened into little points that pressed against her corset. She glanced at her aunt, but that indomitable woman was peering at the cushion cover on her lap trying to decide which shade of blue was best for the feather of a peacock.

After a few silent moments, Aunt Agatha reverted to the topic of Clarissa's marriage. "We need to consider which of the gentlemen who have shown an interest in you would be the most eligible to consider as a husband." Aunt Agatha did not bother to keep the irritation out of her voice. "If you had been a little more encouraging to the many gentlemen who showed an interest in you during your first season, there might be a wider choice available now. As it is, there are some who have not been deterred by your aloofness. Mr. Hemsby could be persuaded that you would make a dutiful wife. There is also Sir Galpin. I have heard that he is needing to marry soon."

Clarissa's shoulders sagged and she forced herself to form a neat stitch. Concentrating on her embroidery meant she did not have to look at her aunt as she ventured to ask, "What about love? Can a lady not expect to find love in her marriage?"

"Love?" Aunt Agatha's voice dripped with disdain. "Love is a sentimental notion invented by writers of novels for the entertainment of idle minds. Respectable ladies eschew such over-wrought emotions as uncouth and should be horrified even by the thought of something so vulgar and foolish. A sensible lady must always be dignified and refined, not given to crass emotions or frivolous passions."

Clarissa took a deep breath. It was not very sensible of her still to be able to feel the pressure of Lord Anthony's strong, capable hand where he had touched her arm in the gallery or for shivers of pleasure to course down her spine whenever she heard his deep, smooth voice. It was not respectable or dignified to tremble with desire each time she saw the outline of his hard muscles encased in his closely-fitted breeches. Perhaps, once she was married, she would learn how to forget the delightful tendrils of pleasure that unfurled in her whenever she was near to the viscount.

Aunt Agatha glared at Clarissa, driving her argument home. "Love leads to excess and causes people to make foolish decisions that expose them to scandal and their families to ridicule."

Clarissa's cheeks flamed. Her shoulders slumped even further and she found it difficult to focus on the placement of her next stitch. She spoke slowly. "My mother and father loved each other. I do not remember them well, but I do know that they were very happy together."

Aunt Agatha made a sound that was almost a snort. "The disgrace of your parents' love led to a scandal that caused much harm to their families." She could not keep the bitterness out of her voice. "I did not have many suitors, but every one of them vanished rather than be associated with a family tainted by disgrace." She controlled the tremble in her voice and continued the lecture. "Over time, the scandal died down and thanks to my father, the family name was rescued from complete dishonor so that now most people have forgotten the scandal."

Clarissa gave up all pretense of sewing. She clasped her hands and exclaimed, "Oh, Aunty, I am so sorry that your life was ruined, and yet you have always been so good to me. I will never do anything to disgrace you." Her voice became brittle as she resigned herself to her inevitable future. "I will marry someone respectable and will be all that is proper in a wife, a very paragon of perfection who will never cause anyone to raise so much as an eyebrow. I will endeavor to keep my unruly emotions under control."

Aunt Agatha's voice softened with tenderness. "You are a good girl, Clarissa, and you will find that being married is not as unpleasant as you fear it might be." She cleared her throat, putting aside emotions and focusing on the business of marriage. "You will need to let the acceptable gentleman know, discreetly, of course, that you would welcome an offer of marriage from him."

Clarissa felt a pit opening up in her stomach. The only gentleman she found acceptable was Viscount Donnington. Like a foolish moth dancing around a candle on a dark winter's night, she was drawn to the bright flames of his presence. It was dangerous to linger on thoughts of him. She tried to smile at her aunt. "Mr. Hemsby has asked if I would like to walk with him at five o' clock in Hyde Park."

Aunt Agatha sighed with relief and brushed her hand over her forehead, dislodging the second letter Mrs. Bedford had brought in. It fluttered across the floor and landed near Clarissa's feet. She quickly picked it up and carried it to her aunt. "We were so focused on Sir Bradley's letter that this was overlooked. It has the Duke of Broadwell's crest on the envelope."

Aunt Agatha slit the envelope open and unfolded the elegant linen paper favored by the duchess for her correspondence. She raised an eyebrow as she scanned the page. "Lady Amelia has invited you, with me as chaperone, to a dinner on Thursday. She wants to thank all the people who offer assistance to the women at Mary's Haven."

Clarissa clapped her hands in glee, all the gloom of the previous discussion forgotten in the delightful prospect. "Oh, we must write to accept immediately. I enjoy making the baby dresses for those poor women and their children, but I have never met any of them."

Aunt Agatha's eyes opened wide in horror. "I should think not. Those women are scandalous, and while it might be acceptable for a young lady to sew garments so that the poor children do not run around without a stitch of clothing on, it would not do to have any interaction with such god-forsaken women! If I thought any of them would be at the duke's house, I would not allow you to be there." She shook her head. "I do wish you could find some less shocking cause to support."

Clarissa couldn't help laughing. "Aunty, if God has forsaken those poor women and their babies, then it is just as well that the duchess has not left them to be abandoned." Her voice softened and her eyes were filled with compassion. "Very few people want to help these girls to improve their lives. Just think what they would have to do to support themselves if it were not for Lady Amelia's help!"

"I try not to think of that or of what led them there in the first place," retorted Aunt Agatha. "There is something very disrespectable about helping fallen women. I have heard that Mr. Hemsby has petitioned to have Mary's Haven closed down because people in the neighborhood do not want such women living nearby. If you are serious about encouraging his attention, then it would be better for you to have nothing more to do with Mary's Haven."

Clarissa felt an icy hand grip her heart. Marriage to Mr. Hemsby was not a pleasant prospect, but it would be better than marrying Sir Galpin, her only other real option. She nodded her head, her voice grim with the knowledge of her grim future. "I will do all I can to be the best wife and not incur Mr. Hemsby's displeasure, but Aunt, please can we go to the dinner?"

Aunt Agatha smiled generously. "We will attend. Fetch me my writing desk."

Clarissa crossed the room with a light heart. The jolt of joy that surged through her at the thought of attending the duchess's dinner had little to do with her sense of benevolence. Lord Anthony was sure to be one of the guests.

CHAPTER 5

*C*larissa stepped out of the Pantheon Bazaar, into the bustle and commotion of Oxford Street. Delighted with her purchases, she tugged open the string around her parcel and peeped at the pretty cerise and chartreuse ribbons she had bought. She would make rosettes from the cheerful pink that would enliven her old evening gown. She wanted to look her best for the duchess's dinner. She wondered if Lord Anthony would prefer the pink or green ribbon, but then shook her head.

Aunt Agatha tutted impatiently. "Come along, dear, don't dawdle."

Clarissa took a hurried step forward and bumped into the bulky form of a large man. The impact catapulted her onto the ground with a hard bump. Her head hit the pavement and she cried out in pain. She lay on the ground, dazed and confused. After a few moments, the buzz of voices around her began to filter through the fog of pain.

Slowly, that buzz of voices began to form itself into words. She was dismayed to hear a sharp voice declare, "What a shockingly unladylike exhibition! I never expected to see Miss Blakeney sprawled on the road for everyone to gawk at."

Clarissa tried to sit up but was engulfed by a rush of nausea and dizziness. She looked up to see the prim, pursed face of Lady Carson staring down at her, shock and disgust evident in every feature. Her usual companion-in-arms, Mrs. Brazington, agreed. "Dreadful, dreadful. I would be mortified if my daughters ever showed their legs in such an unseemly way. I do not know how she will ever show her face in public again."

Tears trickled down Clarissa's face, the pain and humiliation causing her to lose control of her usually carefully guarded emotions. She did not think her face could become any redder and she tugged at her dress as she hastily tried to scramble to her feet. She wavered but suddenly large, competent, comforting hands steadied her, helping her to stand. The sudden rush of blood to her head made her feel sick, and she clung to the arm of her rescuer.

"There, my little rose, you will soon be back to normal." The deep, soothing voice of Lord Anthony Donnington wrapped around her, forming a shield against the horror of the last few moments. She sighed and leaned closer to the reassuring warmth of his solid presence.

The murmurs in the crowd increased and the viscount gently handed her over to the care of Aunt Agatha, who was clucking like an agitated hen. She wobbled on her unsteady legs, and her head throbbed. Tentatively, she touched the bump that was forming at the back of her head. She tried to grab hold of Lord Anthony's supporting arm, but he firmly moved back with a shake of his head. "Not yet, not now, my little one."

Slowly, her awareness of the situation became clearer. The crowds were beginning to disperse, but many ladies of the *haut ton*, and quite a few gentlemen, had seen her humiliating fall. By evening, she would be an object of gossip. The cold hand of despair gripped her heart. The shame of her disgrace ripped to shreds the fragile fabric of her carefully cultivated mantel of perfection.

Slowly, she straightened her shoulders, determined to salvage what dignity she could. She glanced around, looking for her parcels. They lay scattered all around where she had fallen.

She bent down to pick up the nearest one, but Lord Anthony swiftly laid a restraining hand on her arm. "No, little rose. Stay still."

Clarissa responded immediately to the authority in the viscount's voice, but a little frown creased her forehead. Lord Anthony smiled at her. "Do not worry. Your parcels will all be safe."

Clarissa turned her aching head and saw that the viscount's groom was gathering her scattered and torn parcels. She bit her lip and tried to offer her thanks, but the viscount brushed her words aside. "Think nothing of it, little rose. It is my pleasure to help you."

When the groom placed Clarissa's parcels on the seat of Lord Anthony's phaeton, Aunt Agatha began to shake her head. "Thank you, Your Lordship, but if you could procure a hansom cab for us, we will get home safely."

The viscount raised an eyebrow. "I am sure it would be much more convenient and comfortable for both of you to use my carriage, Miss Blakeney."

Aunt Agatha, who was pale and trembling, accepted his offer without further demur, much to Clarissa's relief. The viscount handed both ladies up into the carriage and Clarissa settled back against the comfortable swabs with a sigh of gratitude. Her head was throbbing and tears were slipping down her cheeks. She closed her eyes but they flew open again when she felt Lord Anthony's firm, strong hands tuck a rug over her lap.

"It would be best to summon a doctor as soon as possible. I will arrange to have Dr. Bentley, my usual physician, come to see you."

Again, Aunt Agatha protested. "Thank you, Lord Donnington

but I can send my housekeeper to fetch the apothecary we usually consult."

Lord Anthony ignored her protests, distracted by Clarissa, who was agitatedly searching for something amongst her parcels. "What is it you need, little one?"

"My smelling salts. I am feeling a little dizzy and they should be in my reticule, but it is not here."

The viscount gave his groom a questioning look. He shook his head. "No, milord. That's all there was. There was no reticule on the pavement."

At these words, a man who had stopped unloading barrels from his cart nearby to gawk at what was happening, stepped forward. "Begging your pardon, milord," he began as he doffed his cloth cap, "but I saw what happened."

The viscount nodded, urging the man to continue. He cleared his throat. "The thug who bumped the young lady did so deliberately. He was watching her when she stepped out onto the pavement and he took his chance when she was distracted to push her over. He grabbed her reticule."

Lord Anthony frowned. The carter shuffled but hastened to explain his own lack of action. "I had just hefted a large barrel onto my shoulder when it happened, and by the time I had put it down, the man had disappeared into the crowd."

"Thank you. Could you describe the man you saw?"

The carter frowned. "I didn't see him clearly. His back was to me most of the time but he was a tall man. He was wearing a brown corduroy jacket and had a dark green cap pulled quite low on his face. I think he was swarthy, but the shadows made it difficult to tell."

The viscount nodded his thanks and handed the carter a shilling. Then he bowed to Clarissa and Aunt Agatha. "My groom will see you safely home, but if there is anything that you need, please do not hesitate to ask." He smiled tenderly at Clarissa. "I will call in tomorrow to see how you are doing."

~

WITH A FLIP OF HIS COATTAILS, Mr. Hemsby, his face even more somber than usual, took a seat next to Clarissa at the small worktable. A loud creak from the dainty chair caused Aunt Agatha, who was seated at a discreet distance near the window, to look up sharply, fearing for the safety of her furniture.

He shifted his heavy bulk, but his ponderous tones drowned out the continued creaking of the wood. Clarissa found it difficult to concentrate on her embroidery. Her head still ached from the bump to her head, and Mr. Hemsby's presence was not at all soothing. She couldn't help compare him to the viscount who had shown such sincere concern for her well-being.

In spite of her aunt's protests, Lord Anthony had sent his physician to examine her and when he had visited earlier that morning, he had immediately asked if her head was aching less and whether she had rested well. Clarissa couldn't help feeling somewhat aggrieved that Mr. Hemsby had not even asked if she had been hurt by her fall. She fingered the volume of Wordsworth's poetry that Lord Anthony had brought for her. She had spent a pleasurable half an hour listening to his rich, velvety baritone bring the words to life.

Mr. Hemsby's reedy voice, sharp with disapproval, cut through her thoughts of the viscount. "I was deeply distressed to hear how your behavior was the topic of conversation at Mrs. Brazington's soiree yesterday evening. It is most unfortunate that a young lady who usually comports herself impeccably should have given society cause to gossip about her. Such damage to your reputation will not be easily overcome and it behooves me to point out that it is in my best interests to delay the proposal of marriage I am considering, until the gossip has died down."

Clarissa looked up, a flash of indignation sparkling in her blue eyes, but Mr. Hemsby shook his head and continued to pontificate. "Yesterday, Miss Blakeney, you were the center of a commotion witnessed by many people, including upstanding members of society." He gave an ingratiating smile that caused her to shudder. "It is as well that I am a gentleman of understanding and I can find it in me to pardon your indecorous behavior. However," he continued, ignoring the way Clarissa was bristling at his words, "if no further such incidents occur, I will visit your cousin and request your hand in marriage, once the talk dies down."

He sat up straight and attempted to pull in the bulk of his stomach that was straining against the corset he wore beneath his shirt. "I trust, Miss Blakeney, that you are not unconscious of the honor I bestow on you by such an offer. It is to be hoped that your behavior will give me no further cause to reconsider my offer."

Clarissa had no answer to give. She could not let her only prospect of marriage know that she would not care if he never renewed his attentions to her. She could still feel the warm clasp of the viscount's hands and the solid comfort of his presence.

Silence fell heavily in the room, and after a few moments, Mr. Hemsby leaned forward. Peering through his quizzing glass, he examined the baby dress Clarissa had almost finished. He replaced the quizzing glass in his pocket and then commented ponderously, "That is very fine sewing, Miss Blakeney. However, it seems to me a trifle immodest for a young, unmarried lady to be occupied with making clothes for infants."

A wave of irritation swept over Clarissa but, with great effort, she reminded herself that no matter what she felt about the viscount, Mr. Hemsby was the one who was seeking her hand in marriage. No matter how kind, how caring Lord Anthony had been, it was not an offer of marriage. She would have to learn to tolerate Mr. Hemsby's complacent self-righteousness in the same way that she had learned to conform to society's rules. She would become the image of the perfect wife.

Swallowing the lump in her throat, she answered as placidly as she could. "This is for a baby who has just been born at Mary's Haven."

Mr. Hemsby pursed his lips. "Yes, quite. That is exactly my point. A delicate young lady should not even know of such... unsavory matters, let alone offer assistance to women who have fallen into wickedness." He gave her another ingratiating smile. "Your kindness and sympathy are admirable qualities, well suited to one of the weaker sex. And yet, Miss Blakeney, I trust that you will allow yourself to be guided by my superior understanding of right and proper behavior. Once our betrothal is made formal, I will expect you to abandon your... support of that institution. In fact, considering the disgrace of yesterday, it might be better if you ceased any association with it immediately. Indeed, I am leading a petition to have it closed down. It is situated near some warehouses in which I have a business interest, and I can hardly expect my decent and respectable customers to cross paths with such unsavory women."

Clarissa's heart tightened. She glanced at Mr. Hemsby's somber face and smug expression and for a moment wondered if being an unpaid governess to Sir Bradley's children might, after all, be preferable to marrying such a man.

Aunt Agatha made a low, rumbling noise in her throat and Clarissa straightened her shoulders. She owed it to her aunt to marry decently. Once she was married, she would be able to provide support for her aunt and some comfort in her old age. Her heart heavy, she bowed to the inevitable, but made one last desperate bid for independence. "I thank you for your consideration, Mr. Hemsby, and I assure you that I will be a proper and respectable wife." She shook the little garment out and raised it slightly so that Mr. Hemsby had to look at it. "I ask, however, that you would allow me to finish this dress. I have promised Lady Amelia that it will be done, and I do not like to break my promises."

Mr. Hemsby nodded, attempting to look gracious but succeeding only in looking like a bullfrog that had managed to secure the largest lily leaf in the pond. "Your resolve to keep promises is to be admired."

Taking advantage of his magnanimous mood, Clarissa added, "The duchess has invited my aunt and me to a dinner party on Thursday. She would like to thank all the people who help with Mary's Haven."

Mr. Hemsby tugged at his stiffly starched collar. "It seems that your aunt has accepted the invitation and it is always difficult to extricate oneself from a confirmed invitation." He swallowed as if the next words were distasteful. "Furthermore, I am interested in some of the business ventures that the duke and marquess have established and it would be inadvisable to let them believe that I do not want to continue the association."

Clarissa smiled. But Mr. Hemsby added a caution that sounded the death knell to Clarissa's hope of an evening of happiness. "It is as well to inform you, Miss Blakeney, that once I decide to marry you, you will not spend much time gadding about to endless entertainments. I am content to remain beside my own hearth. Do not forget when you are among people of a rank far superior to yours that your behavior is a reflection of my good name. I expect you to behave with appropriate decorum and respectability. As I said earlier, any hint of inappropriate behavior would be sufficient to force me to change my mind."

CHAPTER 6

*C*larissa followed the dignified butler up the grand stairs to the main drawing room of Montgomery House, the Duke of Broadwell's London residence. As they passed a mirror on the landing, she checked surreptitiously that her white muslin dress had no creases, that every strand of her sleek blonde hair was in place and that her simple pearl pendant had not moved from its position in the center of the velvet ribbon choker around her neck. Satisfied that she presented the picture of a perfect young lady, she brought her roiling emotions under careful control.

She took a deep breath as the butler, Carter, opened the drawing room door. Lord Donnington was most probably already in the room, and she was determined that she would not betray her feelings for him by one look or one gesture. Her betrothal to Mr. Hemsby would be settled shortly and she would have to forget that she had ever found the viscount attractive.

The door opened and light and laughter spilled out into the corridor. Clarissa shot a startled glance at her aunt, but her eyes conveyed her longing to join the animated chatter and unguarded enjoyment of guests who clearly found pleasure in each other's company.

Aunt Agatha's lips straightened into a primmer line than usual. "It is all very well for these people to relax the social conventions, but you must not forget your assurances to Mr. Hemsby. You cannot afford to earn his displeasure," she hissed under her breath.

Clarissa nodded, but a tight hand seemed to be squeezing her heart. She stepped into the elegant but comfortable drawing room, her eyes scanning the little groups of people for a sign of Lord Anthony. He was not here. Despair weighed her down and her feet dragged as she took a few steps into the room.

A few feet from her, three gentleman and two ladies were ensconced in comfortable chairs, leaning against the cushions as if they were in their private boudoirs rather than at a formal dinner. One of the ladies, dressed in an elegant gown of deep green silk, was eagerly explaining how she admired Turner's *The Shipwreck*, and the gentlemen listened to her opinions with deep interest. Clarissa took half a step forward, eager to share her views on the painting, but a sudden memory of Mr. Hemsby's supercilious eyes brought her to a halt. She could not jeopardize her only chance of marriage by earning his disapproval. Even though he was not one of the guests, any minor transgression was sure to be reported to him. She did not want to add fuel to the fire of the gossip that still raged about her incident in Oxford Street.

A burst of laughter in the middle of the room distracted her. The duke, surrounded by three or four guests, was holding court. Clarissa's eyes widened, aghast as his arms encircled Lady Amelia, who was leaning against him, in a tight embrace, her hands resting on his chest. Clarissa's mouth dropped open when the duke tilted his wife's face up and kissed her on the lips.

She felt a blush steal over her cheeks at this blatant display of affection. She knew she should turn away from such an intimate demonstration, but the tender way the duke looked at his wife and the affectionate warmth on her face kept Clarissa transfixed. She felt so awkward that when Aunt Agatha murmured, "Disgraceful!" she found herself agreeing, and yet a twinge of envy shot through her. She could not imagine Mr. Hemsby treating her with such affection, even in private.

The image of Mr. Hemsby's strongly disapproving face was displaced by a wayward thought. She shivered as she wondered what it would be like to have Lord Anthony's arms clasp her so possessively to his side, to feel the brush of his lips against hers, to see such tenderness in his eyes as he looked at her.

She quashed this thought with another shudder, but this time of desire inspired by the image of the viscount's deep auburn hair and broad shoulders. Again, she surveyed the room, hoping to see a glimpse of him. She silently scolded herself at the wave of disappointment that washed over her when she could not see him.

Clarissa straightened her shoulders. It was not for nothing that she was known as the paragon. She knew how to conduct herself in social gatherings. With her chin tilted upwards, she drew on all her training and experience and headed towards the center of the room to greet her hostess. But her stomach had tightened into a hard ball and her fingers were clenched tightly at her sides. She wanted to clutch at her aunt's hand like a little girl meeting company for the first time, but Aunt Agatha had joined a group of elder ladies and was politely exchanging greetings with Lady Danforth.

Clarissa's uneasy progress was halted by the sudden flurry of soft green silk and the clasp of the duchess's hand. Her sweet voice sang out, "Here you are at last! Welcome to my home, Miss Blakeney. I am so glad that you could come!"

The duchess was new in London society, and Clarissa had only met her two or three times, although she had often seen her at the opera and fashionable balls. They had spoken only once, after a meeting at Lady Watford's house to discuss how best they could support the women and children at Mary's Haven. The duchess had led the meeting with grace and dignity and Clarissa had thought her to be the perfect picture of respectable dignity. Lady Amelia's current insouciance was bewildering.

Clarissa smiled shyly at the exuberant duchess and allowed that irrepressible young lady to take her hand and lead her across the room. Lady Amelia weaved her way through her guests, laughing apologies when she bumped into anyone and calling greetings to people they passed. With a very charming grin, she enlightened Clarissa, "You must excuse my enthusiasm. I have not been a duchess for very long and because my dear duke is a bit older than I am, I do not have many close acquaintances of my own age. I make a point of cultivating people who can be my friends."

Lady Amelia stopped speaking only when she reached the comfortable chair where Lady Charlotte was reclining. She let go of Clarissa's hand and dropped down onto the arm rest, flinging her arm around Charlotte in a tight hug. "My dear Charly, what exciting news! My little Bastian will be thrilled to have a playmate almost his own age." She picked up a cushion, plumped it and placed it behind Charlotte's back. "Are you sitting comfortably? I remember how badly my back hurt when I was carrying Sebastian."

Lady Amelia seemed to have forgotten all about Clarissa as she fussed over Lady Charlotte. A sharp dart of jealousy lodged itself in Clarissa's heart. Clutching the soft white muslin of her dress in tight fists, she fought to bring her unexpected ire under control. Straightening her shoulders, she reminded herself that she had to keep her emotions and views hidden behind the thick varnish of societal gloss that she had applied so carefully over the years. Her arrangement with Mr. Hemsby meant she would never experience the kind of agreeable friendship shared by Amelia and Charlotte.

The marchioness settled back against the cushion Amelia had tucked behind her with a cheerful giggle that drew Clarissa's attention to Charlotte's response. "I am very well. Theo is treating me as if no other women in the world have ever had a baby. He decided that this was the most comfortable chair in the room and he made Lady Sherbonne move so I could sit here." Her nose wrinkled as she added, "The only real discomfort I have found so far with being pregnant is that some foods make me queasy."

Shocked, Clarissa forgot her carefully learned politeness as she exclaimed, "Ladies should not mention such things!"

The warm enthusiasm of the young duchess transformed into an icy dignity as she sat up straight and looked at Clarissa. "I do apologize for having offended you, Miss Blakeney. I had forgotten that some society ladies might find it distasteful to hear about such a natural and joyous event as the procreation of children."

The words stung, and Clarissa flinched even though her innate honesty made her acknowledge at least to herself that she had sounded priggish. She bit her lip, trying to think of how best to salvage the situation, to let the duchess know that she loved babies and was happy for Lady Charlotte. In the silence that fell after Lady Amelia's comment, Clarissa could hear Aunt Agatha on the other side of the room, telling Lady Watford why Mr. Hemsby would make an ideal husband for Clarissa. She winced.

Amelia and Charlotte had been watching her closely, and at this reaction, their offended expressions softened. They exchanged a glance, sharing their sympathy and understanding.

Lady Charlotte leaned forward, touching Clarissa's hand. Earnestness and compassion colored her words. "I am very excited about my baby, who was created because of the love that my husband and I share. I am not going to let society force me to behave as if having a child is a disgraceful secret that I need to be ashamed of." She ended with a comment so softly spoken

Clarissa almost missed what she said. "I almost ruined my life because of false shame, and I have learned to value love and pleasure."

Clarissa blinked rapidly, trying to bring order to her disordered thoughts. Her own compassion was roused by the wistfulness in Charlotte's voice, but the sound of her aunt's voice prevented her from letting down her guard.

Lady Amelia, in an attempt to assuage Clarissa's confusion, shifted the topic slightly. The ice in her voice thawed but had not completely melted. "Miss Blakeney, I would like to thank you for the very beautiful baby garments that you have made for Mary's Haven. I wish you could see the delight and pleasure your garments bring to women who have been victims of the hypocrisy in society. The care you have taken to make the dresses so pretty, gives them hope of a better future."

The gentle reprimand in Amelia's words made Clarissa's eyes tighten with unshed tears. She gave a watery smile and was just about to say how much pleasure it had been to sew the tiny dresses when the low sound of a throat being cleared made her look up. Her aunt had moved closer to where the young ladies were talking, and when Clarissa looked at her, her eyebrow shot up so high, it almost vanished beneath her neatly coiffed hair in a silent reprimand. Clarissa's well-intentioned words fled behind a veneer of polite manners, even while her fingers twisted into knots. She parroted words she had heard spoken by Lady Carson. "It is not necessary to thank me, Lady Amelia, for simply doing my duty. Those of us who lead respectable lives need to set an example of decency for those who do not know better and whose behavior is morally questionable."

Amelia's thoughtful expression slid behind a mask of aloofness, but a flicker of hurt in Charlotte's eyes pierced Clarissa's heart. Her cheeks flushed and she wanted to recall her words, but they hung in the air, forming a barrier between Clarissa and the two women who could never be her friends. Mr. Hemsby had made sure of that.

Lady Amelia frowned and Lady Charlotte looked ready to argue, but she sank back again as Lady Amelia gave her a slight shake of her head. "I trust you will have a good evening, Miss Blakeney," she said smoothly, just as Carter announced that dinner was served.

CHAPTER 7

*V*iscount Donnington strode into the drawing room of Montgomery House just as Carter, the butler, announced in ringing tones that dinner was served. The babble of chatter and laughter subsided and guests began to throng towards the door, impeding Lord Anthony's progress. He swore softly as he searched the throng for his paragon, his muse. With a nod, he greeted the Earl of Sherbonne and Baron Loxley, who were putting a book of drawings they had been examining back on a low table, but he did not stop to talk to them.

The Viscount dodged the dowager countess, Lady Sherbonne, as she swept past on the arm of Lord Watford. Lord Anthony swore again and rubbed the fleck of paint that spotted his otherwise pristine gloves. He was not usually late, but his day had been beset by a series of problems. His father's widow. Lucretia, had sent another string of letters, complaining about the will and making all kinds of ludicrous suggestions about her future. Lord Anthony had spent the best part of the day with his solicitor, trying to find solutions to her unreasonable demands. To make matters worse, his steward had sent letters about problems on his estates. It might become necessary for him to return to Dorset to see what could be done.

By the time his solicitor had left, the viscount was so irritated that the only solace could be found in painting. In his studio, he had forgotten his troubles as he became absorbed in the girl on his canvas inspired by the Greek statue. Even now, as he tried to hide the fleck of paint, his eyes lit with delight. The girl in the painting might have the body of the Greek statue, but her face was Clarissa's. The tantalizing glimpses he had caught of shapely ankles, rounded buttocks and firm breasts fueled his dreams. As the picture of the girl on his canvas became more and more life-like, he had contemplated what his muse looked like beneath her sedate clothing. His cock had pulsed with anticipation of seeing her naked body gorgeously displayed for him to admire. Eventually, the ache had been so insistent that he had tossed his brush down, unbuttoned his breeches and taken hold of the hard, throbbing organ. Slowly, his hands had run up and down the length of his hard cock, while he pictured Clarissa's wide blue eyes and soft, luscious lips. Using the juices that flowed copiously from his dick, he had rubbed harder and faster, imagining the heat of Clarissa's pussy gripping him tightly in her silky grasp. He had spilled all over his hand, down his legs and onto the floor of his studio, thankful that none of his sperm had spattered onto his canvas.

But now he was late for Lady Amelia's dinner party. And he could not find the living, breathing woman he was falling in love with.

A tender smile softened his eyes when he caught sight of golden hair glowing under the light from the candelabra near the window. He paused, heedless of the maelstrom of guests who milled around him, transfixed as always by the loveliness of Clarissa. He was so caught up in admiring the perfect form of her face and the graceful way her dress emphasized her alluring figure that, at first, he did not realize that something was wrong. Little by little, he noticed her hands clenched into tightly balled fists, the stiffness of her shoulders, the defiant tilt of her chin.

He frowned as Amelia rose to her feet and nodded her head with the kind of dignity so often seen in the duke himself. Charlotte was gripping the arms of the chair. He had to find out what had caused such tension. He swore lightly under his breath, cursing his tardiness. He should have been here to act as a buffer, a shield, between Clarissa and the bewildering behavior of the duke's guests, who, out of the public eye, let down their guard and disregarded the safe and staid manners of polite society.

He pushed past the duke, who raised an eyebrow but said nothing, his dark eyes taking in the details of the little scene.

Lord Anthony arrived at Clarissa's side just as Theo was helping Charlotte to her feet. His friend was bending low over his wife, whispering words that Anthony could not hear, but Charlotte flashed a look that combined both annoyance and sympathy at Clarissa and then smiled as her husband placed a kiss on her forehead.

The viscount bowed in greeting to Clarissa. A warm thrill of satisfaction flashed through him as relief flooded her eyes. Every protective instinct in him rose to the surface, and he wanted to enfold her in his arms, to shelter her in his embrace and whisper words of comfort to her, but he would have to win her slowly. She was like a nervous filly that needed to be coaxed and encouraged to try new paths, but once she had the confidence to let her true nature shine through the layers of social convention she had so assiduously built up over the years, she would be powerful, strong and poised. She would be a woman who would delight him forever.

With a smile, he offered her his arm. "You are looking remarkably well this evening, Miss Blakeney. It would be my honor to escort you in to dinner."

Clarissa's hand tightened on his arm, and he placed his large hand over hers. He could feel the slight tremble in her body as she murmured, "Thank you, my lord."

As they tagged on to the end of the line of guests, Anthony carefully, gently, sought to understand what had caused the tension that kept Clarissa's chin firmly tilted and her eyes gazing unseeingly ahead of her. "Is your head still hurting? Do you need a cordial?" She gave one quick shake of her head but said nothing. He pursued his questioning. "I am glad that you are well enough to be here this evening. I believe you will find Amelia and Charlotte delightful friends and very similar to you in many ways."

Clarissa winced, but she caught her lip between her teeth and did not answer. Anthony gently rubbed his thumb along her arm, soothing her agitation and offering his understanding of her predicament. She sighed.

They reached the dining room, and Lord Anthony led her to a vacant seat near where his friends were sorting themselves. He held out her chair for her, and she sat down primly, hardly even aware of the people around her. As she shook out her napkin and placed it on her lap, he rested his hand on her shoulder.

She stiffened and then relaxed. She bent her head to adjust her napkin and whispered so quietly that Lord Anthony had difficulty hearing her. "I do not believe that a friendship between those ladies and me is possible. There are many obstacles that prevent such an acquaintance."

Anthony squeezed her shoulder before taking his own seat. He leaned closer to her and murmured, "Many things are possible that seem unlikely at first. Don't despair, only be true to yourself and all will be well. If you allow me to guide you, I will help you find the strength and courage to accept all the pleasures that life has in store for you."

~

CLARISSA SMOOTHED her napkin over her lap, trying to ignore the sensations the viscount's strong, firm hand on her shoulder sent ricocheting through her body. She stared at the neatly laid out, beautifully embossed silver cutlery in front of her and tried to remember that she should no longer indulge in her wild dreams about the viscount.

Lord Anthony pulled out his own chair and sat down, grinning when his friends teased him about being late. Clarissa sighed at this further evidence of Lord Anthony's good nature and general bonhomie. She gave a quick shake of her head. It was all very well for the viscount to suggest she should abandon all that she had been taught and simply follow her heart, but the specter of Mr. Hemsby loomed over her every word, her every action. Like the statue of the Greek girl, she would be forever frozen between her desires and reality.

Clarissa's dismal thoughts were interrupted by Lord Anthony's large, warm hand resting on her back, his fingers brushing against the soft skin at the nape of her neck. She shivered. His touch was soothing, and a warm glow of satisfaction unfurled in her heart. Although the viscount was engaged in a conversation with the Earl of Sherbonne about a horse they had seen at Tattersall's that morning, he was aware of her disquiet, of her need for comfort.

Loxley asked Sherbonne whether he was going to buy the horse, and Lord Anthony took the opportunity to ask Clarissa, "Are you all right, little rose?"

Her eyes were strangely blurred and she blinked a few times before saying, "Lady Amelia has been very kind. Everything is beautifully arranged." She stared straight ahead at the attractive arrangement of flowers in the middle of the table, not really noticing how perfect the dark red and pink roses looked against the soft green ferns.

A glimmer of laughter flickered in Lord Anthony's eyes. His fingers tightened on her neck and his thumb moved in insistent circles. The warmth of his hand seeped into her, melting the tension. She unclenched her fingers that had been tightly curled in her lap.

The viscount's voice wrapped around her like sunshine on a spring morning. "Lady Amelia has learned to be a very good hostess. She delights in making things pretty and has a good eye for color. That is one thing you have in common with her."

Clarissa tried to bring her rioting emotions under control. Lord Anthony's compliments unsettled her. With relief, she accepted a serving of cream of artichoke soup from a footman, not sure how to respond to Lord Anthony, whose hand still clasped her neck and whose eyes still observed every emotion that flickered across her face.

She dragged her spoon through the pale green, aromatic soup in front of her and whispered so softly that Lord Anthony had to lean very close to hear. "I believe that it takes more than a similar taste in décor to become friends, and I do not think that Lady Amelia finds me suitable."

Lord Anthony's finger pressed more deeply into the flesh of her neck, and she gasped at the pressure. The sense of belonging to the viscount, even for a few seconds, was more deeply satisfying than any thought of being Mr. Hemsby's wife. She swallowed. She had to tell Lord Anthony the truth of her situation, and then she would lose forever the little moments of joy that she had gathered over the years like precious pearls.

"Besides," her dilemma came out in a rush, "Mr. Hemsby has asked for my aunt's permission to court me. He is only waiting for the scandal of my tumble in Oxford Street to die down and then he will speak to my cousin and announce our betrothal." Her voice was brittle as she tried to control her emotions. "He has made it clear that it would not be suitable for his wife to count herself as the friend of a duchess or to continue helping with Mary's Haven."

Lord Anthony swore under his breath, muttering something

that sounded like *insufferable prig*, but he abruptly removed his hand from her neck. Clarissa felt bereft, as if a winter storm had blown away the warmth of a summer's day. The corners of his mouth tightened and he sipped his wine slowly, still watching her closely. She took a spoonful of soup, hardly tasting it, and tried to compose herself.

After a few moments, the viscount commented drily, "You do not, if I may be so bold as to say so, Miss Blakeney, have the elated appearance of a young lady about to marry the man she loves."

Clarissa flushed a deep, rosy pink. The viscount's voice sent tendrils of pleasure coursing through her body, but his uncanny ability to see beneath her carefully constructed façade, to understand the impulses of her heart, was unnerving. Never, had anyone observed her as keenly, as closely as the viscount did or understood her so well. She steeled herself to resist his effect on her. She could not let him know that she did not want to marry Mr. Hemsby, that the circumstances of her life had forced her into a place where pleasure was a luxury that she could not allow herself to have. Never could the viscount know that when she closed her eyes at night, it was his face she saw, his voice she heard, his touch she felt.

She braced her shoulders, burying the tattered rags of her dreams beneath her studied politeness. "Mr. Hemsby is a creditable gentleman, well-respected in society and able to provide well for his family. Any sensible lady would feel honored to receive an offer of marriage from him." She could not avoid the hitch in her voice as she answered.

A sound of disgust rumbled in the viscount's throat. He could not understand why Clarissa would want to marry Mr. Hemsby. The viscount knew women, knew how to tell if they were genuinely attracted to him, or if they were interested only in his status and wealth. And even now, Clarissa's face had the faint pink flush of pleasure that indicated her desire for him. Her lips were parted and slightly moist and her eyes gleamed with desire. Clarissa might deny that she was attracted to him, but her body told a different story.

A sharp arrow of jealousy pierced his heart at the thought of his sweet, perfect Clarissa giving herself to Mr. Hemsby in the marriage bed. He had to rescue her. She would suffocate under the insufferable respectability of Mr. Hemsby's self-importance.

He had not missed the catch in her voice when she spoke about her imminent betrothal. She did not love Mr. Hemsby and the betrothal was not final. Between two sips of wine, Lord Anthony's desire to win and woo Clarissa for himself settled into determination. He had given Clarissa too much space, too much time, and he had almost lost her, but it was not too late. His paragon deserved a man who would value her, appreciate her, love her.

He swallowed a spoonful of soup, hardly tasting it, and responded smoothly, "Indeed, Mr. Hemsby is the very image of solid decency and respectability." He only just managed to control the contempt in his voice. "But he is not likely to bring much joy to his wife." His voice softened as he cajoled, "Little one, is your happiness not important?"

Clarissa's fingers tightened around the stem of her glass until her knuckles were white. She spoke quietly, "A lady in my position, with almost no dowry and no real connection in the world, must accept whatever opportunity presents itself to her. To be the mistress of my own home must be sufficient compensation for marriage to Mr. Hemsby."

The viscount noticed the tightness around her eyes and the tiny quiver at the corner of her mouth. A flash of anger surged through him as he thought of how all of Clarissa's gentle beauty and slowly emerging passion would be snuffed out, suffocated by the weight of Mr. Hemsby's solid respectability. His every impulse to protect and nurture her rose to the surface. "It is not necessary to settle when there are other options available to you," he hinted.

Clarissa flushed, but she stared at the bowl of soup in front of her, rather than looking at the viscount. Lord Anthony placed his empty glass on the table and Carter immediately filled it with more of the duke's excellent burgundy. He brought it to his mouth, but thought better of swallowing its contents in one gulp. He swirled the ruby red liquid, releasing its rich fragrance and admiring the deep burgundy color gleaming in the light of the candles.

Clarissa watched him, a slightly puzzled look on her face when he began to speak. "This is a lovely wine, bringing pleasure to all the senses. It would be such a pity if it remained in a dark cellar where nobody could ever enjoy it, where it would do no good because it was simply stashed away and never given the chance to fulfill its purpose."

Clarissa nodded. "It is an excellent wine," she agreed.

The viscount smiled at her. "I see I need to explain my analogy more clearly. There is so much beauty, so much loveliness in the world that people miss out on because they are frightened of how it will change their lives. They fear the freedom of pleasure." He swallowed a mouthful and then took Clarissa's chin in his strong, supple fingers, turning her to look at him. "Little one, you are like this wine, with so much depth, so many nuances to be enjoyed and savored, and it would be a great pity if all that loveliness remained bottled up for the rest of your life. Marriage should be a partnership, a place where a man and a woman together fulfill their potential and find true happiness."

Clarissa was breathing deeply, clearly affected by his words and his touch. Her big blue eyes were wide and he could discern each shift in emotion, from fear to eagerness, anticipation to regret. With each breath, the swell of her breasts rose and fell as she battled to control her agitation. Lord Anthony watched, mesmerized. He wondered if it would ever be possible to paint the soft creaminess of her skin, the tempting curves of her figure hidden under the pure white of her dress and the sheer loveliness of her face. It took all his self-control not to trail his fingers along the silky smoothness of her cleavage and watch how she fought to keep still while he examined every gorgeous inch of her. Her nipples would harden into tight peaks under that virginal dress, and then he would slowly, deftly, unfasten the tight buttons and set her free.

His cock swelled and lengthened at the images of her naked body exposed to his pleasure, and he held back a groan as his breeches suddenly felt too tight. He could feel the buttons dig into the turgid flesh of his swollen manhood. He shifted, trying to ease the ache, but enjoying the pleasure of it at the same time.

Clarissa, unaware of the private battle for control that assailed Lord Anthony, primly answered his question. There was a polite smile on her lips, but her eyes were sad and wistful. "What you describe is the kind of marriage propagated in fairy tales and romance novels. It does not exist in real life. Marriage is a convenient transaction in which a man and woman come together to ensure the stability of society."

Lord Anthony could not let such blasphemy go unchallenged. He leaned towards her, his eyes darkening to the intense green of a forest before a storm. He was vaguely aware that Loxley and Sherbonne had stopped talking about the most recent of Beethoven's symphonies with Theo. All three of his friends leaned forward, waiting to hear how he would answer Clarissa.

The viscount took a deep breath. "I am sorry that you have not had the opportunity to see the beauty, the joy, the pleasure of a marriage in which two souls unite in harmony." His voice became husky with remembered emotion. "My parents loved each other, and when I marry, I will strive for the same depth of passion that they shared."

Clarissa's eyes softened at the vulnerability in Lord Anthony's tone. She was startled into sharing her own experience. "My parents loved each other deeply, too. I remember how happy they were, but I also know how... difficult it was for them."

Lord Anthony took her hand in his, clasping it tightly, and ran his thumb over her wrist in soothing circles. She stared at a fixed point in front of her, but Donnington was gratified that she did not try to remove her hand.

For now, the glint of tears in her eyes called to his need to reassure her. "It is a pity that society condemns emotions as vulgar and uncontrolled and does not admire the beauty found in love. That kind of attitude, I think, often causes more harm than the good that embracing pleasure brings about."

With a low cry, Clarissa pulled her hand away from the viscount's grasp and murmured, "No, please, no. It isn't right." And then, so quietly Anthony hardly heard it, she whispered, "Mr. Hemsby." The panic that flared in her eyes made her look like a fawn startled by hunters.

The viscount fisted his hands, stilling the urge to take her in his arms. He had to lure her gently, introduce her slowly to the ideas that went against all she had been taught about the proper conduct of young ladies.

Baron Loxley, with a sympathetic glance at his friend, changed the subject. "Miss Blakeney, have you ever heard it said that pleasure is the greatest good?" he asked as he sipped his wine.

CLARISSA UNCLENCHED the tight fists that had formed in her lap. This dinner party was quite unlike any she had ever attended. She was torn between her impulsive desire to respond to the viscount's intriguing ideas and arousing touches and the chains of conventionality that kept her bound to society's expectations.

Confusion clouded her eyes. "That is a strange concept, Lord Adam. Pleasure and goodness are usually considered to be at odds with one another."

Viscount Donnington leaned back in his chair, content for the moment to let Adam take the lead in explaining their philosophy to Clarissa. Clarissa needed to be coaxed gently, not stormed like a citadel. Although the thought of storming her, capturing her, seeing her surrender to him, sent blood rushing to his groin. He slid his hand under the table and surreptitiously squeezed his aching cock, trying to focus on what Adam was saying.

"Society would have us believe that pleasure is not good and that goodness has little to do with pleasure." Clarissa nodded in agreement. The baron placed a slice of chicken on his plate and then continued. "But we see things differently. Perhaps an example would help. The baby clothes you make for the women at Mary's Haven do much good. The women who receive them have the pleasure of dressing their babies in pretty clothes, the assurance that there is still hope that life is beautiful. And I believe that you derive pleasure from creating something beautiful while doing good."

Clarissa leaned forward, confusion shading her voice. "Thank you, my lord, but I have done nothing more than my duty. It is the obligation of those in society who have the means and opportunity to alleviate the burdens of the less fortunate."

Charlotte had been thoughtfully following the conversation, drawing comfort from the way her husband ensured his hand was always resting somewhere on her body. She noticed how Clarissa dug her fingernails into her palms and how she blinked hard, as if she was trying to hold back tears. All the young marchioness's earlier irritation dissolved into sympathy. She leaned forward, eager to help Clarissa make sense of these new ideas. "Miss Blakeney, Clarissa," she smiled gently, "duty is such a dry, harsh word for something that brings such pleasure to others, that makes their lives beautiful. It is not a word I like. People always seem to think it is their duty to tell you something unpleasant." She giggled. "I have never heard anyone feel it their duty to tell me something good."

Lord Theo placed a kiss on his wife's forehead but addressed Clarissa, his voice carrying an edge of authority that made her shiver. "Charlotte is right. Far too often, when people feel a duty to do good works, there are so many strings attached, that the good they do becomes a moral burden that is often a very heavy one, for both the person who receives and the person who gives."

Lord Anthony noticed Clarissa's shiver and once again claimed her hand. This time she did not resist, and he gently rubbed her wrist with his thumb. He felt her tension ease under his ministrations and smiled when she leaned towards him, trusting him to support and protect her.

The footmen were setting out the next course and the conversation subsided. Lord Anthony leaned closer to her so that his mouth brushed close to her cheek. "You, my little one, have a soul that is above duty. You delight in all that is beautiful, like the flowers dancing in the breeze or the soaring music of the opera. I am sure that when you find the courage to follow your heart, you will understand why pleasure is the greatest good."

Clarissa looked at him, her eyes wide and her lips slightly parted. His artist's eye admired how the candlelight made her pale skin glow like the finest porcelain, and he yearned to capture her image as she was now, soft and vulnerable as she struggled to understand these new ideas. Every painting of her would be a masterpiece, a work of perfection.

Sherbonne, who had carved the roast chicken that had been placed on the table, winked as he placed a slice on Clarissa's plate. Casually, he remarked, "Have you ever heard the story of how Mary's Haven got its name?"

Clarissa delicately swallowed a piece of roast chicken before answering primly, "Mary's Haven is, I would think, named after the purest of women. Those unfortunate souls who seek shelter would draw inspiration from her to lead chaste lives."

Sherbonne's eyebrow shot right up at this. He ignored the low laughter that rippled around the table at Clarissa's response. "The Mary who found shelter there was a young serving girl who had been dismissed and found herself on the streets because she was the victim of a footman's lust."

Lady Charlotte added, "Mary has done very well since the night we took her in. She is now one of our senior housemaids at Oakdene, and her child is healthy and growing fast."

Clarissa forgot all propriety as she gaped at the marchioness. "You employ a woman who was... who had..." She stumbled to a halt, blushing deep red when she realized she could not complete her thought without referring to subjects that a young lady should not even know about, let alone mention.

Charlotte's eyes met Clarissa's, softening as understanding and sympathy warmed them. Clarissa's bewildered utterance reminded her of her own confusion when the duke had placed Mary into his own carriage and brought her here to Montgomery House. Her voice was low and earnest as she tried to explain to Clarissa. "Mary was not at fault for the dreadful circumstances that she found herself in. I believe society does women a grave injustice when it disparages them for situations over which they have little control." Charlotte's eyes held a plea for Clarissa to sympathize with women caught in the tangles of society's unrelenting morality. "If you were to meet some of these girls and hear their stories, I believe you would feel more than just obligation towards them. They are not wicked, and their children are not a disgrace. We want to give them opportunities that society denies them."

Clarissa listened to the marchioness, her eyes pensive, her

earlier defensiveness slipping away. As Lady Charlotte spoke, Clarissa heard the echo of the words that had haunted her childhood. She was a disgrace, born out of wedlock because of the wickedness of her mother's passion. She was on the verge of blurting out that she sympathized with Mary, understood the unjustness of society's condemnation of love, when Aunt Agatha's voice filtered down the table.

"Yes, Lady Watford, Clarissa is most fortunate to have attracted the attention of Mr. Hemsby. He is such a respectable gentleman. She will be preparing to be his wife and will, therefore, no longer be able to assist with Mary's Haven."

Clarissa gave a little cry, but then she sat up straight, once again pulling her hand from the viscount's grasp. If Mr. Hemsby knew that she was born out of wedlock, or that she had let Lord Anthony touch her so intimately, he would refuse to marry her and then she would be thrown on the cold mercy of her cousin. For the rest of the dinner, she retreated behind her façade of perfectly structured social manners, only speaking when asked a direct question and never once elaborating on her ideas.

The other guests engaged in lively, energetic conversation, even the ladies speaking freely and eagerly about politics, art and life in general. Not once did anyone insinuate that it was unladylike not simply to agree with what the men thought.

The longer she sat there, the more she dreaded her own future as the downtrodden wife of Mr. Hemsby. And her despair was increased by the careful attention the viscount paid to her. He served her portions of the best dishes at the table, carefully noting the ones she liked and those that were not to her liking. Each time he offered her a taste of some new dish, his hand brushed against her and every inch of her body felt alive with new sensations. She felt like a tinderbox, ready to ignite into bright flames. Her heart warred with her head and when Lady Amelia rose, signaling that the ladies should withdraw, leaving the men to their port and brandy, Clarissa fled swiftly. She paused only once to look back at the viscount. But even as she followed the other ladies, she could feel the weight of his gaze on her and longed to flee into his arms, to cast herself on his broad chest and forget all her problems in the safety of his embrace.

CHAPTER 8

*C*larissa idly flipped through the cards of invitation that had been delivered with the morning post. Her aunt was arranging a bunch of dahlias that had arrived with a stiffly worded card from Mr. Hemsby. She sighed. She had certainly not been short of partners at Lady Silverton's ball the night before, but her heart was heavy. Mr. Hemsby had ostentatiously danced with her twice, but she had felt no joy in being with him. She had also danced one brief cotillion with Lord Anthony and then he had disappeared. It was evident that his interest in her was waning. No matter how many times she skimmed through the cards and notes, there was nothing from the viscount.

She tossed them aside, not interested in answering the politely worded invitations to attend further balls and soirees or to join the gentlemen who believed she enhanced the beauty of their curricles when they paraded through Hyde Park during the fashionable hour. A small frown marred the smoothness of her face as she watched Aunt Agatha arrange the dahlias from Mr. Hemsby. She hated dahlias. They were too stiff and formal.

Aunt Agatha, oblivious to the rebellious thoughts rioting through her niece's mind, observed complacently, "Mr. Hemsby can always be relied upon to be respectable and discreet. These flowers convey just the right message of dignity and respect. We will need to have a little dinner party next week, I think, with Mr. Hemsby and his mother and one or two others as guests." She paused as she adjusted the position of a vivid yellow dahlia. "You must do all you can to encourage his attentions. Any little slip now could jeopardize your chances with him. I do hope that he will write to Sir Bradley very soon."

Clarissa's voice was tinged with irritation. "I don't care if he never writes to Sir Bradley at all. He does not care for me at all. He only wants to marry me because he likes people to know that he has succeeded in winning the hand of the 'elusive paragon', where all others have failed. What he doesn't realize is that there was never much competition to begin with. Gentlemen enjoy dancing with me, but my lack of dowry and connections prevents them from seeing me as a suitable wife." She could not keep the bitterness out of her voice.

"Clarissa, such peevish comments are not very genteel and are not appropriate for a young lady to utter, especially about a gentleman who is likely to be your husband," admonished her aunt. "As Mrs. Hemsby, you will have some standing in society. As an unpaid nursemaid to Sir Basil's children, you would not even be allowed to dine with the family, let alone attend any balls or the opera." She sniffed and rammed a stubborn dahlia into the vase.

Clarissa riffled through the pile of cards again. "I am sorry, Aunt. I know I should be satisfied, but I can't help hoping that there will be a little affection in my marriage."

There was a wistfulness in her voice that made Aunt Agatha put the flowers down and cross the room to where Clarissa was sitting. Her voice softened with a modicum of understanding, "Child, it is unfortunate that the circumstances of your life have made is necessary for you to marry Mr. Hemsby. But no good can possibly come from grieving over a gentleman who will never be your husband." She touched Clarissa's cheek. "The viscount has flirted with you, but he has never shown any real interest in courting you. When he marries, it will be his duty to choose a wife who has a large dowry and whose social position is equal to his own. It is better to accept the way the world works than to become bitter and go through life carrying a grievance for something over which you have no control."

Clarissa squeezed her aunt's hand, but she said nothing. There was nothing to say. Aunt Agatha returned to her flowers, shaking her head as Clarissa frowned down at the cards again. No matter how many times she skimmed through them, Lord Donnington's would not suddenly appear. She would have to draw cold comfort from her aunt's bleak words. Now that the viscount knew she was, to all intents and purposes, betrothed to Mr. Hemsby, it was only natural that his interest should shift to new flirtations and she would be forgotten.

She swallowed, trying to forget the sudden image that filled her memory of how Lord Anthony had smiled so sweetly as he led Lady Edith in a quadrille at the ball last night. She would need to get used to seeing him pay attention to other ladies, and to the woman he eventually married. But even as she resolved to better her jealousy, her heart felt heavy. Never again, would she have the pleasure of dancing with the viscount, of engaging in lively discussion about poetry and art. Never again, would he offer her the delicacies she most enjoyed from the supper table.

Her foolishness made one last feeble attempt to assert itself. Holding out a fragile sliver of hope, she ventured. "Aunty, are these all the cards?"

Aunt Agatha placed the vase containing Mr. Hemsby's dahlias on a side table. "Gracious, child, how many would you like? You have more than enough invitations to fill every evening, and Mr. Hemsby has arranged to accompany you to a lecture on the declining morals of modern society tomorrow afternoon. That should suffice."

Clarissa bristled. "Going to any lecture with Mr. Hemsby is not a pleasure, especially not one which will decry pleasure." She fidgeted with the cards in her lap. Her voice dropped, "I just wondered if I might have misplaced a card."

Aunt Agatha pursed her lips and a frown formed between her eyes. "I suppose you are unhappy that Viscount Donnington sent no card or flowers. You are acting like a debutante in her first season, not like a young lady on the verge of entering into a very proper marriage. Mr. Hemsby would be shocked to know how often you think of another man. Indeed, it is not proper or decent for a young lady to mope about any gentleman."

Clarissa swallowed hard, trying to dislodge the lump in her throat that seemed to be growing bigger. She blinked rapidly, keeping the tears at bay that had so inconveniently gathered in her eyes. She refused to respond to her aunt's reprimand, but her disappointment could not be assuaged. Her voice was brittle as she diverted her aunt's attention. "Mr. Hemsby mentioned that he might pay us a visit this morning."

Aunt Agatha sat down with a sigh. "That is good. I was concerned that he might let your unfortunate tumble in Oxford Street keep him away." There was a moment of silence as both ladies remembered how Lord Donnington had so competently, so agreeably, offered his assistance that day. Aunt Agatha continued, "You need to ensure that Mr. Hemsby knows that he will not be making a mistake by marrying you." She pulled out a piece of paper and quickly began writing a list. "It is not too soon to begin to discuss buying the wedding clothes you will need. I think Sir Basil can be convinced to give you an allowance to cover the costs once Mr. Hemsby has spoken to him."

Clarissa tightened her lips and gathered the offending cards into a pile which she dropped carelessly onto the table beside her. "I do not think I will need many new clothes. I doubt that I will attend many balls or dinners once I am Mrs. Hemsby."

Before Aunt Agatha could retort, Mrs. Bedford, the housekeeper, knocked lightly on the door and announced, "His lordship, the Viscount of Donnington."

Clarissa looked up, startled to see Lord Anthony's large frame filling the doorway, an exquisite bouquet of roses filling his arms. He bowed graciously to the two ladies. "Good day, Miss Blakeney, Miss Clarissa. I trust the morning finds you well?"

Aunt Agatha stood up, her eyes suddenly gleaming with approval and relief. She eyed the bouquet with great interest. "We are well, thank you, Your Lordship. Please sit down. Will you have a cup of tea with us?" Clarissa was too flustered by the unexpected appearance of the viscount to notice the hint of a smile that threatened to break out on her aunt's usually stern face.

"Tea would be very welcome, thank you," Lord Anthony accepted Aunt Agatha's invitation. Having fulfilled his duty to his hostess, he moved across the room to where Clarissa had frozen in position on the sofa. He held out his bouquet to her, his head tilted slightly to the left and a soft smile playing around his mouth. His green eyes, reminiscent of a forest in the fullness of summer, roamed over her tightly clenched hands, her stiff shoulders, and then they lingered on her wide blue eyes in which delight, vulnerability and eagerness chased one another.

His voice was as welcome as sunshine breaking through clouds after a storm. "Miss Blakeney, I wanted to bring you these roses." His lips curved up in a bright smile as she relaxed slightly and reached for the magnificent bouquet. His grin made him look like a schoolboy who had hit the winning run in the final cricket match of the season. "I chose each flower here especially for you."

Clarissa felt as if her whole body had melted like frost touched by the rising sun. "You picked the flowers yourself?"

"Indeed, I did. I could not leave such an important task to a servant. I had to make sure that every flower was perfect for you." He did not even glance at the other flowers Clarissa had received that morning, but his next words convinced her that he had seen every stem. "I have heard you say that you do not like dahlias because they are such stiff, formal flowers. You, my little one, are a perfect rose, lush and glorious."

Clarissa took the bouquet the viscount held out to her and buried her face in the fragrant mass, hiding her blush and inhaling their heady aroma. She murmured, "Thank you, Lord Donnington. They are very beautiful and smell so sweet." She examined the bouquet silently for a few moments, conscious that he was still far too near her for comfort or politeness and that his eyes had not moved from her face. Finally, she looked up at him, repeating, "You picked these for me?"

Lord Anthony was grinning broadly now. "I did." He held up his hands as evidence. Clarissa could see a faint red mark where a thorn had scratched him. His voice was light and eager. "I wanted every flower to speak to you." He touched one of the flowers, his sensitive artist's fingers stroking the petals gently. "These white ones reflect the purity of your soul, your innocence. I chose the different shades of pink to express how much I admire your sweet nature."

Clarissa touched the petal of a coral rose. The viscount had not said anything about that one, but she knew it conveyed desire. She caught her bottom lip between her teeth, uncertain of what to say.

Her aunt came to the rescue. "How very poetic of you, Lord Donnington. Give them to me, Clarissa, and I will arrange them for you. I believe they will look very pretty in your boudoir." Clarissa was puzzled by her aunt's smile and show of approval when she had just been discouraging Clarissa's interest in the viscount. Lines of bewilderment creased her forehead as Aunt Agatha took the roses with a smug nod.

Her aunt moved swiftly to the door, saying, "Clarissa, dear, why don't you show the viscount our garden?" She explained to

Lord Anthony, "It is only a little one, but our roses are commendable. I will arrange refreshments for when you come in from your walk."

Bewildered, Clarissa stared as her aunt swept out of the room carrying the roses. Lord Anthony took a step closer to her, and suddenly she realized that she was alone with him.

Swiftly, she rose from the sofa, ready to obey her aunt's instructions but also feeling the need to put some distance between herself and the viscount. She did not understand what had just happened but her whole world seemed to have tilted out of orbit. However, the viscount was standing so close that the aroma of sandalwood and bergamot overwhelmed her senses. She stumbled slightly, trying not to brush against him, but he reached out and steadied her, his hand circling her arm, securing her close to his side.

She fixed her gaze on his dark green waistcoat, tracing the embroidered gold decorations with her eyes. She did not want to look at him, but Lord Anthony had no intention of letting her avoid facing him. Still holding her arm, he placed the fingers of his other hand under her chin and tilted her head up so that she had to look into his eyes.

His eyes roamed over her face until she began to squirm. Finally, he spoke. "My little rose, I prefer you to look at me and not try to hide. You have hidden for too long, from society, from me, but mostly from yourself. It is time to begin to trust me so that you can find the courage to be yourself."

Clarissa took a deep breath, trying to calm the panic that flooded her. She did not know why the viscount had come to visit her or what he meant by his strange comments. Her heart was beating very fast and her hands felt clammy. A knot tightened in her stomach. But her body heated at his touch and she wanted to mold herself against his strong body.

Lord Anthony kept his eyes on her, and she knew that he was aware of every emotion that flashed across her face. Her uncertainty, her diffidence, her fears were clear to him, but so was the yearning to yield to his guidance. She caught her breath, suddenly realizing that his eyes reflected her desire.

She could only take a proper breath when he stepped back half a pace, held out his arm and said, "Come, little one, let's go and view your garden."

CHAPTER 9

The viscount's artist's soul recoiled at the prim symmetrical paths, precisely laid out flowerbeds and strictly trimmed hedges of the Blakeney's garden. Here, nature had been so severely regulated that all the joy of riotous colors and complementary shapes he loved in the wildness of untamed nature had been eradicated. He glanced at Clarissa. The garden explained much of her character. If she had been regulated and trimmed as much as this garden had, it was no wonder she struggled to follow her heart's desires.

He paused before a neat row of roses, all the same height, each color separated from the others as if blending them would be somehow improper, indecent. Clarissa had withdrawn behind her polite façade and had said very little since they had left the drawing room. She needed to be coaxed out from behind the walls of fear that surrounded her heart.

"These are beautiful roses," he began. He reached toward a deep red rose that had not fully opened and let his fingers trace its petals. "You might have noticed that there were no red ones in the bouquet I gave you," he added, the casual sound of his words not reflecting the depth of his desires, "but I believe that ultimately the red suits you best. When you are ready, I will shower you with the deep red roses of passion and pleasure."

Clarissa's face flushed almost as red as the rose. His words caressed her just as his fingers did the rose, and she could not suppress the desire to feel the touch of his fingers on her cheek, on her arm, on her swollen breasts. Even though the viscount was not looking at her, she felt desired, beautiful, passionate. She felt like a woman who could stir men's passions.

But his intensity also frightened her. She could almost feel the brittle armor of her perfectly constructed social demeanor shatter as he spoke. She clasped her arms around herself, in a vain attempt to keep her passionate desire for romance from spilling out.

Lord Anthony turned from the rose and looked at her in that way he had that seemed to know every nuance of her soul. Her voice was tight and high as she tried to ignore her response to him. "My aunt is particularly proud of her roses," she deflected.

The viscount stepped closer to her, shaking his head. "No, my little flower, you are not going to use that social tone on me. It is time for us both to admit our true feelings, to put aside social niceties and be honest with ourselves and each other."

Clarissa shivered. Lord Anthony stepped closer to her and the heat of his body made her heart beat faster. He caressed her cheek with a gentle sweep of the back of his finger down her face. The touch sent tendrils of pleasure right down into the deepest parts of her.

Clarissa ran her tongue over her dry lips and tried to focus, but her voice was very soft, so low that Lord Antony had to lean even closer to hear her. "Why? Wh-why are you so intent on unsettling me?"

Anthony chuckled, a low, warm sound that sent another shiver ricocheting through her body. His fingers continued to stroke her cheek and she found herself leaning into his touch with a little sigh.

Every pore of her skin was tingling with awareness of Lord Anthony. He was watching her in the same thoughtful way he had perused her face that day in the museum, but his gaze was even more focused, more intense. There was nowhere to hide from his penetrating eyes that pierced through her careful façade and laid bare the vagaries of her heart. She tried not to squirm as the heat of his body furled around her.

She gave a little jump when Lord Anthony covered her hand with his. Her hand felt so tiny, so delicate as he engulfed it in his warm, comforting clasp. His voice reflected the same strength and reassurance. The viscount's deep green eyes glinted with humor and compassion. "What's the matter, little rose?" he asked with a smile. "Do you not like to have your hand in mine?"

"I-I do. Like it. B-but I don't think I should."

He chuckled, brushing his fingers over her knuckles, and she shivered. "Why should you not?"

With a wild glance around the garden, she muttered, "Mr. Hemsby."

Lord Anthony's eyes hardened. "I suppose he must be dealt with if we are to make any progress."

In spite of her churning emotions, Clarissa couldn't help giggling at this. The viscount continued. "I blame myself for your hasty acceptance of his attentions."

The blue of Clarissa's eyes deepened at the unexpectedness of Lord Anthony's words. She was not used to men admitting they were at fault for anything, let alone something as absurd as her imminent betrothal to Mr. Hemsby.

She blinked and tried to turn her face away. "Look at me," he insisted, cupping her chin with his long, firm fingers, and tilting her head so that she had no choice but to follow his command. "It is so much easier to communicate when you do not hide those beautiful eyes." He smiled as those brilliant eyes widened with arousal and the beginning of trust.

Her skin was tight and breathing was something of an ordeal.

Her body felt hot and tingled in unmentionable places. She knew she should flee from the viscount, but her body involuntarily leaned closer to him.

The viscount's eyes were as dark as the leaves in a forest just before a storm. She shuddered. He continued inexorably. "I do not believe that I have mistaken your response to me. You find pleasure in my company. You desire my touch. And yet you have attached yourself to that absurd Mr. Hemsby." He watched her face silently for a moment before continuing. "If I am wrong and you tell me now that you do not like me, that you find me intolerable, unpleasant, undesirable, then I will walk away and never bother you again."

A little cry of dismay fell from Clarissa's lips at the thought of never being bothered by the viscount again. A smile lightened his eyes. "Just as I thought," he said. "So why is it that you have tried to keep me at a distance?"

Clarissa took a deep breath. She could not avoid the intensity of his gaze. "It is not that, my lord, only..." she petered out.

His eyes did not waver even when a large white cat prowled out from under a rose bush and curled itself around his legs. "Only..." he prompted.

"This, now, how you look at me." Her words had become as confused as her thoughts.

The viscount continued to look at her steadily, silently compelling her to explain herself more clearly. She tried to shift her gaze so that he could not see the very core of her being. A low rumble from his throat brought her eyes back to his face. "No one has ever watched me as closely, seen me so clearly." Her voice was little more than a whisper.

"I do indeed watch you closely," agreed Lord Anthony. "You are quite exquisite and I find much pleasure in looking at you."

Clarissa's face turned a soft pink. She could not break away from his gaze. "Th-thank you," she managed, and then rushed on. Again, she squirmed. Her voice was very low. "When you look at me, it feels as if you can see right through me, that you know my deepest desires and understand my secret thoughts."

The glint of humor had faded from his eyes. "I have only just begun to know you, my precious flower. It will take a lifetime to know you properly. You are like one of these roses; with every petal that unfurls, there is more to admire, more to understand."

The tip of her tongue moistened her lips. "But, y-you cannot."

A flicker of confusion clouded his eyes. "Because of Mr. Hemsby?" he asked.

She nodded. "Yes, no. Not really."

He raised an eyebrow. "Are you saying that you *do* want to marry Mr. Hemsby?"

She shook her head vigorously, almost managing to dislodge the tight grip of his fingers on her chin. "I c-can't. Marry."

"Little one, you need to explain more clearly. Who is it you cannot marry?"

"Y-you. I cannot marry you." The words rushed out.

The viscount took a step backwards. His forehead creased in a frown. "You do not want to marry me? You would prefer to become the wife of Mr. Hemsby?"

Again, she shook her head. "N-no. But you cannot marry me."

He stepped closer again and placed his arms around her shoulders, drawing her close to his firmly muscled chest. She struggled and then subsided against him. "I am used to making up my own mind about what I can and cannot do," he assured her. "Why should you think I cannot marry you?"

Clarissa was bewildered to feel tears bite at the back of her eyes at the viscount's words. She took a deep breath to hold them in place. "You have to marry someone who is equal to you. A lady with a title and a large dowry and good family connections."

Lord Anthony's clear laughter rang out across the little garden. Clarissa's face turned an indignant red. "I am pleased that I can give you such cause for amusement," she snapped.

His large hand splayed out across her back and his thumb moved in slow circles. "Oh, my sweet little one, you are such a perfect delight. What makes you think that I am making fun of you or that I care a fig for what society says?" His hand continued its comforting movements. "It is you I care for, you I love. Neither your family name nor your background is of any interest to me. It is enough that you are a gentleman's daughter and can hold your own in society." His voice was tinged with humor as he answered her final points. "And I am not in need of bolstering my fortune with my wife's dowry." He paused for a moment then dropped a kiss onto her glossy hair. "I have come to understand that when I follow my heart, it guides me to do what is best. And I want to marry you."

Clarissa raised her face to him, her eyes so wide they seemed to fill her face. "I-I am not sure I really understand. You like… love me?"

In answer, the viscount pulled her closer so that her breasts brushed up against the hardness of his chest. "Yes, I love you, and I like you," he affirmed. And then, without another word, he grasped her neck and bent closer. He kissed her.

Clarissa felt herself growing soft, melting like jelly left out in the sun at a picnic. The viscount's lips were soft but firm as they pressed against hers. At first his touch was light, sending shivers of pleasure down her spine, and then he moved against her mouth with such forcefulness that she yielded to his insistence and her mouth opened softly against his. She parted her lips, silently begging him to go further, to heighten the sensations that were already colliding in her body. Tingles and ripples ricocheted right through her, collecting in a pool of fire in her core.

His tongue traced the outline of her lips and she pushed against his hard body to find support. Her hands clung to his arms. Her knees were unsteady, weak, and if he did not hold her, she would collapse into a shuddering heap at his feet. She stopped thinking and surrendered to the pleasure of his mouth on hers.

A very long time later, he drew back and grinned at her. She was panting and her hair was tousled. But she didn't care. Shamelessly, she tilted her face towards him and the word "please" fell shamelessly from her lips.

Lord Anthony perused the face of his beloved. Her eyes were wide and glazed, her mouth swollen and pink and her cheeks flushed. Her softly spoken plea shattered the control he had left, and he responded. This time there was nothing tentative about his kiss. He claimed her with his lips, with his tongue. The taste of her was as addictive as opium and he needed more of her. His mouth moved over her cheek, along the line of her jaw, and when he reached the hollow below her ear, he nipped. She squealed but dug her fingers more deeply into his arms, urging him to continue. He lapped the skin along the side of her throat and then caught the lobe of her ear in his mouth and sucked, enjoying the low moans and sighs that she was making.

His hands roamed over her back, until he cupped her bottom, relishing the softness of her as he lifted her more securely into his embrace. Her hands let go of his arms and she wrapped them around his neck, nestling her face against the hollow below his shoulder.

After thoroughly exploring her mouth and placing kisses all over her face and neck, Anthony raised his head. His hands drew soothing circles over her back as he crooned soft words into her ear.

Clarissa had never been as happy as she was in that moment, as she rested her head against Lord Anthony's shoulder and relished the warmth of his hands on her back. Her body was limp with pleasure. She felt complete, whole, as she never had before. Her heart was overwhelmed with feelings she could not name but she expected might be akin to love. The viscount's declaration of love reverberated in her heart, radiating contentment. She could stay like this forever.

A sharp voice shattered her peace. "Miss Blakeney, your aunt said you would be here, but I did not expect to find you in such a compromising position." Mr. Hemsby was standing a few feet away, a look somewhere between horror and disgust on his face.

Clarissa scrambled out of Donnington's arms and hurriedly straightened her gown. Her throat hurt from the panic that arose. She could feel her face burning with shame as she tried to move away from the viscount, but although he let her tidy herself, he kept his hand on her back. It was both reassuring and a reminder of the indiscretion she had been caught in.

Her brain did not seem capable of forming sentences, but she was saved from having to respond to Mr. Hemsby's bristling indignation. Lord Donnington's voice was calm, pleased, triumphant. "Good day, Hemsby. You are just in time to be the first to congratulate us. Miss Blakeney is to be my wife."

Mr. Hemsby snorted. "I have been gravely mistaken in the character of Miss Blakeney. I had thought to do her a favor by offering a Little Miss Nobody the protection of my family name, but her recent conduct has been highly questionable. I would not tolerate such a wife. You are welcome to such a brazen hussy."

With that, he stalked back towards the house, leaving Clarissa on the verge of tears. She stepped farther away from the viscount. "Oh, what have I done? What will happen to me now?"

Anthony moved closer. His voice was hard although his eyes reflected his tender concern. "You are well rid of such a self-righteous prig. Dear little one, surely you know that I have admired and loved you for many months. You are perfect in every way." When she began to shake her head, he took hold of her shoulders. "I love your sweet, caring nature, your intelligence, your passion. You are everything I want in a wife."

"Y-you love me?" She burrowed her face against him, fearing

to look into his eyes that could see how her own longing mirrored his words.

"I do love you, little rose. When you surrender to my love, offer yourself wholly to me, you will bloom like the finest rose. When you surrender to me, promise to obey me, you will be the most exquisite woman in the world."

A cold hand gripped Clarissa's heart at these words. All her objections to being married rose to the surface. She stiffened. Her voice was clearer, harder. "Thank you, my lord, but I do not think I can accept your offer."

Although Lord Anthony was bewildered by her response, he said nothing, simply holding her close to him, giving her time to sort through her thoughts. When he felt her body soften against him, he spoke quietly. "What is it that you are afraid of?"

Her voice was muffled against his light woolen coat. "I just want the chance to be myself. I think it is unfair that ladies are expected to obey their husbands always and must always agree with their husbands in everything."

"That would truly be a dreadful way to live," he agreed. "Do you really believe that I would insist that you always agree with me?" Clarissa nodded. His voice was hard, almost cold as he continued. "I had not thought that you had such a low opinion of me."

Clarissa felt the blood rush to her face. She shuffled uneasily, her heart heavy because she did not want to disappoint Lord Anthony, because in spite of what her head was telling her, her heart wanted to surrender to him.

Tears pricked the back of her eyes. She clutched at the soft material of his coat. "B-but you said that I would need to let you control me."

A soft huff of laughter brushed over the top of her head. "It is a matter of semantics. You have seen Amelia and Charlotte with their husbands."

He waited for her to murmur, "Yes," before he continued. "Do you believe that they are forced to accept everything their husbands say?"

"N-no. I have heard them both disagree quite avidly with things the duke and the marquess have said."

"And how do Sebastian and Theo respond?"

Clarissa looked up at Lord Anthony. "They listen to their wives' points of view. But I don't understand how that relates to what you expect from a wife, that you want me to surrender all that I am to you, to obey you."

He cupped her face again and lingered over a kiss, showing with his body how eagerly he desired her, how much he admired her. When he brought the kiss to an end, he tilted her face so she could not avert her gaze from his. His eyes were filled with compassion, tenderness, care. Her breath caught in her throat.

His voice dropped even lower and there was a husky depth to the smooth honey of his words. "My lovely rose, you do surrender so beautifully to me, and when you do, you find the freedom to be more yourself. I will help you to become all that you are meant to be, a perfect wife for me."

CHAPTER 10

*C*larissa took a step backwards as Lady Charlotte brought the chestnut mare to a stop in front of Aunt Agatha's house. She took a deep breath, trying not to let her fear of the large beast show. Lord Theo, on an even bigger animal than Charlotte's, was leading a third horse. She gulped. That was the creature she was expected to ride!

Clarissa took a deep breath and wished she had not agreed to this outing. A quiet tea in her aunt's drawing room would have been more than adequate for spending time with her new friends, but Charlotte had insisted that the only way to enjoy the planning of a wedding was from the back of a horse. And so here Clarissa was, preparing to ride to Richmond with the marquess and marchioness of Oakdene. And her betrothed.

She tugged her seldom-used habit straight and ran the leather of her riding crop through her fingers. "Good day, my lord, my lady."

Charlotte slipped off her horse and came forward with a laugh. "No need to be so formal, dear Clarissa. We are going to be almost sisters, and so we should be allowed to call each other by our first names." Her smile disappeared for a moment and her voice was slightly hesitant, as if she was afraid Clarissa would reject her offer, so well-known for always obeying the rules of etiquette. "If that is all right with you?"

The marchioness's vulnerability, and a desire to allow her feelings more freedom, stirred empathy in Clarissa's heart and she swept aside protocol. After all, she had been caught in a compromising position with Lord Donnington and was now betrothed to him. A simple matter of names could not damage her reputation further. Besides, she liked the young marchioness and wanted to be friends with her. "Oh, I would be delighted if you did."

Charlotte's face lightened and she turned to her husband, who was still holding the third horse. "Then, Clarissa, I would like to introduce you to April's Maiden, one of the horses I keep in London."

Clarissa took a hesitant step backwards and Lord Theo, noticing her fear, assured her with his deep voice, "April's Maiden is the gentlest horse I have ever known. Come closer and let her greet you."

Clarissa stepped forward, finding some comfort knowing that Lord Theo could protect her from this large beast. Tentatively, she patted the horse's neck. Even through her gloves, she could feel the smoothness of the mare's glossy coat and her strokes became more confident. The horse bent her head towards Clarissa, clearly enjoying the attention. A small smile hovered on her mouth. She found herself cooing to the horse. "What a pretty lady!" Suddenly the horse huffed and nuzzled her shoulder. She laughed, reconciled to the ride.

"She is indeed a pretty lady," a new voice offered just behind her, a deep, rich voice like the hot chocolate she enjoyed at breakfast. Lord Donnington had arrived while she was making friends with the mare. She turned to greet him and blushed as she realized he was looking at her, not the horse.

She held her breath as the viscount's large, capable hands

settled on her waist and he tilted her face up. He placed a light, teasing kiss on her forehead.

"No, please not here. Anyone could see," she protested, even as her body heated and her skin tingled at his touch.

Lord Donnington touched her nose with his finger tip, an affectionate smile on his lips, but he stepped back. "It's all right, my little flower, I am not going to let any harm come to you from foolish gossip."

He lifted her into the saddle and the riding party set off, Clarissa beside her new friend, Charlotte, while the two gentlemen brought up the rear.

When they reached the more open roads near Richmond, Charlotte began to urge her own horse into a faster trot, but the marquess called out a sharp warning. Charlotte reined her horse in but wrinkled her forehead and turned to Clarissa. "It is so frustrating to have to walk Lady May so slowly. She wants to run as much as I do!"

Clarissa, who was still perched a little awkwardly in the saddle of her horse and was only just managing to control April's Maiden at a sedate walk, raised a questioning eyebrow. "I think we are going quite fast enough." She added apologetically, "I am not used to riding. My aunt and I spend most of our time in London and I have not been on horseback much since I left the schoolroom."

"Oh, I could not live without my horses!" exclaimed Charlotte. "The marquess keeps horses in town for me so that when he has to be in the city, I do not hanker too much for the country."

Clarissa glanced at the gentlemen as they passed the ladies, urging their own horses to a canter. "From all that I have seen, I would not have thought that the marquess would insist that you keep to a sedate lady's pace. Or that you would so readily obey such an injunction."

Charlotte laughed. "You are right, although there are interesting consequences if I do not listen to my husband." The young marchioness ignored Clarissa's questioning glance at the emphasis she placed on the word interesting. "He is usually very encouraging about my love for horses. We have had some very exhilarating gallops across the fields at Oakdene, and I have even beaten him once or twice when we race." Her hand rested lightly on her stomach for a moment. "But for the moment, it is necessary for me to be more sedate, more ladylike. He was simply reminding me that he does not want me or the baby to come to any harm." Her face lit up. "I like to be reminded about how much he cares for me."

With a sudden blush, Clarissa remembered the conversation Charlotte and Amelia had had at the duke's dinner party. Charlotte was expecting her first child. She wondered if she would ever be able to talk so freely, so easily, about her feelings for the viscount and about such intimate matters as passion and pleasure. She had not even told him that she loved him, even though he had said those words to her many times in the last few weeks.

Clarissa was not sure how to answer the marchioness and so just leaned forward to pat the neck of April's Maiden.

Charlotte watched the young lady who was soon to be Anthony's wife and decided she needed to try to help her overcome her reserve. It hadn't been all that long since she herself had faced similar qualms about the marquess and his world and she remembered vividly how shocked she had been.

She rode thoughtfully alongside Clarissa for a few minutes. Finally, with a deep breath, she explained, "Do you know, sometimes I provoke Theo to show me that he cares. It sounds silly, but we faced a few... difficulties when we first married and sometimes, I just need to be reassured of his love for me."

Clarissa turned puzzled eyes to Charlotte. "Really? The marquess looks at you with such open affection that it tends to make me feel uncomfortable," she admitted. "When I first began spending time with you, I envied the kind of love you share."

She blushed as she thought of the tender touches Lord Anthony lavished on her, and she shivered, once again conscious of how her restraint kept her from responding to him.

Charlotte simply giggled and urged Lady May to walk a little faster. The two ladies drew up beside the gentlemen who had stopped at the entrance to Richmond Park. Clarissa looked around her appreciatively. Large trees shaded a broad path through the park and birds sang as they never did in the middle of the city. She breathed in the peace of the countryside.

They entered the quiet park, and once again, the gentlemen broke into a canter, leaving the ladies to follow more sedately. Charlotte picked up the conversation from earlier, her eyes lingering on the handsome form of her husband on horseback. "I will tell you my story one day, but I thought today, I could help you understand the viscount a little more, just as Amelia once helped me to accept Theo's unusual ways."

Clarissa bristled and then relaxed, realizing that the marchioness was right. She did find it difficult to understand her betrothed. Her voice was so soft that Charlotte had to lean forward to hear her say, "None of the previous gentlemen of my acquaintance were as... forward as Lord Anthony is. It is not usually considered proper for a gentleman to touch a woman, even his wife, in public, except in the formality of dances or when they offer their arms as support." Her breath caught in her throat. "And yet, when he touches me, kisses me, I am ready to abandon all the rules I have ever known. He makes me feel things I never dreamed possible."

Charlotte smiled with understanding. "Pleasure is something that society does not understand, but it leads to good; it is good. Anthony will help you to experience the heights of pleasure if you surrender yourself to his guidance, as I have learned to do with my dear Theo." She glanced around at the beauty of the park. A deer and her fawn were just visible under the trees. "Oh, look how wonderful that is! Let's leave the horses here and see if we can get closer."

Clarissa was dubious. "Are we allowed to leave the set paths?"

Charlotte had already dismounted and was calling to her husband to look after the horses. She spun around to answer Clarissa. "As long as we do no harm, it is sometimes better to leave the well-worn paths."

Clarissa hesitantly followed Charlotte deeper into the woods. A small smile hovered on Charlotte's mouth. "That is a lesson that applies figuratively to so much in life if you want to experience the full joys the world has to offer."

Clarissa bit her lip. "My aunt believes the paths are there to guide us with the wisdom of our ancestors. She does not approve of leaving the tried and tested ways."

Charlotte placed her hand on Clarissa's arm as they wandered along the path. "Your aunt has brought you up well. Your meticulous concern for all that is right is a credit to her, and yet she so clearly approves of your betrothal to Anthony. I believe she wants your happiness more than you realize."

Clarissa thought back to the day the viscount had announced that he was going to marry her. She had been so bewildered by Lord Anthony's kiss and embarrassed when Mr. Hemsby had come upon them in the garden that the next few hours were a blur in her memory. Everything had happened so quickly that she was still reeling from the shock of being affianced to the viscount.

Lord Donnington had led her indoors and Aunt Agatha served him tea, almost cooing when the viscount asked for Clarissa's hand in marriage. Clarissa had been so overwhelmed that it wasn't until after dinner when she was heading upstairs that she thought to ask her aunt, "You are happy that the viscount has asked me to marry him, and yet just this morning you said I should forget all about him. What happened to change your mind so completely?"

Aunt Agatha patted her hand, a slight smile on her face. "Ladies are allowed to change their minds. My dear, I know that you do not really admire or respect Mr. Hemsby. To be honest, I also find him a bit dull."

As they entered Clarissa's bed chamber, she asked, "Why were you so insistent that I encourage him, then?"

She sat at her dressing table and removed the pins from her hair. Aunt Agatha picked up her hairbrush and began to brush out the long locks. She looked at her niece in the mirror. "I encouraged you to accept Mr. Hemsby's offer when I believed that Lord Donnington's intentions towards you were not serious. I am not too proud to admit that I was wrong."

Clarissa smiled but said nothing. Her aunt continued the vigorous brushing of her hair. "I am also aware that you have a strong personality and very decided opinions. You would soon lose respect for a man, especially your husband, if he was not as strong as or stronger than you are." She quirked an eyebrow. "I believe that Lord Donnington has the strength to manage your whims and foolishness." Her face broke into an unexpected smile. "Besides, any woman would be impressed by the romantic way he delivered his flowers to you."

Charlotte's soft exclamation brought her back to the present. "Oh, look, the fawn is coming towards us."

The two ladies moved towards the deer and her baby, but Clarissa stepped on a twig, which snapped. The noise startled the creatures and the deer fled silently farther into the woods, her baby following her. Charlotte laughed, but Clarissa was disappointed. She was not used to walking so quietly through the woods.

Charlotte was leaning against a grand old oak tree, her hand resting protectively on her stomach. "I do miss the countryside. If it were at all possible, I would never come to London." She spoke wistfully and then brightened a little, turning to Clarissa. "Sometimes, when I am surrounded by all this beauty, I wish I had spent more time learning to paint as well as the viscount does."

Clarissa, who had been scrambling through the under-growth, following in Charlotte's wake, the long skirts of her deep blue riding habit hitched up over her arm, came to a sudden halt. "Lord Anthony paints?"

Lord Anthony himself answered. "I do, my little love." He brandished a sketchbook in his right hand. "I am seldom without my sketchbook, and there are some who admire my paintings."

Charlotte slipped away, with a softly muttered, "Sorry," to Lord Donnington, leaving Clarissa alone under the trees with her betrothed.

Lord Anthony slid the sketchbook into one of the large pockets of his coat and stepped closer to Clarissa. She took a step backwards, suddenly nervous of this man she was betrothed to marry yet who was in so many ways a stranger to her. He matched her steps one by one until she was backed against the huge solid trunk of an ancient oak tree.

Lord Anthony grinned. He stepped so close to her that his coat brushed against her dress and she could feel the heat of his body. He placed one hand on each side of her head, caging her against the tree. Her breath was hard and fast, as if she had been running. Her eyes were wide and anxious, and yet her desire burned strongly in their blue depths.

"Still trying to flee, my little rose," remarked Lord Anthony, so mildly that Clarissa could be forgiven for thinking he had no real interest in her answer. Except that his eyes were focused on her with a force of passion she had never seen before.

She shook her head. "N-no, not exactly. It is -j-just that I am realizing how little I really know you."

Lord Anthony tilted her face upwards and looked steadily into her eyes. "You know me well enough to understand that I would never harm you, that I will do all in my power to protect you, that I will love you till the end of time."

Clarissa's eyes grew even wider. The viscount continued, a wry edge to his voice. "I do apologize, though, for not having told you about that I paint and sell some of my works."

Clarissa studied her husband-to-be's eyes. She was startled to see the vulnerability that hovered behind his confidence. Eager to assure him of her support for a hobby that was usually considered a pastime for ladies, she touched his jaw, saying, "I would like to see your paintings. You are so observant and appreciate beauty with such passion that I am sure they must be excellent."

Donnington studied her eyes silently and then said, "You have already seen some of my work. I noticed you admiring a picture of Broadwell Castle in the duke's drawing room."

Clarissa's mouth dropped open. "You did that? But I thought only working artists painted in oils. I thought gentlemen were above the kind of dirty work required for professional painting."

Donnington's face hardened and his green eyes darkened to the color of a pine forest at night. Even though he had not moved an inch, there suddenly seemed to be a wide chasm between them. Clarissa flushed a deep red.

"Is it a problem for you that I paint, that people buy my works? You would prefer a husband like Mr. Hemsby who has never dirtied his hands with any kind of grubby work?"

The heat of tears tightened Clarissa's eyes. She blinked rapidly. "I-I am sorry. I did not mean to offend you. I-it's just all so new and different."

Anthony's posture relaxed and he leaned a little towards her. "Painting is part of who I am. I am seldom more at peace than when I am bringing an image to life on my canvas." The lines around his mouth deepened, making his face look harsher. "There are those who believe a gentleman should not indulge even in idle sketching, but my painting is more than a hobby for me. It is part of who I am. I do not sell my paintings to earn a living, but I believe that people appreciate my art more when they pay to own it."

Clarissa's eyes could not grow any wider. They filled her face. Slowly, she ran her finger down the viscount's cheek. "It must be magnificent to have such a gift, to be able to bring beauty to life."

Donnington was silent for a few moments, wondering how Clarissa would respond when he told her about the kind of painting for which he was best known. He traced her face gently with his finger as if he were painting her. "I have found a new source of inspiration, a new muse, in you. Your beauty draws me, urges me, compels me to produce images I had not thought were possible."

Clarissa looked up at him, wonder and awe brightening her face. "Th-that is a compliment I did not expect. Would you let me see your studio?"

A smile flickered at the corner of his mouth. "You will. But before I take you there, I need to tell you a little more about the kinds of paintings I most enjoy creating."

She did not move her gaze from his face. Her fingers rested gently against his cheek. "Oh, do you think I am not able to understand art? I did admire the painting in the duke's house." Uncertainty, anxiety clouded her eyes.

Anthony brushed her face softly with his fingers, enjoying the slight tremble that rippled through her body and the faint pink flush of desire that colored her cheeks. "You have heard us talk about pleasure, about how pleasure is the ultimate good?"

Clarissa nodded, and when the viscount's finger outlined her chin and then swept down towards her décolletage, she bit her lip but leaned deeper into his touch. A slight frown creased his forehead. "At a later date, we will discuss why I like it better when you answer clearly and verbally. But for now, I want you to understand that my paintings convey my view of life." He dropped a kiss onto her forehead. "I am looking forward to painting you, my little love."

Clarissa frowned at him. "I am not sure how a painting of me could show pleasure and goodness."

A low chuckle rumbled in Anthony's chest and Clarissa shivered again. She tried to step away from the overpowering intensity of his presence, but the tree kept her firmly in place. His fingers continued to trace her, as if she was the canvas on which he would paint his pleasure. "I will find great pleasure in finding a thousand ways in which to capture every fleeting emotion that fills your eyes, of showing how the light changes the hue of your skin, And you will have the pleasure of letting me explore you, examine you, observe you until I know every part of you."

He continued to touch her as he spoke, and pleasure rippled through her body until she was overwhelmed by the sensations. She could hardly concentrate on the words Lord Anthony was saying. His hand followed the shape of her body, then hovered over her breast. She gave a startled cry when he cupped her breast in his hand and squeezed.

His other hand had been busy unfastening the buttons of her riding habit, and now he pushed it open. Beneath, she was wearing a tight corset that held her breasts firm and pushed them up, so that their creamy mounds were temptingly displayed for his pleasure. He bent down and with a long sweep of his tongue, savored the taste of her skin. With a half-strangled mewl, she tried to push him away, but he merely grabbed her wrists in his right hand and held her firmly in place while he continued to lap her breasts in long, firm sweeps of his tongue. Her breasts tightened and swelled. The nipples hardened into sharp little points that poked against the soft linen of her corset.

Lord Anthony held her steady against the tree trunk, concentrating on running his tongue in long sweeps over the exposed part of her breast. He caught her soft skin between his teeth and bit softly. She groaned. He moved to the swell of her other breast and repeated the same actions. She bit her lip, trying to silence the sounds that fell from her mouth, moans and squeals. All coherent thoughts vanished like clouds on a summer afternoon. All she knew were the sensations produced by the viscount, the firm press of his tongue, the pressure of his shoulder against hers, the brush of his hair along her skin and the heat that coursed through her veins. She could feel herself growing hot and wet between her legs.

Soon her squeals of protestation shifted to little cries of delight. Lord Anthony grinned. When he raised his head from her breast, the soft breeze brushed over the wetness and she shivered. He watched her response for a moment and then, still holding her hands tightly against her waist, said, "My little flower, this is only a tiny taste of the pleasure we will find together, and it is very good."

Clarissa wriggled and then, realizing she could not and, if she was truthful with herself, did not want to break free from the viscount's hold, stood still, her breasts proudly displayed for his pleasure. In a strange way, being held so firmly by him was empowering. She flushed a deep pink when he pressed against her and even through the fabric of her riding habit, she could feel the hard ridge of his manhood. A surge of pride and pleasure rushed through her and she smiled.

Lord Anthony had taken off his supple leather gloves and was caressing her with his bare fingers. She could feel the slight hardness of callouses from where he held his brushes and the gentle abrasiveness sent shivers through her. With one of his gloves, he began to slap her already too sensitive skin, just where her breasts rose above her tight corset. She could hardly breathe but arched her back so that her breasts were more easily available for him to play with.

While he continued to slap his glove rhythmically on the soft mounds of her breasts, he began to explain, "I strive to express this kind of pleasure in my paintings, which is why most of them are not available to public view. And when I paint you, all your loveliness will be caught forever on my canvases, and then I will always have you displayed for my enjoyment." He kissed her mouth with a possessive passion that left Clarissa with no doubt about his feelings for her. "And I will have you always ready and available for my pleasure, too."

Clarissa blushed. The viscount's words and actions suggested that the paintings he wanted her to pose for were not the sedate portraits usually seen in the public galleries of stately homes. She tried not to imagine just what the paintings would show. With a low groan, she leaned against him, partly to hide her face and partly to soak in his aura. Her body was both hot and cold and she snuggled closer to him, drawn by the powerful magnetism of his presence. She settled into his strong arms, holding on to his shirt, relishing the solidity of his strong torso, the comfort of his arms, the fragrance of citrus and greenwoods and something that was uniquely him that enveloped her.

CHAPTER 11

*I*t was some moments before Clarissa became aware of the viscount's voice, rumbling deep in his chest where her head still rested against him. "One day I will create a painting of you that will surpass anything I have ever done." The viscount reached into his pocket and took out his sketchbook. He flipped over a few pages and then handed the book to Clarissa, open to one of his drawings. "You have been my inspiration since I first saw you at the opera three years ago. And I already have pages and pages of drawings of you, some from when I have sketched you at balls or parties and others derived from my imagination."

Clarissa stared at the sketch in front of her. It was the body of the Greek girl, but it had become something so much more. It was her, surrounded by deep red roses in a garden. A figure of a man could be seen dimly in the background, and she was ready to flee from him, but was also half-turned to face him, to lure him, to will him to catch her. The expression on her face, her posture, reflected all the fears, all the uncertainty that she tried so hard to keep hidden. She bit her lip. "I... you... this... This... It's who I am... my whole being." Unexpected tears tugged at the back of her eyes. "No one has ever seen me so clearly." She closed the book quickly, trying to cover her nakedness of both body and soul.

The viscount's arms tightened around her. "It's all right, my little flower. You do not need to hide yourself from me. I will keep you safe. You can face your fears and pursue pleasure because I am here to protect you. I promise I will never let anything harm you." His fingers stroked her exposed skin. She trembled at his touch but it was not sufficient to distract her from her thoughts.

Tears trickled down Clarissa's cheeks. She knew that a lady should never display any emotions and yet Lord Donnington had a knack of uncovering the depths of her heart and soul. She tried to push him aside and wrap her arms around herself. He stepped back, allowing her some space to regain control of her dignity.

Pulling out his soft linen handkerchief, he wiped the tears from her face. "It's all right, my little rose. I like to see everything that you feel. Tears are not a disgrace."

Clarissa tried not to sniffle, but the word 'disgrace' pierced through her thoughts as if the sword of Damocles was about to fall on her head. "I... oh what have I done?" she cried out in distress, pushing against the immoveable mass of his body. "Oh, I will be disgraced and then no one will marry me because of my tarnished reputation."

Lord Anthony traced the path of tears down her cheek. "Foolish little flower. Do you not know that nothing will change my mind about wanting to marry you?"

The viscount's voice was so confident, so warm and reassuring that Clarissa believed his promise, but she had to tell him the truth. "I-I live under a cloud of disgrace. I am sorry. I should have told you the truth before I led you to believe that I am a perfect young lady."

Lord Anthony suppressed a smile at her overwrought words

but waited quietly, patiently, all the while caressing her cheek. Long experience had taught him that people often spoke more freely when they had to fill a silence than when prodded by questions that might not get to the heart of the issue.

Clarissa's face was a picture of misery and her posture was stiff. After a few moments of silence, she buried her face in the folds of Lord Anthony's soft coat. "My reputation... oh, I should never have allowed you to take such liberties with me." She sniffed again and them pulled back, "I will bring disgrace, dishonor to my family. Already, Mr. Hemsby believes that I have abandoned all good sense."

Lord Anthony gave a disgusted snort. "If Mr. Hemsby had his way, all pleasure would be eradicated from the world. He does not understand the beauty of pleasure, the goodness of it." His voice was low, soothing, encouraging. "Besides, he is not the one you should be seeking to please."

Clarissa straightened her shoulders. "I have worked very hard to overcome the disgrace of my birth. I have strived to become the paragon of all that is decent and proper because I do not want anyone to think I am not good enough." Her eyes drifted down and she scuffed at the acorns scattered around her feet. "And yet when I am with you, I forget everything I have tried so hard to achieve. Deep down I am just as wanton as my mother was. I have been tainted by the same disgrace."

Lord Anthony's strong hand cupped her neck in a possessive clasp. "Your reputation in society is impeccable, my little rose. But at what cost? You have denied the very essence of your soul and were in danger of become nothing more than an empty puppet, letting society pull the strings to make you behave according to its narrow rules."

Clarissa's eyes widened, and the viscount could see her struggle to accept the truth of his words. Her upper lip was caught between her teeth and her hands moved restlessly at her side.

"B-but..." she began to protest and then stopped, unsure of how to answer.

Lord Anthony shook his head, a soft smile lighting his face. "I did not fall in love with your impeccable reputation. It is you, a woman of passion and intellect, whom I desire. And no matter what disgrace you believe you have inherited from your mother, I will not judge you and neither will my friends." With a brief laugh, he added, "We all have our own peccadilloes."

Clarissa concentrated for a moment on the steady movement of the viscount's hand as he stroked her back. Reassured by his calmness, she took a breath and confessed her secret. "I was born out of wedlock." Her voice was little more than a whisper and even through the thickness of his coat, he could feel the heat of her blush.

Silence greeted her confession. Lord Anthony did not recoil in horror, declaring that she was dishonorable and unworthy to be his wife. Clarissa waited. The viscount continued to hold her close, his hand never ceasing its soothing caress.

Clarissa sighed with relief and the tension in her shoulders began to soften. She snuggled closer to the comfort of Lord Anthony's broad chest, aware of the firmness of his muscles which came from long hours of boxing in Gentleman Jack's studio and other similar activities.

She found herself filling the silence with the details of her childhood. "My mother, who was the daughter of a vicar, was estranged from her family because of her... condition. But my father, who was the second son of the local squire, loved her. In spite of his family's objections, he eloped with my mother shortly after I was born. But they both succumbed to fever when I was little and my father's family reluctantly took me in." The matter-of-fact way she outlined the distress of her childhood only thinly disguised her pain.

The viscount's soft murmurs encouraged her to continue. "My childhood was... uncomfortable, unpleasant. My cousins were taught to despise me and so I learned to be independent. When I was twelve, Aunt Agatha, who by then had resigned herself to spinsterhood, invited me to live with her in a cottage on the estate. She has been very kind to me and done all she can to ensure that I would always behave impeccably so that my past could somehow be redeemed."

Lord Anthony held her quietly for a few minutes, allowing Clarissa to sort through her turbulent thoughts. With a rueful laugh, she looked up into his face. "And yet, here I am giving in to the same passions that led my mother into trouble."

The viscount cupped her chin and tilted her head up. His eyes were filled with affection, with understanding. Again, Clarissa shivered, as his eyes saw the very depths of her soul in a way no one else ever had.

"My little love, I am sorry that you had such a difficult childhood. Your parents loved one another and yet society condemned their love. But I do not believe that passion and pleasure are wrong. You have inherited your mother's sensitive nature, and that is to be commended. If you allow me to, I will show you that when you yield to pleasure, you will discover much good in life."

As he spoke, he moved Clarissa backwards so that her back was pressed against the hard trunk of the oak tree. He was so close to her that the slightest movement caused her breasts to brush against his solid chest. Already, her nipples were puckered into hard little points threatening to poke through her bodice. She was grateful for the good quality of her clothes that covered her indecent response to being maneuvered by the viscount.

But her comfort was short-lived. Lord Anthony ran his hands over her shoulders and down towards her breasts. She took in a deep breath. He reached for her arms and raised them above her head, holding both her wrists in place with one big hand. He was so close to her that she could feel every breath he took, the heat that radiated from his body and the slow, steady beats of his heart.

She squirmed, fighting the trepidation that swamped her even as she raised her eyes to his face, silently begging for more of him.

"Do not move," he cautioned. His other hand began to seek the ties of her corset. She shivered, arching to the insistence of his touch. He began loosening the ties, slowly, deliberately, his eyes focused on her face as his hand uncovered her nakedness.

When the corset began to fall open, Lord Anthony slipped his hand beneath the heavy linen and brushed his hand over her eager nipples. She let out a little cry, somewhere between a mewl and a squeal. His eyes lit up but the rest of his expression remained intense as he focused on her.

He crushed his lips against hers, hard and intense. She hesitated for a moment and then her lips parted slightly, allowing Anthony to draw her into his mouth, to nip at her lower lip, to slide his tongue into her mouth and explore her, taste her, devour her. His kiss took possession of her and she willingly let him. She surrendered to his power.

In the heat of the kiss, Clarissa moved her hands seeking to echo the way the viscount was exploring her. Her hands clutched at his shirt, beneath his waistcoat, wanting to touch his skin, to feel his nakedness against hers.

Anthony found his way to the alluring curve of her breasts. A tremble ricocheted through her body as he stroked her, kneaded her flesh, rubbed her areole.

Suddenly he pulled back from kissing her but was still close enough for her to feel the brush of his breath against her cheek.

"Naughty girl," he admonished with a half-smile, "I instructed you to keep your hands above your head, but where are they now?"

With a guilty start, Clarissa glanced at where her hands

rested on Lord Anthony's chest. Hastily, she moved them back into the position the viscount had placed them in earlier.

"That's better," he approved. His fingers gripped her nipple tightly and twisted. She squealed at the sharp pain and then squirmed as the pain sent tendrils of pleasure through her body.

Lord Anthony slid a hand around her throat, holding her, possessing her. She trembled, wanting more of his touch. Her body was radiating the heat of her passion. Her thighs were clenched tightly, trying to contain the wetness that dripped from her core. Her breasts ached, wanting more of the viscount's rough caresses. Her mouth tingled with the feel of his mouth on hers. Her heart beat so rapidly, it felt like a bird fluttering against the bars of a cage.

The viscount pushed against her until the full hardness of his body was against every part of her. His leg pushed between her thighs, forcing her to open herself to his strength. The hardness of his thigh thrust against her aching pussy. She began rubbing herself against him, wantonly, passionately, trying to increase the sensations that were consuming her. She abandoned all politeness. She needed this, needed his touch, needed his body.

The viscount pushed his thigh against her pussy as she rode him. He continued to kiss her and his hands increased in their fervency to examine her body. She felt her breath catching in her throat, she felt the fire raging inside her, she felt herself clench around an emptiness in her private places. Her breath hitched higher. Her blood pounded in her head, raced through her body. Suddenly the intensity built to a peak and she shattered with a loud cry that echoed through the woods.

Red flashed behind her eyes and then darkness settled around her. She drifted on a warm cloud of bliss. She was anchored to the earth only by the strong arms of the viscount that still held her tightly.

CHAPTER 12

*I*t was some minutes before Clarissa became aware of her surroundings. She heard the gentle words of the viscount as if they were a distant pattering of rain. She snuggled against his solid chest, feeling safe and secure. She took a deep breath and smiled as she realized her hands were once again resting on his body, but this time he did not seem to mind.

His words became more distinct. "Welcome back, little flower. Did you enjoy your ride?"

Clarissa was engulfed in blushes, but she had to be honest. She nodded, unable to find the words to answer her betrothed.

"Hmm," he murmured against her hair. "We'll soon work on the right way to give answers. But it is time to begin our ride back to London. If we don't leave soon, you will not have time to change for Lady Davenport's soiree this evening."

Lord Anthony placed his hand on the small of Clarissa's back as he guided her back to the main path. Clarissa pushed aside the niggling voices that accused her of impropriety, of unladylike behavior. She felt like a bird whose cage door had been opened and all she had to do to be free was to flap her wings. If she soared into the wide, welcoming skies, she would be what she was created to be. She would discover the pleasure of being herself.

She walked beside the viscount, her head held high even though her cheeks were still stained with the blush of embarrassment. The viscount chatted casually about the scenery and she murmured answers, hoping that she was making sense.

It was not long before they were back on the main road that ran through the extensive park. Lord Theo and Lady Charlotte were talking quietly near the horses. The marquess raised a quizzical eyebrow as Clarissa and the viscount emerged from the woods, but he said nothing.

Quickly, the party remounted their horses and began trotting down Queen's Ride, admiring the beauty of the park. It was idyllic and Clarissa soon allowed the tranquility of the park to settle into her heart.

The party was about a quarter of a mile from the gate. The loud bang of a gunshot cracked through the air, shattering the tranquility of the afternoon. Clarissa screamed as the startled horses panicked. April's Maiden whinnied and reared. Clarissa fell to the ground with a hard thud.

All went dark. She couldn't breathe. Her arm lay limply at her side and excruciating pain lanced through her. Vaguely, she became aware that Lord Anthony was kneeling beside her, running his hands over her to assess her injuries. He was speaking but she could not make sense of his words. Blood pulsed in her ears and the ache in her head dimmed any other sounds.

"Clarissa, where are you hurt?" he repeated, his voice husky with concern.

Clarissa winced as his hands ran over her shoulder. She had landed on her back, her shoulder taking most of the impact of her fall. She felt nauseous and dizzy. Lord Anthony looked grave as he continued trying to determine where and how badly she was injured. When his hands circled her ankle, she could not hold back a cry of pain that shocked her out of the wooziness.

Lord Anthony rose onto his haunches and eased her into a sitting position. When she winced and gave another sharp cry of pain, he pulled her into his lap and cradled her throbbing head against his chest.

He looked at Theo, who was also now crouching next to her. Charlotte, who was a competent horsewoman and had managed to keep control of Lady May when the sound of the gun being fired had frightened the animals, was holding the reins of all of the horses. "She's very pale," she commented. "What are we going to do? She can't ride and there are no doctors nearby. She needs a doctor."

Theo smiled at his wife. "She does, my little lamb, and we will get her to one as soon as possible."

While Theo was speaking, Anthony scooped Clarissa up in his arms and stood. The blood rushed to her ankle, sending sharp jabs of pain through her. She felt faint but bit the inside of her mouth to keep from swooning. He spotted a fallen log a few feet away and settled her on it.

Clarissa bit her lips, trying to hold back the tears. Lord Anthony loosened the buttons on her boot, and as the blood rushed into her ankle, the tears she had been holding back fell. The viscount ran his fingers gently over the swollen foot, but she winced even though his touch was light.

His eyes darkened to the color of moss as he comforted her. "I need to wrap your ankle in some kind of bandage. It will hurt, but it will feel better if it is properly supported."

Clarissa gave a brief nod as the viscount quickly removed his cravat and wrapped it around her ankle. She clung to his arm as the pain throbbed insistently, but as the makeshift bandage was wound around her, she did feel some relief. "Brave lass. You're doing very well. We'll soon have you home."

When the viscount rose to his feet, Theo drew closer. His

face was grim. "How is it possible that a gun could be fired here?" His voice was hard. "I thought the rangers were dealing with the problem of poachers."

Anthony shook his head slowly. His face hardened. "That was definitely gun shot, but if those were poachers, they are very stupid. There are no deer along the main road of the park and that shot was fired in this direction." He opened his hand to reveal a bullet casing. "This was lying on the ground right here."

Theo looked around, trying to see if there was anyone hidden among the trees. "You're right. That is very odd. But for now, if Clarissa is more comfortable, we need to move."

Clarissa felt nausea rise in her throat as the viscount eased her to her feet. She had barely listened to the exchange between the two men, and everything around her was blurred. She winced in pain as her foot touched the ground and immediately Lord Anthony scooped her up into his arms, murmuring softly.

Lord Anthony handed her to the marquess while he mounted his horse and then Lord Theo settled her onto the saddle in front of the viscount. She was too distraught by the pain to consider the impropriety of her position. She leaned against Lord Anthony's chest, his arms around her, resting her hand on the bare skin of his torso where he had removed his cravat.

The ride back to Aunt Agatha's house was agonizingly slow and the group of friends was much more somber than they had been on the way to the park. Theo walked his horse next to Lord Anthony while Charlotte brought up the rear, leading April's Maiden. The viscount was very careful not to jostle Clarissa, but even so, her ankle throbbed continuously and her shoulder ached.

They rode silently for a few miles, but when they reached the busier streets, Theo raised the matter of the shooting again. "Why would anyone want to shoot at us?" he mused.

Anthony shook his head. "We need to ask which one of us was the target and then perhaps we will know who is behind it and why." His frown deepened. "But it is interesting that the shooter didn't seem to aim at any one if us in particular, rather just generally in our direction as if he wanted to scare us, not harm us." Clarissa shuddered, and he nestled her closer to his chest. "It's all right, pet. You will be all right. No one is going to harm you. I'm going to make sure that all is well."

Theo shook his head. "I am not sure the shooting was random. And it is strange that twice in the last few weeks, Clarissa has been involved in strange incidents that have led to her being injured."

Clarissa gave a startled cry, and the viscount hushed her with soothing sounds. She settled again into his embrace and let the voices of the gentlemen wash over her.

"Could you see anyone?" Anthony asked.

The marquess shrugged and tilted his head at an angle. "My first thought was to see if Charlotte was all right, and I didn't think to look for the shooter."

The party rode in silence for the rest of the trip, all of them wondering why anyone would want to unsettle them, frighten them, and particularly why Clarissa had been targeted on two separate occasions. The only sounds were the steady clopping of the horses' hooves and Anthony murmuring words of comfort and reassurance to Clarissa from time to time.

CLARISSA SIGHED as she leaned back on the *chaise longue* that had been drawn up beside the window in her aunt's drawing room. Her foot was raised on a pillow and cushions supported her bruised shoulder. It had been four days since the incident in the park, and she was confined to the house while her foot and other injuries healed.

The headache that had raged since she fell off the horse had eased and she could think more clearly. She even had enough energy to attempt sewing, but the baby garment she had begun before that eventful day lay limply on her lap.

Aunt Agatha set a cup of tea down on the low table next to Clarissa. "There you are, dear. A good cup of tea will cheer you up. Do try to eat a little of that bread and butter, too. I am concerned that your appetite is still so poor. You need some nourishment to help you get better."

Clarissa smiled her thanks and wrapped her hands around the comforting warmth of the cup. She drew the heat into her, hoping that the icy cold fear that gripped her, freezing her innermost being, would lessen with the familiar comfort of tea.

She had not told her aunt the full story of what had happened. Lord Donnington had cautioned her not to mention the gun shots to her aunt. As far as anyone who had not been with them knew, April's Maiden had been startled by something they had not seen and Clarissa had fallen. She tried not to think of that horrible moment when a bullet had rushed past her and the horse had reared, throwing her to the ground, but her sleep was constantly disturbed by horrid images.

Aunt Agatha sat down on a chair near to Clarissa and sipped her own tea. "It might be expedient to postpone the wedding," she remarked.

Clarissa jerked in surprise, almost spilling her tea. "Why?" was all she managed to say.

Aunt Agatha pursed her lips. "This injury of yours makes it difficult to be fitted for wedding clothes and a bride hobbling down the aisle on a sprained ankle will be a very odd sight. Just think of what people will say."

Clarissa scowled. "My foot is getting better. I could put some weight on it this morning. I'm sure that within a week, I will be able to run, and the wedding is still two weeks away."

Aunt Agatha looked ready to argue, but the ladies were interrupted by the sudden and unexpected appearance of Clarissa's cousin and *de facto* guardian, Sir Bradley Blakeney. He stalked into the room, irritation bristling from every pore.

Clarissa was so surprised that she tried to stand up and then squealed when pain shot through her ankle. She sat back down hastily.

Sir Bradley scowled. "Ladies," he greeted them curtly, looking only at Aunt Agatha. He wasted no time in getting to the reason for his sudden and unwelcome visit. "Your letter detailing Clarissa's upcoming nuptials has brought me to London as soon as I was able to leave the work on the estate. As her dowry is still my responsibility, I thought it my duty to oversee the marriage settlement and not leave it to two naive women who will accept any paltry arrangement. These city gents can be very subtle in how they manipulate business matters to suit their own ends and it takes a man to know how to deal with them." He sat down on the edge of a chair, sweeping his coat tails aside. "It would have been more appropriate if the viscount had discussed all things pertaining to the wedding with me. He didn't even think to ask my permission to marry Clarissa."

Aunt Agatha's lips straightened into a grim line, but she answered politely, reminding herself that once Clarissa was married, she would have to rely on Sir Bradley for support. "It is kind of you to come. I have the papers here and I believe they are in order. The viscount is a gentleman of the highest order." She stood up and walked briskly across the room to her bureau but opened a drawer with a little more force than necessary.

As she handed the documents to Sir Bradley, the housekeeper announced the arrival of the viscount himself. Clarissa bit her lip, nervous about the meeting between her cousin and her betrothed. But the viscount was full of charm as he greeted Sir Bradley and her cousin could not fault the viscount's impeccable manners. He had to respond with equal politeness.

"Ah!" Lord Anthony remarked as he saw the papers the other

gentleman was holding. "Sir Bradley, it is very conscientious of you to review the legal aspects of your cousin's marriage."

The viscount sat down next to Clarissa, taking her hand in his, his eyes softening with affection as he perused her face and asked if she was feeling better. Clarissa was too tense to answer and she just gave Lord Anthony a quick nod. He said nothing, just squeezing her hand and letting his fingers caress her in slow circles, offering comfort and understanding.

Clarissa eyed her cousin anxiously as he sat down at a table to examine the documents. He said nothing as he read, but grunted once or twice when something particularly interested him.

Lord Anthony accepted the cup of tea Aunt Agatha handed to him with an insouciant smile. He chatted quietly to Clarissa, ignoring Sir Bradley's presence as if he was nothing more than an annoying fly. Clarissa felt herself begin to relax, although Aunt Agatha was still sitting stiffly with her back rigid and her shoulders squared, prepared to defend her actions if Sir Bradley raised objections.

After a few minutes, Sir Bradley looked up, his face hardening as his eyes traveled down to where Clarissa's hand lay in Lord Anthony's one. He glared at the viscount, but his voice held grudging approbation. "Well, this is an exceedingly generous agreement. I cannot see any necessity to amend it, unless you were to reduce the allowance it provides for Clarissa." He tapped the marriage settlement with his forefinger.

Lord Anthony tilted his chin and his lips were set in a hard line. His voice was low, almost casual, but there was an authoritative edge to it that reinforced his superiority over the country squire. "The allowance I have arranged to give Clarissa is fitting for someone in the position she will have in society. She will never feel stifled or obligated as my wife, or that she has to beg and scrape. Someone as lovely, as perfect as she is, deserves to have everything of the very best, and I will cherish her."

Sir Bradley looked flustered, his face flushing an angry red. He folded the pages, running his hand sharply down the fold. A cruel look flashed through his eyes when for the first time since his arrival, he looked directly at Clarissa, although his words were addressed to the viscount. "My lord, I wish you well in your marriage. I trust that you have chosen wisely and will not be disappointed in my cousin. She has earned a reputation for being a paragon, but I know how difficult, stubborn and opinionated she is when she is not parading herself among members of society. Even this," he gestured vaguely at Clarissa who was still lying on the sofa, her foot raised on a cushion, "is typical of her constant attempts to be in the limelight, to have people fawn all over her. The intractability of her character is not unexpected in a girl with her background."

Clarissa's heart clenched tightly and her breath caught in her throat. All the feelings of inadequacy, of desperation to be accepted, of unworthiness that she had experienced as a child flooded through her at her cousin's words. All her efforts to be a perfect young lady crumbled to dust. She focused on her hands, still held by the viscount, unable to look at him or at her cousin.

Lord Anthony, however, squeezed her hand lightly, sending a trickle of warmth into her icy body, and then stood up. He looked powerful, even a little menacing, as he stalked towards Sir Bradley. Although her cousin was only eight years older than she was, about the same age as the viscount, he looked stodgy and almost middle-aged next to the energetic, athletic viscount. Clarissa could believe the stories she had heard about the viscount's proficiency at the sport of boxing as he towered over the man who had treated her so cruelly when she had been a child. She almost laughed when Sir Bradley cringed.

Lord Donnington, every inch the viscount, snatched the folded pages from Sir Bradley's hand and seemed not to notice how the paunchy man flinched, trying not to cower. His voice cut through the room like a knife. "My judgement is not often questioned, especially by country gentlemen who know nothing about me. Clarissa is everything, indeed more than I could hope for in a wife. I have admired her strength, her intelligence, her sensitivity for many months, and each day my regard for her increases. I love her and she is now under my protection. She is no longer your concern and I would thank you not to express your bigoted opinions about my wife."

Clarissa wanted to applaud but her manners and her long-standing fear of her cousin kept her still. The trickle of warmth that had stirred in her heart became a flood of sunshine, bringing light and joy to her heart. Never had anyone defended her as the viscount now did. She was not in the least upset when Sir Bradley stood up, his face red and his fists tightly clenched, sputtering, "Well, I wash my hands of the girl. I will ensure my solicitor settles the matter of her dowry and then I will return to my country manor. I had thought to offer to walk the girl down the aisle, but I will leave these women to their own devices."

Aunt Agatha held the door open and smiled at Sir Bradley's back as he stalked from the room. Clarissa looked up at her betrothed, her beloved, and had to wipe away the tears that had gathered in the corners of her eyes as relief washed over her.

Lord Anthony came back to her couch and took her hands in his. Even though Aunt Agatha was still in the room, he bent down and kissed Clarissa softly on the lips. "I believe the duke is more than happy to walk you down the aisle," he said, "unless you would prefer someone else?"

Clarissa laughed. "No, no. I would be honored to have Lord Sebastian look after me. Thank you for dealing with my cousin. He has always treated me as if I was something of a nuisance." Her voice softened with wonder. "Thank you for protecting me. It is a strange experience for me to have someone care enough to defend me."

Lord Anthony studied her for a few moments. "I will always care for you, my little flower," he promised. Then he turned to

Aunt Agatha, who had resumed her seat, her face softer than it had been since Clarissa's accident. "Miss Blakeney, I wanted to invite Clarissa to come to my house for lunch today. She has not yet seen Donnington House and I would like to introduce her to some of the staff who will be responsible for her well-being once we are married."

Aunt Agatha shook her head, but her words were gentle. "She is not yet well enough to gad about, and, besides, I am not available to chaperone her today. It will not do to have her exposed to even more gossip. Someone is bound to discover if she is alone with you in your house before you are married."

Lord Anthony quirked an eyebrow, but he answered politely, "I will ensure that Clarissa's reputation is not compromised. The duke and Lady Amelia will be joining me for lunch, and so she will have a suitable chaperone. I will also see to it that she does not over exert herself." He glanced at Clarissa, who was listening to this exchange with her mouth slightly parted and her eyes wide and shining. A rush of blood to his groin made his cock jerk at the pretty sight. "I have a perfect sofa which she will find very comfortable."

CHAPTER 13

"Oh, you poor darling," cried Lady Amelia as she rushed into the intimate sitting room Lord Anthony preferred to use when he was entertaining his friends. The duchess was followed more slowly by her husband, the Duke of Broadwell, who smiled warmly at Clarissa.

Amelia sat down next to Clarissa on the large, comfortable sofa where Lord Anthony had settled her a few minutes earlier. Clarissa tried to look dignified, but with her leg raised on an ottoman and pain throbbing through her ankle, her usual self-possession had vanished. "I'm feeling much better," she lied, although she grimaced as Amelia jostled her on the sofa.

Amelia shook her head. "You don't need to try to be polite and correct. You're with friends and we want to help you." Her pretty face grew more serious. "It must have been horrid to have bullets flying at you. I would have been terrified."

Clarissa's face turned even paler and she shuddered as she tried to control her memories.

The duke cautioned his young wife, "Amelia, that's enough. Rather, tell Clarissa about how little Sebastian is trying to stand on his own."

Amelia pulled a face at her husband, who raised a warning eyebrow, but she obeyed him, and Clarissa was soon laughing as the duchess regaled her with the latest antics of her little son.

The duke watched the two ladies settle into a comfortable coze, and then he turned to the viscount. "Have you been able to find out anything more about what happened?" he asked.

Lord Anthony, his eyes lingering on Clarissa, shook his head. "Theo and I have sent people to ask the park rangers and others who were riding that day if they saw anyone with a gun, but no one can say anything definite." He shook his head, a frown reflecting how much the shooting had disturbed him. "Poachers are not usually active at that time of day and definitely not on the main thoroughfare."

The duke concurred. "It seems unlikely that poachers were involved. This feels more personal."

The viscount closed his eyes for a moment, reliving that dreadful moment when Clarissa was lying motionless on the ground. He took a deep breath. "It all seems rather improbable that anyone would shoot directly at a group of people, at us, in broad daylight. And yet Theo and I have discussed what we remember, what we heard and saw, the bullet casing we found, and we both agree that someone deliberately, purposely, fired a gun at us."

The duke's clear blue eyes darkened. "Perhaps it would help to consider the problem from the opposite angle," he suggested.

Lord Anthony frowned. "What do you mean?"

"There are two, perhaps three, questions that can be asked. Firstly, was the shot fired at the four of you generally, or was one of you a specific target? Secondly, who would want to frighten and upset all of you, or one of you? And why?"

Lord Anthony was quiet for a few moments. He shifted uneasily in his chair, perturbed by a sudden unwelcome thought. The duke had been watching him closely and now asked, "What is it?"

The viscount wanted to shrug the thought off, almost laughing at how preposterous it sounded. But the duke's piercing eyes insisted that he explain his reaction. "It's probably nothing, but..." he wavered.

"At this stage, nothing is too ridiculous to consider. We need to examine all the possibilities until we find the truth." The duke's deep voice was more grave than Anthony had ever heard as he said, "Would Clarissa's spurned suitor feel aggrieved enough to want to harm her?"

Anthony shrugged his shoulders impatiently. "Mr. Hemsby? I shouldn't think so. He claimed he would have nothing more to do with her, although I suppose he might feel slighted, especially if anyone has commented on how he lost the paragon to me." Anthony swirled the tea in his cup. "As I said, it is probably nothing to do with the situation, but Lucretia's letters to me have been increasingly desperate. There is an odd mixture of vitriol and pleading in them, but Lucretia has never met Clarissa and I cannot imagine her skulking behind trees and taking pot shots at anyone."

The duke was thoughtful. "Shooting someone does seem rather drastic, even for Lucretia, but be careful. Do you plan to go to Dorset after your wedding?"

Anthony glanced at Clarissa, who was chatting enthusiastically with Amelia. He nodded. "Yes, yes, I want to take my bride there, introduce her to my estate and enjoy the summer in the country."

Fotheringham, Donnington's butler, entered the sitting room to announce that lunch was ready and the gentlemen brought their discussion to an end. There would be time to think more about the matter later, but for now they turned their attention to entertaining the two ladies.

∾

CLARISSA LOOKED AROUND as she leaned on the viscount's arm on the way to the dining room. She smiled, delighted by all she saw. Lord Anthony's house was elegant but was at the same time very comfortable. Much of the furniture had been passed down through the generations of Donningtons who had lived here and had the air of long-standing comfort. Some modern pieces attested to Lord Anthony's taste and blended in well. Beautiful rugs covered gleaming floors and fascinating ornaments were displayed on well-chosen tables and bureaus. She wanted to stop to admire a large painting of a waterfall cascading down a mountainside, but Anthony moved her quickly on to the dining room, saying, "There will be plenty of time to examine everything to your heart's content. For the moment, we need to get your weight off your foot."

A pleasant meal was set out on the long table and Clarissa found her appetite returning as she nibbled a slice of delicious, light honey cake spiced with ginger that accompanied fresh grapes and other fruit that had been grown in the viscount's own gardens.

She was beginning to regard the viscount's friends as her own and enjoyed the banter that accompanied the meal. Although the duke at first appeared formidable, Clarissa soon found herself in a lively debate with him about whether gardens should be picturesque, as Repton favored, or more rugged and natural.

She relaxed, enjoying not having to remind herself that young ladies were not expected to offer their own opinions but meekly accept whatever they were told. A vivid smile, quite unlike the placid image she usually showed to the world, lit her face, softening her prim appearance and enhancing her beauty. She liked just being herself. If this was a foretaste of her married life, then great pleasure awaited her. She was all the more eager for her marriage to take place quickly, no matter how much her foot hurt.

During a lull in the conversation, her eyes were drawn to a painting of a group of four men indulging in a picnic near a river that hung on the wall opposite her seat. The viscount's eyes followed her gaze. "What do you think of that picture?" he asked, his voice deceptively nonchalant.

"I like it very much indeed," she answered spontaneously. "It is so different from the rigid formality of the usual posed portraits one sees. It is a very happy picture. The artist's brush strokes are exuberant, free, as if he rejoiced in the beauty of the trees and liked the people he was painting."

Lord Anthony was grinning widely by the time she finished speaking. The duke huffed but could not hold back a smile. It was Lady Amelia who exclaimed with a laugh, "That is one of the earliest paintings of the much sought-after artist, Roland Alexander."

Clarissa glanced around at her lunch companions and then her eyes widened. She looked at the viscount. "You painted that?"

"Yes, I am R. Alexander. That's a depiction of Theo, Sherbonne, Adam Loxley and me when we were still at Oxford."

Clarissa rose from her seat and hobbled closer to the painting. "You have captured each of your friends well, showing something of their characters. The earl looks complacent and content with the way life treats him, the marquess is alert and focused, yet delighted with life, while Baron Loxley is pouring wine for the rest of you, as always ensuring that everyone is taken care of. But you have done yourself a disservice, my lord. Only your back is visible."

The viscount had risen from his seat while Clarissa was examining the painting and he now stood close behind her, his body brushing against hers. His voice was low, mesmerizing. "You are very perceptive, my little flower. However, the image of me is quite accurate in many ways. I am observing the others, something that I often do." He paused as his eyes flickered over the painting, a smile on his lips. "This is a favorite of mine, although not really the kind of subject matter I usually paint." He ran his finger lightly over the soft skin of her neck and down to where her shoulders just peeped out from the white muslin of her dress. She shivered and leaned back against him. "After lunch, I will show you my studio and some of my paintings. I might even begin a portrait of you," he promised.

~

WHEN THE FOOTMEN had cleared the lunch from the table and Fotheringham was serving coffee, Donnington leaned back in his chair. "I think it is time for me to show you my studio."

Clarissa turned to him, her eyes bright with anticipation and her cheeks glowing a pretty pink as she recalled the images she had seen in the viscount's sketchbook. She wanted to see the life and color his paints gave to his ideas. She remembered his earlier promise to paint her, and her blush deepened. She nodded. "Yes, please, I would like that very much," she said, her voice bright with the anticipation of discovering more about this fascinating man who was soon to be her husband.

Lord Anthony felt a surge of blood flood his groin, thickening his already throbbing cock. A slow smile quirked his lips upwards as he noted how eagerly the lady he loved was to discover the world of pleasure he would lead her into. He set down his half-finished cup of coffee. "If you have finished, we can go now." He glanced at the duke and Lady Amelia, silently asking whether they were going to leave him alone with his bride-to-be.

The duchess rose to her feet. "I think that is an excellent idea. Come, Clarissa, you can lean on me."

The viscount's studio was situated towards the back of his grand house, away from the rooms guests usually had access to. Lord Anthony led the way upstairs, his steps quick and light. Clarissa's sprained ankle made it difficult for her to walk too quickly and he was impatiently tossing the key from hand to hand when the two ladies finally joined him outside the solid wooden door which shielded the secrets of his soul. The duke trailed behind with a smirk on his face.

Eagerly, Lord Anthony unlocked the door. "Welcome to my studio, little flower. You can look at everything in this room and ask as many questions as you want to, but do be careful about touching. Paint can be messy."

He stood aside and Amelia led Clarissa into the room. Clarissa halted just inside the studio and gazed around her, her hands clenching and unclenching as the room revealed new insights into her beloved's soul. Dozens of canvases were stacked against the walls, some were completed while others had been set aside in the middle of the work as new inspiration had grabbed him. In one corner, a stack of new canvases, stretched and blank, were waiting to receive his ideas. A few easels around the room displayed some of his work. The room was redolent with the acridity of paint and solvent, mingled with the heavy linen aroma of canvas and an indefinable something that Clarissa whimsically thought of as creativity.

In the middle of the room, facing a large midnight blue sofa, the main working easel held the painting that the viscount was currently working on. In easy reach of the canvas, was a small table, cluttered with the paraphernalia of painting, brushes, jars, tubes of paint, cloths smeared with the colors he used most. Clarissa glanced from the canvas to the sofa and then stepped closer to the easel.

Her cheeks turned the color of the deep pink roses that Lord Anthony had brought her the day he proposed. The painting was of a man standing near a window in what could be a bedroom, but much of the background was as yet incomplete. A woman knelt at his feet, looking up at him. Both were completely naked and positioned so that the viewer could see the plump curves of the woman's bottom, the pale slope of her back, and the swell of her breasts. Clarissa gasped as her eyes followed the luscious lines of the woman up to where her hand was resting on the man's thigh. His manhood was clearly visible, large and turgid and darker than the flesh of his stomach as it jutted up towards his navel.

Clarissa gave Amelia a startled glance, too embarrassed to look at Lord Anthony who was standing in the doorway, watching her. She could find no words to articulate her response. Her well-trained inclination was to condemn such explicitness as profane and obscene, but her honesty compelled her to concede that the image was beautiful, alluring. In some strange way, she could identify with the woman and wondered what it would be like to kneel at Lord Anthony's feet, waiting for him to guide her into pleasure. The painting expressed her deepest desires, the ones she usually pretended did not exist. As she studied the painting, her body became uncomfortably warm and the air in the room seemed to grow thin. Her clothes felt too tight and it was difficult to breath.

Amelia, with her usual insouciance, eased the tension. She ignored Clarissa's response and turned to the viscount. "This is exquisite!" she declared. "Is it a commission or something you are doing for your own pleasure? If it is for sale, I would love my duke to buy it. It would look very good in his dressing room at Broadwell Castle."

Clarissa was able to even out her breathing as the young duchess praised the painting. She even turned to look at the viscount as he walked farther into the room. His voice was wry as he answered, "I am not going to sell this one. It has a personal significance and I will keep it for my own dressing room."

Clarissa glanced at the painting and then back at her husband-to-be. A tight fist clutched at her heart and blood rushed to her head, causing a faint buzzing in her ears. Her stomach felt as heavy as a stone. Who was the woman who allowed herself to be painted in such a way by the viscount and who had special significance for him? Pangs of jealousy pierced her soul. She blinked rapidly a few times.

Suddenly the viscount was right beside her and his large, sensitive hand was splayed against the small of her back. She wanted to pull away, to demand an answer to the questions that raged in her heart, but the warmth of his nearness eased her jealous response and she leaned against him.

Lord Anthony's voice was low and rough as he answered her unspoken questions. "This painting reflects one of my most personal fantasies. The woman was based on elements of the Greek statues, but most of her is drawn from my imagination."

Clarissa heaved a sigh of relief and tilted her head so she could see his face. A little smile played at the corners of her mouth. Once again, she examined the painting, this time able to be a little more objective, although she trembled as she was beset with a sudden desire to kneel at the viscount's feet, as the woman on the canvas was kneeling before the man who was clearly her lover. "It is a very interesting painting," she remarked primly.

She looked at the woman again and then raised querying eyes to Lord Anthony. "She, the woman, the lady, her hair is in a style similar to the way I usually arrange mine." She was flustered by the realization that the viscount had been thinking of her while he painted this erotic image. And then she was even more startled when a closer perusal of the man revealed him to be the viscount himself. Blood rushed to her face as she wondered if he really looked like that without his clothes on. Her eyes lingered on the protruding manhood. She gulped and her hand involuntarily reached towards the painting, wanting to touch that strange organ.

A strong hand wrapped around her delicate one, preventing her from touching the canvas. "No, little one. I did warn you not to touch anything. The paint is not quite dry and I would be upset if you were to smear it." As Anthony spoke, he shifted even closer to her and she was suddenly aware of the very real, pulsing rigid length of his male organ pressing against her buttocks. She froze.

The viscount continued talking, as if the closeness of their bodies was not making it almost impossible for her to think clearly. "However, little flower, your response pleases me. I am glad that the picture stirred you so deeply, that you are so eager to engage with it. I am looking forward to showing you the pleasure you so clearly desire." His hand moved slowly up her back and then down again, and her body trembled with anticipation, with yearning that she no longer wanted to suppress. The viscount's next words sent her senses reeling. "This is one of my favorite fantasies, having you kneeling naked at my feet. Soon, we will explore the passions that I have so far only imagined."

Clarissa felt a surge of heat pulsate through her body as his hands surrounded her waist, pulling her even closer to him. The thick ridge of his manhood rubbed against her more insistently. She said nothing. She did not know how to tell her betrothed how deeply she longed to have him show her the pleasure he promised. She did, however, lean against him more completely, silently conveying her desire for more of him, but also shifting her weight to ease the ache in her foot.

Lord Anthony turned her around in his arms and his eyes showed concern when he saw how pale and peaked her face was from the pain of standing on her hurt foot for so long. "I promised your aunt that I would not let you stand for too long." He slid one arm around her shoulders and then dipped slightly to place the other beneath her knees. He scooped her up into his arms and, in half a dozen quick strides, was standing in front of the midnight blue sofa.

Before Clarissa had become engaged to the viscount, she had thought the descriptions in novels of gentlemen lifting ladies into their arms was nothing more than fiction, that it could not happen in real life, and yet she was becoming accustomed to being carried so close to the viscount's chest. There was something quite thrilling in surrendering herself to his physical dominance like this. She huffed as the viscount carried her the few paces to the sofa, her hands clinging to his coat, but her eyes gleamed with their unspoken satisfaction at being so nurtured, so cherished, so desired.

Gently, Lord Anthony placed her on the sofa, moving a cushion behind her and easing her foot onto a small bolster. She wriggled, searching for the most comfortable position.

He leaned over her, his face so close to hers that she could feel the whisper of his breath. "I am sorry I did not look after you better. I should have insisted that you sit down as soon as we entered the studio. Does that feel better, my pretty flower?" he asked.

She nodded but winced slightly, and the viscount wrapped his sensitive fingers around her aching ankle, soothing the pain with slow tender strokes. "It will feel better soon, I promise. You do not need to move again for a while. Not once I have everything arranged to my liking." The viscount's voice carried a hint of amusement as Clarissa wriggled again, this time as she anticipated what his words suggested.

She looked up at her betrothed, her lip caught between her teeth. Uncertainty and desire chased each other across her face. He bent closer and his lips brushed across hers in a soft kiss. Tingles rippled through her body and she bit back a moan, frustrated when he did not respond to the parting of her lips by claiming her mouth.

He stood up with a laugh and Clarissa suddenly realized that the duke and duchess had left. Her breath caught in her throat in a moment of panic. Lord Anthony followed the direction of her eyes and then studied her face for a moment. He took her hand in his, saying, "My little love, there is no need to fear being alone with me. I will not harm you, but I might, indeed I will, challenge you. I want to begin to show you some of the pleasure that we will enjoy once we are married, and at times you might feel a little uncomfortable, until you understand the goodness of pleasure and will beg me for my caresses. Do you trust me to lead you into pleasure?"

Clarissa found it difficult to breath. Her mind cautioned her, listing all the objections a proper young lady should have to being alone with a man, even one she was about to marry. His words should have alarmed her, but her heart beat fast, encouraging her to submit to the viscount's promptings with the kind of natural grace he had depicted in his painting. His fantasy was quickly becoming her fantasy too.

She gave a quick nod, but the viscount was not satisfied with such a vague response. He straightened his shoulders as he stood next to the sofa. His posture, every line of his face, was stern and uncompromising. "Clarissa." His voice was harder than she had ever heard it before and she dropped her eyes, shivering at the displeasure she heard. His voice hardened even more, sounding like a whip cracking across the large room. "Look at me," he insisted.

He waited while she struggled with her uncertainty, her apprehension knowing she had to yield willingly or neither of them would find pleasure in their encounter. It took a few silent moments before Clarissa summoned the courage to raise her eyes to his.

Lord Anthony's heart softened at the sight of vulnerability warring with bravery in the vivid blue depths of Clarissa's eyes. It almost made him cast aside his intentions and simply sweep her into his arms, showering her with kisses and soothing words. But he wanted her to explore new territories of pleasure, and that required her to learn to follow his instructions.

He kept his face as impassive as possible and held her gaze

with his intense eyes. "Clarissa, it is much more effective for you to answer me with words. I need to know that you fully understand what I am saying to you, that you agree to every one of my suggestions. This is not the place or time to be coy."

Clarissa's breath came out as a light hiss as she considered Lord Anthony's words. It took her a moment to recall what he had asked. Her eyes were wider than usual and her earnestness was clear. "Yes, my lord, I do trust you and I would like to know more of the pleasure you can teach me."

Anthony almost groaned as his cock jerked at her answer. She was delightful, perfect, and would soon be the paragon of his pleasure. His face softened as he contemplated what he was about to ask of her. With a brief nod, he slid his hand into her neatly arranged hair and tugged at the pins that held it in place. She gave a startled gasp and lifted her hands as if to object, but then subsided and allowed him to loosen the silken mass.

"Are you comfortable on this sofa, little one?"

Clarissa began to nod and then quickly recovered, finding the right words. "I am. Thank you. The cushions are almost as soft as the pillows on a bed and with my foot raised, the pain has eased."

A smile flickered through the viscount's eyes. "Good. I want you to remain like that while I prepare for your portrait."

CHAPTER 14

*C*larissa breathed a deep sigh of satisfaction and let the tension in her shoulders flow away, like rubble carried by a slow stream. She watched as Lord Anthony shrugged off his well-fitted forest green coat and dropped it onto a chair near the door. He loosened his cravat and rolled up the sleeves of his fine white linen shirt. Clarissa was riveted by the smooth ropes of muscles on his forearms that she had until now only vaguely been aware of beneath his well-made clothes.

Then he lifted the half-finished painting off his main easel and placed a large blank canvas in its place. His muscles rippled as he moved around the room and heat pulsated through Clarissa's body, gathering in a pool of fire in her most intimate places. She tightened her thighs, but the heat increased and her nipples bunched into hard points of desire. She tried to focus on the artist at work as disinterestedly as possible, but nothing in her response to Lord Anthony could ever be objective.

He sorted through his paints slowly, glancing at her from time to time as he selected some and discarded others. A small piece of charcoal was sharpened to a point. Finally, he pulled a deep blue smock over his clothes, which still left his forearms bare.

Placing a few small brushes in his pocket, he surveyed Clarissa and glanced at his blank canvas. A smile lit up his face. "Now I need to prepare the most important part—you!" he smirked as he crossed over to the sofa.

Clarissa gave a little start. She had been mesmerized watching the viscount set out his things, admiring the graceful, controlled movements of his body, and for a moment she had forgotten that he was doing it all so that he could paint her. Now her cheeks burned with bright spots of color and she shifted uneasily. What would he want her to do? The thought of being naked before him thrilled and appalled her. She glanced past him to where the painting of the kneeling girl now rested against the wall. She couldn't kneel. Even sitting up for a while sent blood rushing to her foot, increasing the pain.

Anthony shook his head as he noticed the trepidation fill Clarissa's eyes. "It's all right, my little love. I did tell you that you would remain on the sofa, and you will. Even if you had not damaged your foot, I would have posed you here. It is something I have imagined since I first saw you."

Clarissa said nothing, but her face relaxed and she managed a little smile. The viscount was now right next to the sofa, and he tipped her face up with his index finger. His eyes were intense. "My little flower, my muse, did you see the statue of Aphrodite reclining at the museum?"

Clarissa took a deep breath. She had stood in front of that statue for many long minutes, fascinated by the sensuousness of the goddess' naked body, only a small cloth draped over her lower limbs. She had looked so seductive, so alluring, and so satisfied with herself. Clarissa had found herself wondering what to would be like to be so confident and unashamed of her nakedness.

But now she squirmed. Thoughts she could foster in the

silence of her imagination were very different from following through on those ideas in broad daylight. She remained silent for a few moments, but when she saw the viscount's lips straighten into a firm line and his eyes harden, she swallowed and murmured, "Yes, yes, I did see her."

Lord Anthony's eyes lit up with approval and anticipation. He ran his fingers over her face and then slowly down her neck, to where her buttons were tightly fastened. "My sweet little love, my muse, I have often imagined you lying on this sofa, and I have contemplated what treasures I will uncover beneath your clothes. Now I will have the delight of seeing you in all your natural beauty, naked and unashamed." Clarissa squirmed again and the viscount almost purred. "There is no dishonor in letting me see how exquisite your body is." He gave a low chuckle. "I see that the thought of being displayed for me excites you. One day, I will show off your beauty to others, but I have anticipated this for so long that for now, I am going to keep it all to myself."

Clarissa's heart was beating so fast she thought it would burst through her chest. She balled her hands into fists, trying to calm her racing nerves. The light brush of the viscount's fingertips as he began loosening her buttons sent shivers through her, but she kept her eyes focused on his face, drawing courage from the tender fire in his eyes.

Slowly, assuredly, Lord Anthony loosened her dress. His capable, strong hands slid under the material and eased the material from her shoulders. Then he began working on the fastenings of her petticoat and stays. She took a deep breath as her breasts bounced free from their tight confinement. The viscount smiled, but his eyes did not waver from her face. When all of her garments were untied, he took all the layers in his hands and dragged them down her arms. Clarissa was a deep red when he uncovered her breasts.

Lord Anthony paused for a moment and examined her luscious tits, his eyes glazed with approval and desire. Her dress, held in his fingers, was caught on her arms and she couldn't move. She couldn't cover her nakedness or push him away as he lowered his mouth to her breasts and, with a long, slow swipe of his tongue, licked her.

A sound somewhere between a groan and a mewl emerged from her throat. The viscount's tongue lapped at first one breast and then the other. Her skin was tight and hot and her nipples were bunched into hard points that lewdly pointed at his mouth, begging for more of his touch.

Clarissa could hardly think any more when he took her one nipple into his mouth and began to suck on her breast. His tongue was still lapping her in quick, short strokes. Heat and ripples of arousal, such as she had never known, trembled through her, not only where he touched, but also all the way to the very deepest parts of her body. She felt as if she was melting, like butter left on a warm windowsill in summer. Lord Anthony suddenly released her breast with a popping sound and protests rose to her lips, but he was not finished with her. He gazed greedily at her other breast for a few seconds and then gave it the same kind of attention. Clarissa shivered. The wetness on her first breast was cold as the air brushed her, but the second breast was hot from the heat of his mouth. The contrast was disconcerting, and she gave another long, low moan.

Eventually, the viscount, satisfied for now, pulled away. He tugged at her clothes, which were pooled around her waist, and lifted her as he slid the mass of material down her body, leaving it bundled at the bottom of the sofa. She was naked to his gaze, except for her white stockings, tied with simple blue ribbons just above her knees.

Lord Anthony sat back and admired her beauty, his eyes raking her from the gentle curves of her legs, over the soft rise of her stomach, the luscious swell of her breasts, to the sweet beauty of her face. She shifted under his gaze but a quick, "Stay still," from him held her in place. His eyes wandered back along the path they had taken, this time lingering at the dark shadows between her legs. His finger gently stroked the silky blonde curls that covered the top of her mound. Her thigh muscles tensed but a sharp slap from him caused her to relax, splaying her legs slightly open and he caught a glimpse of the sweet pink petals that guarded her most private place.

With a laugh, he reached for one of the brushes in his pocket. Her body was a canvas on which he would paint his pleasure. Clarissa watched him, anxiety clouding her eyes. Lord Anthony gave a low chuckle. "My little flower, perhaps it would be better if you could not anticipate what I plan to do to you." He reached over her to access a small table on which various items had been arranged. The sleeve of his smock touched her breasts and a quiver ran through her. He riffled through the objects on the table and then sat back, a long strip of azure blue linen in his hands. He stretched it, pulling it taut.

Clarissa bit her lip and blinked rapidly. Deftly, Lord Anthony placed the blue linen over her eyes and tied it securely at the back of head. "There, that will help you to focus on the sensations and not worry about what will happen next."

Clarissa gasped. She reached up to drag the blindfold off her eyes, but Anthony caught her hand in his. He raised it to his lips and placed a kiss on her knuckles. "Do you trust me, little flower?"

Clarissa lay still on the sofa. Her betrothed let her consider the immensity of the question, not rushing her to give an answer. After a few moments, Clarissa nodded.

He brushed his finger down her cheek. "Clarissa, I mentioned earlier that it is necessary for you to articulate your answers clearly. If you cannot remember to do so, I will have to help your memory."

He could see her jaw tighten and then relax. She nodded again and then quickly added, "Yes, my lord."

Anthony ran his hands down her arms, along her hips, and

then rested them on her waist. His voice was quietly amused. "I think a tangible reminder will help." He quickly turned her over so that her bottom was facing up and her breasts pressed into the soft velvet of the sofa. Her head rested on her arms. She huffed.

Lord Anthony stroked the pretty curves of her arse, admiring the heart-shaped globes. His hands were deft, strong and firm. She squirmed and then relaxed as he gently massaged her. "There," he soothed, "all ready for me." He removed his hands from her buttocks, and she gave a little cry of loss. "It's all right, my little one. This is just a quick *aide de memoire*." With that, he brought his hand down in a sharp slap across the center of her bottom.

Clarissa cried out and raised her head, half-turning towards him, although the blindfold prevented her from seeing him.

He smoothed his hand over the slight pink mark where he had smacked her and the movement sent the heat deep into her. She relaxed, letting the sensations calm her.

The viscount nodded. "A count of five should suffice." And then, just as Clarissa clenched her buttocks, he added, "And that one didn't count. It was just for fun."

Clarissa gave a little groan. He thought he heard her murmur something that sounded like, "Not much fun." He grinned, while running his hand over her soft skin.

He raised his hand and brought it down hard against her right buttock. She squealed. This time he did not wait for her to settle, but quickly repeated the action on her left buttock. The next three followed in quick succession, the final one being placed right across the center.

Her bottom had turned a deep pink, a very pretty color, like roses coming into their first bloom of spring.

Clarissa buried her face in her arms, trying to hide the tears that leaked from her eyes. Her bottom stung and she felt awkward, uncomfortably exposed. She could feel the viscount's eyes on her, but she could see nothing.

For a moment, she was engulfed in misery. She wanted to push herself off the sofa, find her clothes and flee as far as she possibly could from this strange scene. But then the large, comforting hand of the viscount began stroking her back, sweeping from her shoulders down to her buttocks, and then back again. The regular rhythm soon lulled her.

Lord Anthony was making soothing sounds, and soon she could make out his words. "My sweet, brave girl. You are so beautiful when you surrender yourself to me for your pleasure."

Slowly, Clarissa began to relax and enjoy, letting the warmth of the spanking she had received seep into her. The obvious pleasure and acceptance in the viscount's voice eased her anxiety, and the knots of fear that had bound her so tightly for many years began to loosen.

She smiled.

Lord Anthony watched his beloved, admiring the soft flush of pleasure that colored her skin and the gentle curves that promised so much pleasure. When her body lost the earlier tension, he reached into his pocket and pulled out one of his favorite paintbrushes. He ran the soft bristles over the palm of his hand and then slowly, surely, stroked it over her back.

Clarissa squealed. "What's that? It tickles."

Anthony placed his hand on the small of her back, calming her. "Let that very active mind of yours rest and simply enjoy the sensations."

Clarissa giggled and then rested her head on her arms again. Anthony dragged the brush over her soft skin, enjoying the way her skin tightened and little goosebumps appeared along her arms and shoulders. He drew the brush down her body and then prodded it into the crease between her buttocks.

"No. no, not there," she protested, but Anthony ignored her, simply using his other hand to part her cheeks so he could see more clearly. The little hole was puckered and a deep pink color. He moved the paintbrush around her hole. She caught her breath and her body clenched. Then he shifted her legs farther apart and dragged the brush through the sweet juices that were pouring from her pussy. He dipped the brush into her wetness as if he were loading it with paint.

He stopped for a moment, studying her as if she were a painting and the next stroke of his brush were crucial to the image he was creating. With a nod, he began to color over the faint pink marks left from her spanking. She moaned as the wetness covered her skin. Lord Anthony bent closer to her. His tongue imitated the movements of the brush. Patiently, he lapped up her sweet juices that now painted her bum.

When he was satisfied with his work, he deftly turned her over. Her hands flew down in an attempt to cover the nakedness of her breasts and pussy. "No, little flower. You are not going to stop me from enjoying myself. Place your hands underneath you, and keep them there, no matter what I do to you."

She hesitated and then arched her back as she slid her hands beneath her body. As a reward, the viscount caressed her with long, sure strokes of his hands. He used the movement to splay her legs more widely apart. She tensed and tried to close her legs, but he tutted and she subsided, submitting to his desires, letting them guide her own.

He placed one hand on her stomach, a large, heavy hand that kept her in the position most convenient to his needs. His other hand continued its exploration of her. She let out a startled cry as one of his fingers entered her hole. The tight muscles stretched painfully as he probed her depths, his large knuckle pushing past the tight muscles at her entrance. She held back a sob. Then, as her body grew accustomed to the rude intrusion, she felt waves of pleasure wash over her. His finger wriggled and twisted inside her, opening and stretching her even more. She clenched her innermost muscles, trying to hold on to his intrusive finger, but with a quick pull, he with-drew it.

"No! No. More, again, please, please," she muttered, over and over again, yearning for more of him. The emptiness in her core needed to be satisfied, needed him to enter her, fill her up, make her whole.

He smiled and filled her again, this time with two fingers. The stretch burned and ached, but she wanted more. He began thrusting his fingers in and out of her in steady, controlled movements and soon she was squirming and raising her hips to meet his hand. Then his finger pressed a place inside her which seemed to be the very source of all her pleasure. She groaned as her body struggled to contain the pleasure. He continued thrusting his fingers inside her, deliberately working over that spot with each sure movement. When she felt as if her body would explode with pleasure, he pulled his fingers out. She sank deeper into the softness of the velvet cushions with a long sigh.

She was breathing fast, suddenly aware of the embarrassing wetness seeping from her core that left glistening marks on the tops of her thighs. The viscount placed his finger at the top of that glistening triangle and trailed it down between her legs, sending currents of shock ricocheting through her. His finger-tips slid down the middle of her folds, parting them slightly and causing more wetness to surge from her.

"Very pretty. Quite the most exquisite flower I have ever seen," he murmured, almost as if he was not talking to her, as if she was simply a work of art that he was admiring. In an odd way, Clarissa felt empowered by the viscount's perusal of her private parts and she opened herself to more of his touches.

He buried his face between her legs and began to eat her hungrily. His sucked at her folds and then took one between his teeth. He bit down hard and her body jerked. She wriggled, but with her hands trapped beneath her body, she could not push him away. He continued to explore her sweetness with his mouth and tongue, paying particular attention to the very center of her, running his tongue around her hole and up between her folds to her nub, but he didn't linger there.

When his tongue ran over her nubbin, she groaned and tilted her hips higher, silently begging for more. Lord Anthony ignored her plea. Using his tongue, he began to paint a picture of the furls of a rose. The flat blade of his tongue created the shapes of the unfolding petals, moving closer and closer to the little needy nub that was aching with desire.

After many minutes of meticulous work, he focused on her nub. It had hardened and poked out from the hood, red and throbbing. He traced its shape with his tongue, moving along the sides in regular circles. Then he lapped over the top and she screamed as the sensations overwhelmed her. He held her thighs apart and continued to lick with quick, hard strokes of his tongue. Her body tensed. Using his thumb, he circled her hole, and then plunged it into her.

Anthony continued to lick and nibble at her clit while using his thumb to stretch the tight muscles of her entrance. When her body began to move restlessly, chasing the pleasure that was just out of reach, he sucked her nubbin into his mouth and then bit it.

Clarissa screamed. She exploded in a paroxysm of shaking. Her breasts were tight and the nipples hard. Juices flowed from her eager cunt. She was flushed a deep pink and her breathing was ragged.

Her body was primed, pushing towards an explosion of sensations that she couldn't control, but neither could she reach the peak that she knew was waiting for her. She jerked her hips harder, trying to force his hand to move faster, harder. His thumb flicked over the top of her clit twice, three times. She shattered with a loud cry, a white light exploding behind her eyes. Then there was darkness.

Clarissa did not know how long it was when her breathing

began to slow down to its normal sedate rhythm and her eyes began to clear. Slowly, she became aware of the viscount's voice, gently saying things she could not understand. He was also licking his fingers, sucking the wetness off them that her body had made.

A flush of uncertainty swept over her, but Lord Anthony quickly lifted her into his arms and his murmurs became more distinct. "I am so proud of you, my beautiful goddess. You have pleased me with your unbridled passion. I have never seen anything more wonderful than the gift you have just given me. Watching you climax, knowing that you trusted yourself to my care, gives me such pleasure."

Clarissa nuzzled his chest, faintly aware of the aroma of oil paint and solvent that clung to the soft folds of his deep blue smock. His hands roamed over her naked back, reminding her of the pleasure he had given her. The wetness on her thighs was cooling rapidly but she didn't care that she might be leaving a mark on the velvet of the sofa. She gave a deep sigh of contentment.

"That's just a taste of the pleasure to come," the viscount promised. "But now I want to begin your portrait." He eased her back to the cushions, kissing her on the lips as he did so. She could taste the salty sweetness of her own juices that he had licked off his fingers. It made her squirm again, but he gave a quick command for her to settle, and she did.

The viscount stood, the artist battling with the lover as he considered how best to position this perfect woman who had surrendered herself so delightfully to him. He moved two cushions behind her, so she was almost sitting, and then placed her one arm along the back cushions of the sofa. Her other hand instinctively moved to cover her pussy, and he smiled. That was a perfect place for it, suggesting both innocence and wantonness. Her legs were stretched out on the sofa, the one slightly bent so that it was possible to glimpse the dark shadows of her pussy. He smoothed her hair and drew most of it over her one shoulder. It cascaded over her breast, but just enough of that beautiful mound peeped out to cause his mouth to water.

Delighted, Lord Anthony stepped back and admired her. "Perfect! You really are a paragon of art, my loveliest lady." Clarissa smiled at him, feeling as powerful as the goddess he had called her. Lord Anthony walked quickly to a low chest of drawers she had not noticed until now and returned with a soft chiffon throw, almost the color of her eyes. He draped this over her legs, ensuring that everything above her knees remained uncovered. The softness of the material was sensuous against her bare flesh. Finally, he set a deep red rose on top of the chiffon throw, its half-open petals pointing to her genitalia.

With a final nod, Lord Anthony asked, "Are you comfortable? Will you be able to hold that position for a while?" When she quickly assented, his smile broadened. "Good, because it will take more than this one sitting for the painting to be complete."

CHAPTER 15

DONNINGTON ABBEY

Clarissa shifted against the cushions in her husband's chaise and four, trying to stretch her legs without disturbing the viscount, who was sitting on the opposite bench. Even though the carriage was the most comfortable Clarissa had ever traveled in, after almost three days of travel, her legs were stiff and her head ached slightly. They had left London the morning after the wedding, and Clarissa was eager to reach Donnington Abbey, the viscount's main country seat where they would enjoy their honeymoon.

The first two days of the journey had been full of delightful promise of a passion-filled honeymoon. Lord Anthony had sat beside her, touching her, playing with her breasts and teasing her with kisses. When he hadn't been arousing her passions, he had read poetry to her and they had chatted comfortably about all manner of things.

But something had changed this morning. When she woke up, stretching languidly in the bed, she realized he was already dressed and had eaten breakfast. He had scarcely greeted her, instead urging her not to dawdle as he wanted to get on the road quickly.

As the carriage sped along the road, Clarissa watched her husband make a quick note on a piece of paper and then unfold another letter. He frowned as he perused its contents. Clarissa squirmed but when his eyes flickered towards her, she sat still and he returned to the documents that had occupied his attention since they had left the posting inn.

Clarissa frowned. She twisted her hand and looked at her wedding ring, her disquietude momentarily replaced by the thrill she always felt when she thought about the unexpected turn her life had taken and the pleasure she was learning to enjoy with her husband.

She stole another glance at him. His thick auburn hair was tousled from where he had been running his hands through it, and his finely-formed features were set in grim lines that made him appear formidable and unapproachable. Clarissa did not dare interrupt him, not even to ask the questions that tumbled through her brain.

He sighed, put aside a letter written on elegant cream paper, and scrawled something on the page on his writing table that was now filled with all kinds of notes that Clarissa could not read from her position on the other side of the carriage.

She twisted the ring on her finger and thought back to the night before, wondering if she had somehow displeased him, somehow failed to bring him the pleasure he expected from a wife. She gave a quick shake of her head. He had seemed very satisfied when, after having made love to her, he wrapped his arms around her and nestled her body close to his.

Clarissa knotted her fingers together in her lap, forcing herself to be as still as possible. Her eyes rested on Lord Anthony's hands, and a faint blush stole over her face as she remembered everything that those strong, capable hands had done to her in the last few weeks.

A quick stroke of his pen on the page called to her mind how skillfully he had wielded his brush while he worked on the painting of her and taught her to enjoy the pleasure to be had between a man and a woman. It had taken ten days for him to finish the painting and she had spent glorious hours each afternoon at his London house. She had appeased her aunt by explaining that Mrs. Barlow, the housekeeper, was showing her how the very large household of a viscount needed to be managed. But each day, after Mrs. Barlow had gone over the lists of which merchants sold the best produce, what duties each of the servants was required to fulfill and how the housekeeping budget was properly managed, Clarissa had made her way to the studio for a blissful hour.

As soon as she opened the door, Lord Anthony put aside his brush and paint and began the long, slow, sensuous process of disrobing her. She had quickly overcome her initial qualms and now delighted in the way he touched her, the way he roused her to heights of pleasure she had not imagined possible.

The painting, now resting in the studio as the varnish dried, showed a woman who had discovered the pleasures of surrendering to the love of the man she respected and admired. Clarissa bit back a little sigh, remembering how, each afternoon, while Lord Anthony painted and she reclined like Aphrodite on the blue sofa, they had talked comfortably and easily about music and art and how they had shared stories of their childhoods. Those long, languorous afternoons had brought them closer, connecting them in heart and soul and mind as well as body. Every day she had fallen more deeply in love with Lord Anthony.

Her wedding night had been a feast of delights, a celebration of love. Lord Anthony had led his willing bride into his bedchamber, where the large wooden bed had been covered in red roses. Slowly, he had unrobed her, kissing every inch of skin on her body as she lay on the bed, the soft light of the fire making her body glow. Her new husband had taken hours to worship her body, bringing her to her peak, over and over again, before finally claiming her fully as his wife, thrusting his hard, hot shaft into her warm, willing pussy and breaking through the barrier of her virginity. Even now, sitting in the carriage, she could feel the impression of his heavy manhood in her depths and longed for him to claim her again.

Clarissa was roused from her reverie as the coach slowed down to turn off the road. Massive wrought iron gates displaying the crest of the Donningtons in the center were laboriously opened by a pleasant looking man and his young daughter. Clarissa smiled at them as the carriage swept past and began to move up a long avenue which was lined with beautiful trees and woodland that stretched for miles on either side. She let out a little cry of delight and admiration.

Lord Anthony, responding to her for the first time since they had entered the carriage that morning, raised his head from his pile of papers and smiled, his eyes soft with affection. "The grounds of the Abbey are beautiful. In spring, bluebells carpet the woods, and in autumn, the red and gold of the leaves turn it into a fairyland. I like it in every mood, every season."

Clarissa peered through the window at the great oaks and elms that rose majestically for almost a mile along the avenue, exclaiming in delight at the deep green of the leaves and the patterns of sunlight that shimmered through the branches. She laughed when a tiny red squirrel scuttled up the trunk of a tree.

The road rose up through the woods and suddenly the way before them opened to the sunlight. Lord Anthony banged on the roof of the carriage, urging his coachman to halt. He nodded to Clarissa, pointing out the window opposite the one she had been looking through. "There," he said, his voice filled with pride, "that's the first view of the house itself."

Clarissa slid along the seat and looked through the window. "Can we get out so that I can see it properly?"

"Of course," Anthony said, already opening the door as a footman let down the steps.

Clarissa scrambled out of the carriage and gazed at the view spread out before her. Meadows and fields, verdant and lush in the summer sunshine, rolled over low hills to where a large lake glimmered in the afternoon light. Just beyond the lake, the light grey stone of the house blended into the landscape rather than imposing upon it. Tall chimneys rose from the steeply angled roofs and long windows on each of the three floors suggested an open, airy ambience. Clarissa turned to her husband who had been watching her response and smiled. "Oh, how beautiful. I don't think I have ever seen a house so well-situated, so pleasant and inviting."

Lord Anthony slid his arm around her waist and dropped a kiss onto her forehead. Clarissa leaned into his embrace, flooded with happiness. All would be well.

Suddenly the peace of the afternoon was shattered by the loud crack of a gunshot. Clarissa cried out in fear and shock, her head suddenly light and her throat tight. Lord Anthony bundled her back into the carriage, with curt instructions to the coachman to hurry to the house. Two groomsmen were already running back to the woods to see if they could find the perpetrator.

It took another ten minutes, even with the coachman urging the horses as fast as they could go, for them to reach the front door. Clarissa sat in anxious silence next to her husband. Lord Anthony held her close as they drove the last half mile to the house. He said nothing, simply murmuring soft sounds to soothe her, but she could feel how rigid his muscles were, how tense he was.

Shivers rippled through Clarissa's body and her eyes were tight with unshed tears. Swallowing was almost impossible because of the large lump that had formed in her throat. Her heartbeat didn't slow down as thoughts tumbled through her mind. It was improbable, impossible that guns should have been shot so close to her twice now, but that gunshot had been very real and very near.

Eventually, the coach drew to a stop in front of the steps that led up to the imposing entrance of Donnington Abbey. Clarissa stared with blurry eyes at the rows of servants lined up to greet the viscount and his new bride. She took a deep breath as she stepped out of the carriage, drawing on all her skills as a paragon of proper behavior to face the people who constituted her new household.

Fotheringham, the butler, had arrived at the Abbey ahead of Lord Anthony and Clarissa. He greeted them with a bow, and then he gestured to Mrs. Riggs, the housekeeper, to come forward, but she was brushed aside by another woman who forced her way through the lines of servants.

Clarissa gaped, bewildered at the striking woman, dressed in fine lavender silk with her red hair swept up in the most elegant style, who walked straight up to Lord Anthony, her arms stretched out and a dazzling smile on her impressive face. "Anthony," the woman gushed, her voice low and husky, "it is so good to have you home again. Poor darling, you look quite tense but now that you are home and finally able to rest, you will have nothing to worry about. I will take care of you."

Clarissa drew in a deep breath. Who was this woman and what was the connection between her and Lord Anthony? There was something vaguely familiar about her, but Clarissa was sure she had not met her. Clarissa clutched awkwardly at her dress, not sure what to say or do. None of her training as a paragon had prepared her to handle a lady who ignored her while paying lavish attention to her husband with a friendliness that suggested a long acquaintance and intimacy.

The viscount, conscious that every one of his servants was

149

within hearing distance, tightened his lips and asked, as calmly as he could, "Lucretia, I thought you had gone to Bath?"

The strikingly handsome woman gave a sultry laugh. "I had thought of opening the house there, but I realized that I would be needed here to ensure that you lack none of the comforts that you desire and to which you are accustomed when you return to the Abbey." For the first time, Lucretia looked at Clarissa, a smirk on her lovely face. But it was the look in her eyes that made Clarissa take a step backwards. Never had anyone, not even her cousins when she was young, looked at her with such derision, such intense hatred. Clarissa took a breath and then wondered if she had been mistaken. The venom in the other lady's eyes had vanished quickly and now she was looking at Clarissa with condescending pity. "The new Lady Donnington's reputation as a social belle precedes her, but things are different in the country and I know what pleases you, dear Tony," the elegant lady almost purred.

With a quick shake of his head, Lord Anthony muttered, "We will discuss this later." He gave a little tug and Clarissa, whose hand was resting on his arm, stepped forward. He cleared his throat and smiled at his assembled household. "Good day. Let me introduce you to my wife, Lady Clarissa." There was a flurry of curtsies and bows that made Clarissa blush, but the viscount simply nodded and turned to the housekeeper. "Mrs. Riggs, will you show Lady Clarissa to her rooms while I meet with Mr. Wallbridge in my study." He smiled at Clarissa, lowering his voice so that only she could hear him say, "I will be with you soon, my little flower."

Lady Lucretia gripped Clarissa's arm so sharply that it hurt, which belied the sweetness of her words, "No need to bother Mrs. Riggs. I will help the new countess to settle in." She hustled Clarissa up the steps and into the large hallway, not allowing her a moment to take in her surroundings. Mrs. Riggs followed closely behind, and within a few minutes, Clarissa was standing in front of a large white double door.

Lady Lucretia stepped back, looking smug, with her hands clasped lightly behind her back. Mrs. Riggs opened the door, her mouth drawn into a tight line. "These are your rooms, my lady. I trust that you will be satisfied. We have attempted to follow your instructions and ensure that all is as you requested, but we did not have much notice and it is sometimes difficult to transport items from London."

Clarissa stared at the housekeeper, her mouth slightly open and her eyes showing her confusion. She had given no instructions about her room; she had not even thought of her new home in the whirlwind of preparation before the wedding. But she answered as politely as she could, "Thank you, Mrs. Riggs. I am sure you have made the room as comfortable as possible." Then she followed the housekeeper into the room and stumbled to a standstill. She blinked, not daring to believe the testimony of her eyes. The room was large, light and airy, but Clarissa hardly noticed the proportions of the room. She turned her head slowly, trying to understand what she saw in front of her. The walls were papered in a green wallpaper with elaborate gold designs that swirled around the room in a dizzying display of pattern. The bed was canopied in a gold fabric and the curtains were the same ostentatious design. The bed itself was made of japanned ebony, covered in gilt patterns.

The bright red carpet continued the gold patterns, and chairs and tables and chests of drawers filled the room, all also made of enameled wood and painted in garish designs. Large gilt ornaments were set on some of the tables. Clarissa almost gasped when her eye caught sight of the legs of a chaise longue that were shaped like the feet of crocodiles, also in gold.

She turned to Mrs. Riggs, bewilderment clear on her face. The housekeeper was standing stiffly near a window, her hands clasped in front of her and her face looking grim. Her shoulders stiffened further when Clarissa moved towards her. Her voice was clipped and disapproving although she was trying to sound polite. "My lady, I trust this meets your approval. It was rather difficult to obtain all the pieces you requested, but no expense has been spared to fulfill your wishes."

Clarissa listened in stunned silence. Surely, there was a mistake, a misunderstanding, but the housekeeper had done her best to prepare for her arrival. Clarissa forced a smile. "Thank you for all your hard work. I am sure I will be very happy at the Abbey." She was saved from further prevarications by the arrival of footmen carrying her boxes and trunks. Her lady's maid, Rose, bustled in behind them, ready to help her remove her travel-stained clothes. Quickly, she dismissed the housekeeper, noting that Lady Lucretia had already vanished.

JUST OVER AN HOUR LATER, Clarissa, refreshed and feeling more relaxed now that she was in clean clothes, wandered out into the charming gardens she could see from her bedroom window. She was still bewildered by the strange events of her arrival, but the same kind of determination that had made her a paragon in society possessed her now. She was going to be the most perfect wife the viscount could have hoped for and she was eager to become acquainted with the house and gardens.

She draped a light shawl around her shoulders and walked slowly, admiring the abundance of flowers that bordered the paths. The merry singing of birds flitting from bush to tree and the dance of little blue butterflies filled her heart with song. Just beyond this garden, was a grove of trees similar to the larger woods they had driven through on the way through the estate.

She had seen nothing of the viscount since her arrival, and she wondered what was occupying his time. A slight frown creased her forehead in spite of the loveliness of the afternoon.

All the flurry of her arrival at the Abbey had taken her mind off the gunshot, but now as she wandered through the gardens, her thoughts free to roam, the fear of that moment reasserted itself. Her arrival here had not been the pleasant, tranquil start to her honeymoon she had anticipated. She still had no answers about Lady Lucretia or the strange matter of her bedroom, and a shudder shook her body as the memory of the gunshot forced its way into her thoughts.

As she stepped from the brightness of the afternoon sunshine into the shadow of the spinney, she pulled her shawl more tightly around her shoulders, shivering slightly at the coolness beneath the trees. A rustle of leaves and the sound of footsteps deeper in the woods brought her to a halt. She looked around anxiously but could see nothing. She was just about to turn back to the house, the thought of people shooting at her spoiling her pleasure of the afternoon and her delight in the woods, when three figures appeared on the path in front of her.

A startled scream caught in her throat when she recognized her husband, but the anger that distorted the handsome lines of his face made her take a step backwards.

"What are you doing out here?" he barked. Without waiting for her to answer, he turned to one of the other men who was with him. "Mr. Wallbridge, could I trouble you to escort Lady Clarissa back to the house, where she should remain. She has no business wandering through the woods."

The viscount turned back under the trees, followed closely by the third man. Clarissa stood uncertainly on the path until Mr. Wallbridge stepped forward, offering his arm. "My lady, this is not the most fortuitous way for me to be introduced to you, but come, let us go back to the house." He began walking with her back through the garden. "Let me introduce myself. I am the viscount's secretary. Of course, I know who you are."

Clarissa nodded but said nothing. She could not ask this stranger, pleasant as he was, what had made her husband behave so harshly towards her. Her already overwrought emotions were in complete turmoil and it took all of her self-control to hold back the tears that glistened in her eyes.

~

LORD ANTHONY STALKED into the dining room, his face hard and grim. He glanced at the long, formal table and his frown deepened. Clarissa was already seated at the distant other end of the table, far from his seat. Lucretia was settling herself in a chair to his right and Mr. Wallbridge was opposite Lucretia. The arrangements were not conducive to the kind of intimacy he wanted to share with his wife, but he said nothing as he took his place.

He glared down the length of the table, but the harsh lines on his face softened when his eyes rested on Clarissa. She was as exquisite as always, dressed in a simple blue evening dress, her hair kept in place with a bandeau. A single strand of pearls wrapped around her delicate neck was her only ornament, and she needed no other. But her eyes were slightly ringed with red and her lips were pinched tightly. The viscount's lips narrowed. This was not the happy bride he wanted to shower with pleasure as they began their life together.

With an irritated snap of his serviette, he reached for his wine glass. He should have returned to Donnington some weeks ago, rather than loitering in London, painting and indulging in the amusements offered in the metropolis. Too many things had gone wrong here on his estates in Dorset in his absence and he was inundated with tenants and farmers who needed his assistance. This was not the way he had planned to spend his honeymoon.

Mr. Wallbridge cleared his throat and Lord Anthony turned to him. The secretary's voice was low but urgent. "I know that dinner is not the time to discuss problems, my lord, but were you able to track down the poachers after I returned to the house?"

Anthony glanced down the table to where Clarissa was prodding a piece of beef. He was well aware of how his secretary, a man he had known since they had been students at Oxford, and whom he trusted implicitly, had avoided mentioning the peremptory way he had dismissed Clarissa in the spinney. He would need to console his wife later, but for now he answered his secretary. "There was no sign of them, but we did find some of the traps that they have been setting. There is an inordinate number of them and it will take us a while to find them all." He gave a shake of his head. "It is unheard of for poachers to be bold enough to come so close to the house. It isn't even as if there is much game in that little copse. The few poachers who do venture onto the estate, usually confine their activities to the woods nearer the common."

Mr. Wallbridge slowly sipped his wine. "Poachers also do not usually operate during the daytime. If it was a poacher who shot at you this afternoon, then they have become very bold and we will need to do something very drastic to stop them."

Anthony stabbed at a piece of beef on his plate. "We need to catch them first. In the meantime, they have made it dangerous for anyone to venture too far from the safety of the house."

Lucretia, who had been following this conversation with a smirk on her face, now turned a concerned face to the viscount. "You look quite exhausted, my dear. I am sure that Mr. Wallbridge and Trevett, who is, after all, a fairly capable steward, can handle the issues on the estate. You should relax and regain your strength."

Lord Anthony shot her an exasperated glare. "I am not an invalid in need of pampering. I am fit, healthy and more than capable of handling all that must be done. Furthermore, I am responsible for the estates and much as I trust Mr. Wallbridge and Mr. Trevett to do what I employ them to do, I will not rest until the problem with the poachers and the other issues that have arisen are settled."

Lucretia delicately swallowed the pureed potato she had taken a bite of and looked earnestly at the viscount, her eyes wide and guileless. Her voice oozed sympathy and a hint of admiration. "I know that I am only an ignorant female who knows very little of these matters. You are even more conscientious than your father was." She took a sip of wine. "I would like to offer you the same support and comfort I gave your father. After all, I have lived at the Abbey for many years now and am well-acquainted with its ins and outs. What issues apart from the poaching need your attention?"

The viscount placed his knife onto his plate with a clatter that caused even Fotheringham to shudder. His eyes focused again on Clarissa, and his lips pursed when he saw how she was staring at her plate and that she had eaten almost nothing. His new marriage was one of the issues that he needed to focus on, but he did not mention that to Lucretia. "The roofs on almost all of the tenants' cottages are leaking, even though they were all checked and repaired at the end of winter."

Mr. Wallbridge continued the litany of problems. "One of the streams has dammed up and is flooding some of the lower fields that have just been planted and there has been a spate of small, fairly random fires causing all kinds of damage."

Lady Lucretia tutted sympathetically but said, "Those seem to me to be nothing more than the normal problems on an estate this size. It seems to me to be a little beneath the dignity of a viscount to be so personally involved in helping the tenants deal with problems that are most likely due to their own neglect and carelessness." She glanced at Clarissa, who was still staring at her plate intently, and as she finished her point, her voice was light and amused. "There are all kinds of pleasures offered in the countryside in summer. A number of people have house parties and there are numerous dinners and picnics and even some balls to attend."

Lord Anthony did not reply, simply resuming his meal. Lucretia had never been very interested in the estate and she would not understand the severity of the problems he now faced. He took a deep breath, hoping that Clarissa would understand how necessary it was for him to spend much of his time in the coming weeks setting things right on the estate. Their honeymoon would be a little delayed.

CHAPTER 16

*C*larissa sat in front of the magnificent pianoforte in the drawing room. Her fingers idly picked out a tune but her thoughts were elsewhere. It had been five days since she had arrived at Donnington Abbey and she was lonely and a little bored.

Each morning, long before she was awake, Lord Anthony left their bed to go out in the fields or visit farmers and tenants with Mr. Trevett, leaving her to amuse herself. If she had been allowed to spend time outdoors, exploring the gardens and wandering through the woods, she might find inspiration to dabble with her watercolors. But the viscount, on that horrid first day at the Abbey, had curtailed her freedom to leave the house on such pleasant excursions. She did not want to disappoint him, and her memory of the shots that had been fired were enough to keep her obedient to his instructions, even though they had been expressed so peremptorily.

Every morning she took some exercise by walking up and down the long gallery of the house, and some days she even ventured onto the terrace, but she went no farther. In spite of the grandeur of the house and the wonders it contained, she felt stifled, constricted.

Her fingers slipped and the piano keys jangled horribly. She shuddered, but before she could resume her idle practice, Lady Lucretia, who had entered the room so quietly that Clarissa had not heard her arrive, exclaimed, "Do be careful. That is a very fine instrument, and it is usually only played by those who have been under the tutelage of the finest masters." She sauntered up to the pianoforte and placed her hand possessively on the keys. "It was bought for me by the viscount."

Clarissa raised startled eyes to Lucretia, but her mouth was suddenly dry and she found it difficult to speak.

Lucretia gave a hard chuckle as she deigned to explain. "I mean the late viscount, Lord Alexander, Tony's father. I was the late viscount's second wife." Her fingers played random notes on the keyboard. "When the viscount was widowed, people claimed he would never remarry, but I was very persuasive. I have had a very good life as the countess. People defer to me because of my position and the reputation of the Donningtons." She gave a light laugh. "As you know, the Donningtons are very admired men, extremely wealthy, and even though my husband was quite a bit older than I, he was still a handsome man who knew how to please a woman." Her dark eyes glittered with derision. "And now that Anthony has married you, I am the *dowager* countess." Her lips straightened with annoyance. "I am not old enough to be a dowager. The word is so suggestive of fussy, staid old ladies, while I am only two years older than Tony and have my life ahead of me. I will not go and sequester myself in the dowager's house, but it is rather tedious to have to re-enter the marriage mart and compete for another husband."

Clarissa remained silent. Some of the mystery of Lucretia was solved in this offhand explanation, but Clarissa was uneasy. The dowager countess was not as affable as the friends she had made in the last few months. She was not likely to become friends with this hard, bitter woman. There was something supercilious about Lucretia, something that Clarissa found disturbing in her cold beauty and insidious comments.

Lucretia played a chord on the pianoforte and snapped out, "As I said, this instrument is only for those who are skilled and I will not allow it to be ruined by clumsy hands." She closed the lid abruptly, forcing Clarissa to move her fingers quickly so that they were not caught by the heavy wood.

Still, Clarissa said nothing. Lucretia cast a scornful look at her. "You are a little mouse. So insipid. Tony is hardly likely to remain besotted with you for long. He needs something much more passionate than a paragon of social behavior. He is a man of intense emotions and physical prowess. He needs a woman who can match his... stamina."

Clarissa shifted uneasily on the piano chair, not sure how to defend herself against such an attack. Lucretia huffed impatiently as she changed the subject. "It seems that news of your marriage to Tony and your arrival here has spread throughout the district. A number of invitations and notes have been sent to you. You will need to reply. I have left them in the morning room." With that, she swept from the room, leaving Clarissa to wipe back the tears that threatened to slide down her face.

After a few moments, Clarissa made her way to the pretty morning room, decorated in soft blues and creams, where the countess was expected to deal with her correspondence and household matters. Clarissa had not used the room much. Lucretia dealt with all household matters with Mrs. Riggs and Clarissa had not been in Dorset long enough to have much need to write letters. She now sat at the satinwood escritoire and stared at the pile of letters addressed to her. There were so many that Clarissa, for a moment, wondered if they had been there for a few days and had not all arrived by that morning's post.

With a shrug, she opened the first one. By the time she had opened a dozen and a stack still waited for her attention, she felt overwhelmed. In London, Aunt Agatha had always dealt with the correspondence, had instructed her on how to reply to the many invitations she had received, had sorted through them, deciding which ones needed immediate response and which could be ignored altogether.

She did not know many of the people who had invited her for tea or to soirees and dinners. There were even invitations to two balls. She did not know how to answer, which to prioritize, who the viscount counted as his special friends among them, and which were mere acquaintances. With a shake of her head, she gathered all of them into a pile and decided she needed to consult Lord Anthony.

Quickly, she walked down the long corridor where the viscount's office was situated. She slowed when she saw a footman standing in front of the closed door. She bit her lip and shuffled the letters in her hand.

She stopped at the door, squaring her shoulders, and raised her chin. She would not be daunted by the rituals in an aristocratic household. She was, after all, a countess, and she could deal with footmen, even those who looked at her with disdain.

"I would like to speak to the viscount," she declared, her voice not quite as authoritative as she had hoped it would sound.

The footman, who towered over her from his six-foot height, flicked his eyes over her, but his face remained impassive. She forced herself not to shuffle. "His lordship is extremely busy," the footman, whom Clarissa thought had been introduced to her as Hubert, pronounced ponderously.

Clarissa stood her ground. Surely, her husband could spare a few minutes to help her? She tried to stare sternly at Hubert, but she faltered at his continued implacable manner. "I know that the viscount is busy, but I need to speak to him."

With a slight twitch of his lips, Hubert rapped lightly on the door and opened it no more than an inch. His voice was a little louder, but still ponderous, impassive as he announced, "The honorable lady countess wishes to see his lordship."

The murmur of voices in the study ceased and Clarissa took a deep breath. The papers in her hand rustled as she prepared to enter the room, and then she stopped, brought to a standstill by Lord Anthony's sharp response. "That woman is not to enter my study, under any circumstances."

Hubert turned mocking eyes to Clarissa as he closed the door.

~

CLARISSA STUMBLED to the terrace and dropped the pile of letters onto a table as if they were a fire that burned her. She began to pace along the length of the terrace, her hands clenching and unclenching in agitation. She was about to make her second turn when Mrs. Riggs appeared at the door. Clarissa stopped her pacing. The housekeeper raised an eyebrow, but her voice was as businesslike as usual. "Lady Margaretta Bascombe is waiting for you in the white room."

As Clarissa made her way to the small formal drawing room, she recalled that one of the dinner invitations had come from Lady Bascombe. Clarissa opened the door, expecting to see a matronly woman, probably plump and somewhat homely. She was surprised to see a young lady, not much older than herself, wearing a fashionable yellow gown, with laughter filling her eyes as she came towards Clarissa, her arms outstretched in welcome.

"Good day, Lady Clarissa. I am so glad to meet you. You are quite as lovely as gossip painted you!" Lady Margaretta enthused.

Clarissa was quite taken aback and a smile broke out on her

face, banishing the gloom she had carried for so many days. "Thank you for calling on me, Lady Bascombe. Let's sit down and we can chat."

She quickly arranged for tea to be brought in, although Lady Margaretta protested, "I have come to make a polite social call. I should not stay more than a quarter of an hour!"

Clarissa bit her lip, trying to disguise her disappointment. Lady Margaretta reminded her of Amelia and Charlotte and she was in desperate need of a friendly face. "Oh," she began, "I know that it is proper to restrict the length of a first call, but I was hoping we might spend a little more time becoming acquainted."

Lady Margaretta's lively expression became a bit more serious as she contemplated the young bride. She sat back against the cushions of the settee. "Yes, perhaps a longer visit is in order. You must tell me all that is happening in London. I have not been back since I married Lord Bascombe in my first season, and that was four years ago."

Clarissa gave a quick nod. "That explains why I have not met you. This is my third season and I did not arrive in London until long after you left."

"I do miss the bustle of the city, although the quietness of this district is very pleasant, too. Lord Bascombe is not often able to get away from the work on his estate." She giggled. "And so, I have become used to being a country wife. Although there is not much in the way of lively company, my husband and the viscount have been friends for a long time. We are hosting a little dinner party next Tuesday and it would be a wonderful opportunity for you to meet everyone."

Clarissa felt a niggle of uncertainty about simply accepting any invitation without her husband's approval, but she had warmed to this young lady and it would be very pleasant to be in company again. "We will be there," she promised, "if the viscount is available."

~

Clarissa sat on the window seat of her ostentatious dressing room. She was dressed in an elegant green evening gown with a light wrap draped over her shoulders. Through the window, she could see glimpses of the beautiful gardens surrounding Donnington Abbey. She longed to explore its various nooks and crannies. The chiming of a small carriage clock on her dressing table brought her attention back to the room.

She glanced down at the long driveway, an agitated frown pursing her lips. She could see the carriage waiting at the door, but there was no sign of the viscount. He had, as on most days, left the house before she was awake, and he had not yet returned although he had seemed enthusiastic when Clarissa had mentioned Lady Margaretta's dinner.

Clarissa was not sure whether she should send a footman with a note excusing them or wait another few minutes. Her stomach twisted nervously and she almost ran her fingers through her carefully arranged hair. Her agitation was interrupted by a loud rap on the door, quite unlike the usual polite, gentle tap she had come to expect from the servants. She stood up hurriedly, convinced that something quite dreadful must have happened to Anthony.

"Come in," she called out, as impassively as she could manage.

The door opened to reveal the footman Hubert. Clarissa frowned slightly but kept her voice polite. "What is it?"

"Ma'am, I have come to tell you that you are not to wait for the viscount."

Clarissa was so agitated, she hardly noticed that the footman's manner was bordering on being offensive. "Did his lordship say why?" she asked.

"His lordship said it is easier for him to get there on his own."

Clarissa bit back a hiss of irritation. Lord Anthony was usually much more polite and it was not like him to neglect her in this way. If something had delayed him, could he not at least have taken the time to write a quick note to her rather than sending a surly footman to deliver such a brusque message? But the same training that had taught her to expect more polite behavior from her husband kept her from letting the servant see her frustration. She gathered her gloves and wrap, saying, "Thank you. Please tell the coachman that I will be down directly."

~

LORD ANTHONY TUGGED at his dinner jacket, hoping that he was at least presentable. His manservant, Symes, had brought his clothes to Mr. Meech's farm where the kindly farmer's wife had given him a can of hot water and allowed him to change in the best bedroom.

A clock chimed on the landing of the Bascombes' pleasant house. He hoped the guests had not yet entered the dining room. He might not be a paragon of correct behavior, but he had been brought up to believe that punctuality was a sign of politeness and he did not like to be seen as rude.

He was brought to a halt outside the drawing room by Lucretia's simpering voice. "Tony, I am so glad you are here. It seems that we were both a little delayed."

Anthony stared at her, his face wrinkled by the frown that was becoming habitual. "Did you not come in the carriage with Clarissa?"

She placed her hand on his arm, giving a light laugh that was almost sultry. "Oh dear, there was some kind of a mix-up. I am sure Clarissa did not mean to leave me behind but she raced off so quickly that I had to arrange for another carriage to bring me." She gave another little laugh. "At least I am not late on my own!"

The frown on Lord Anthony's face deepened to a scowl, but

the butler, who had opened the door, was announcing their arrival. "The Viscount and Countess of Donnington." He hardly took a breath and added, "Dinner is served."

Anthony glanced around the room at the twenty or so guests who were arranging themselves to lead into the dining room. He caught a glimpse of Clarissa, her sleek blonde hair gleaming in the candlelight. She looked just as he had seen her many times in London drawing rooms, with her face composed into a calm mask and her head held high, but he knew her well by now. It did not take more than a second for him to notice that her lips were drawn into a straight line and her eyes were sad even though she smiled politely as Matthew Bascombe offered her his arm.

The viscount shook his head but could not refuse to lead Lucretia, who was still attached to his arm, to the dining room. It took a few minutes for the guests to assemble around the long dining room table. Anthony tried to hold back his annoyance when he realized that he was seated next to Lucretia, and his precious Clarissa was at the other end of the table near Lord Bascombe. He had to fight back the urge to stride over to where Clarissa was quietly accepting Matthew's help as she took her seat. Anthony wanted to sweep his wife into his arms and find somewhere very private where he could spend some time alone, reacquainting himself with her gorgeous body. It had been too long since he had made love to her, even though each night he slipped into bed beside her sleeping form and held her close to him while he tried to get some rest from the problems on the estate that seemed to grow worse each day.

He was forced into politeness by Margaretta who was seated at his right hand. "I'm so glad you managed to arrive before dinner began," she said.

Anthony smiled politely. "It was a narrow squeak, but here I am."

Margaretta tilted her pretty head and looked at him quizzically. "I have grown very fond of your wife in the short time that I have known her. There is so much more to her than rumor suggested."

Anthony's face softened with tenderness. "Clarissa is one of the finest women I have ever known."

Margaretta gave a triumphant smile. "I am glad to hear you say so. Such a defense is just what one would hope for from a loving husband." She accepted the mushroom soup a footman was offering and then continued. "I have noticed, however, that she is not brimming with the kind of happiness one would expect in a young bride."

Anthony picked up his soup spoon, but his eyes wandered down the table to rest on Clarissa who was taking delicate sips of soup, more from politeness than enjoyment, even though the Bascombes always kept a very good table. However, his answer to Margaretta sidestepped his wife's emotional state. His lips straightened with irritation. "Margaretta, it appears that your lack of boundaries is an issue. I think I will need to mention your impertinence to Matthew."

Margaretta almost grinned at this. Her eyes were bright and eager. "I'm sure Matthew will think of a very interesting way to show me where I have crossed the boundaries." She ate a little of her soup and then, in a more serious tone, said, "Why were you late this evening? It isn't like you not to be on time. And although you are as elegantly dressed as always, there is a faint whiff of smoke around you."

Anthony glanced around him at the other guests who were all chatting quietly to their dinner partners. He answered quietly. "A part of an elm tree came down on the roof of the cottage of one of the tenants. It caught in the fireplace and most of the cottage was burnt to the ground."

Lucretia, who, on his other side, had been listening to some of the exchange between Anthony and Margaretta, now joined the conversation. "My poor Anthony. It is quite dreadful for you to be exposed to such dangers. You really should have left them to sort it out as it was an accident caused, I am sure, by their neglect. I do hope you are going to charge them for the damages caused."

"What?" Anthony was unable to hold back his irritation. "I have spent most of today helping them to move into a new cottage. They are good tenants and deserve my support, not my condemnation."

Lucretia let his words roll off her as if his frustration was nothing more than a polite enquiry about the weather. She gave a little laugh and placed her hand on his arm. "Dear Tony. Always so noble and righteous. You need to think of your finances before indulging all the peasants who come begging and pleading for your mercy because they do not have the sense they were born with."

The viscount bit back a further retort and joined the conversation about art that Margaretta had encouraged Sir Bentley, on her other side, to begin.

∼

CLARISSA HAD ENJOYED dinner more than she expected. Matthew Bascombe was an intelligent and lively conversationalist and the general chatter around her had been invigorating. Although Lord Bascombe was not one of Lord Donnington's closest friends, they had spent much time together in their youth and they shared similar outlooks on life.

Now, however, the ladies had withdrawn, leaving the gentlemen to their cigars and brandy and all of the anxiety she had felt earlier flooded back. As the ladies gathered in small groups, she overheard one stout, middle-aged woman, whom she had seen at some functions in London, declare, "I am sorry my own Matilda was never able to capture Donnington's interest. I had hoped to marry her off this season, but she is still young and I will find her a suitable match soon enough."

Clarissa stiffened her shoulders as the ladies nearby cast surreptitious glances her way. The woman who had spoken reminded her of Aunt Agatha and, for a moment, she was homesick.

Another lady rustled her fan. "I have heard that the Earl of Sherbonne might be looking for a wife."

A third lady raised her eyebrow. "His mother, Lady Lydia, despairs of his ever settling down. He has an eye for a pretty petticoat and is much too interested in pleasure to think of marrying."

The first woman, Matilda's mother, gave a polite little snort. "Still, he is extremely eligible and with a little persuasion could be convinced to consider Matilda. Matilda is hoping to secure the interest of a rich and titled husband, and she is quite prepared to accept that he will not be the kind of husband to crowd his wife with unwanted attention. He will let his wife live her own life, satisfied with what she gains by marrying him. And Matilda has a good dowry."

Clarissa suppressed a cold shiver as she moved out of earshot of these ladies. A surge of despair clutched at her heart. The conversation about Matilda's prospects reminded her of her declaration of independence, given so boldly to Aunt Agatha at the beginning of the season. She had not wanted a husband to curtail her independence, and yet now that Lord Donnington was treating her the way she had thought would make married life tolerable, she was deeply disappointed. Marriage was not living up to her deepest yearnings. She wanted her husband to pay her the kind of attention she had become accustomed to from him, that she had enjoyed so much, when he had painted her portrait. Her eyes wandered over the paintings in Lady Margaretta's drawing room. Perhaps Lord Anthony was true to his nature as an artist. He was focused, intent, when he was painting, when creativity inspired him, but once the work was complete, he began to look for a new source of inspiration.

As she roamed the room, lost in her thoughts, she stopped just behind a settee which two older ladies had occupied. One flicked a fan towards Clarissa as she spoke to her companion. She did not seem to care that Clarissa could hear every word clearly. "That's an interesting little set-up the viscount has going for him."

The other lady looked across the room to where Lucretia was demanding that the piano should be opened. "It is, indeed, He has managed things very well, but then the Donningtons have always known how to settle things to their best advantage."

The lady with the fan scoffed lightly. "I do believe that the inimitable Lady Lucretia was expecting to continue her role as the Countess of Donnington. She had her eye on the young Lord Anthony even when she was married to his father."

"But my dear Lady Cunningham, just imagine the scandal if he had married his father's wife, even if they are almost the same age! He has it all now—a perfect society wife and his mistress all living under the same roof."

Neither lady paid any heed to Clarissa's little shocked cry at this. She clutched at the edge of a chair, afraid that she might fall as blood drained from her face. The ladies continued as if she was not there.

"Of course, the proper thing for Lucretia to have done was to remove to the dowager house, or to Bath where, I believe, she has a house."

"That would be inconvenient for the lovers. They might not have actually married, but they are quite unashamed about flaunting their relationship. Did you notice how they arrived together this evening, separately from the new bride, and they managed to have themselves seated together all through dinner? I couldn't see him clearly, but I noticed how she ogled him quite scandalously."

The sound of the piano made it difficult for Clarissa to continue to follow the conversation, but she had heard more than enough, more than she wanted to hear. Her heart felt like a heavy stone weighing her down. Her stomach was twisted into knots. It was almost impossible to breath.

She was startled to feel a hand on her arm and to hear Lady Margaretta saying, "Are you all right?"

She had not noticed her friend approaching, but now she forced a smile onto her face and answered politely, although her voice was brittle. "I am well, thank you. I was admiring the paintings in this section of the room."

Lady Margaretta huffed skeptically. "I know some of Lord Bascombe's ancestors are quite formidable, but none of these paintings put that look on your face. Do tell me if there is anything I can do to help?"

Clarissa shook her head. "Thank you, but I just felt a little dizzy for a moment. I am fine now."

Margaretta looked unconvinced, but her drawing room after dinner was not a good place to pursue the kind of personal conversation she would like to have with Clarissa, so she smiled and, taking Clarissa by the hand, said, "If we are to have music, then I insist that you play the wonderful ballad you showed me when you came to tea yesterday."

Clarissa glanced at Lucretia as she answered, "I am sure there are many more skilled players here. I will sit and enjoy their music."

"You play with such feeling, such a sensitivity to the music that no one would ever notice one or two technical deficiencies. Please play." She lowered her voice so that only Clarissa could hear her. "It will be pleasant to hear someone who understands the sense of the music rather than simply flaunting her proficiency." She looked at Lucretia whose fingers were flying over the keys but whose face was expressionless.

Clarissa gave her friend the beginning of a smile. "I do love that song, and it suits my mood this evening. Besides," she spoke almost to herself, "the viscount has said that he enjoys hearing me play."

Margaretta nodded. They had reached the piano where Lucretia was bringing her piece to an end with a flourish. Lucretia looked up at the two ladies who stood beside her. There was a smirk on her face. "I see the paragon has come to display her skills. I am not sure that this gathering is ready for her London ways. It is not as if she needs to impress a prospective husband with her tedious playing." She played a quick succession of chords. "It is sometimes more suitable for those who are not very proficient to give way to those better able to entertain an elect group such as this."

Clarissa felt the heat of blood rushing to her face. She had spent many hours perfecting the accomplishments a young lady was expected to have in the hope that her achievements would deflect attention from her tainted background. Her watercolors and embroidery were exceptional, but she knew her limitations. She enjoyed music but was not quite as skilled at the piano and harp as so many other young ladies were. She had no answer for Lucretia's taunts and took a step back.

Lady Margaretta, however, was made of sterner stuff. She rushed to the defense of her new friend, ignoring Lady Lucretia and coaxing Clarissa. "Oh, but you must play that ballad. It was one of the loveliest I've heard in a long while, and I will be so disappointed if you do not sing it."

Clarissa tried to protest, but one of the other ladies, who had been about to take Lucretia's place in front of the piano, moved aside, smiling warmly at Clarissa.

Clarissa sat down and flexed her fingers. To continue to demur, would suggest a false modesty, so she ran her fingers over the keys and drew on her memory to play the ballad Lady Margaretta had requested. Although she might not be as technically proficient as some young ladies, her voice was sweet and plaintive and she played with all her heart. She soon forgot the audience that had gathered around the piano, as she lost herself in the music.

Her voice rose clear and true as the words of the refrain echoed her own troubled heart.

"O my heart, my heavy, heavy heart!,
Swells as 'twould burst in twain!
No tongue can e'er describe its smart;
Nor I conceal its pain."

The last few notes echoed into the now quiet room. Clarissa's fingers rested on the last keys and she took a deep breath as the gathered guests applauded. She was about to get up when a large hand rested on her shoulder, keeping her in place. She felt the familiar comfort of Lord Anthony's touch. He leaned closer to her as the other guests resumed their chatter.

"That was a very touching rendition of the song, my little flower. Won't you play me another?" His fingers trailed across the back of her neck as he spoke. "Perhaps the Bach prelude that I enjoy so much."

The viscount handed her the music that had been lying on top of the piano. His fingers brushed against hers and she looked up at him, her eyes wide and pleading for more of his touch. She was confused, uncertain, and the conversations she had heard played in her mind, but she wanted him near her, longed to feel his hands on her. She would take whatever he offered.

She was vaguely aware that the other guests, now that the men had joined the ladies, were being served tea and coffee. A hum of conversation filled the room. But Lord Anthony blocked her view of most of the room and she was consumed by his closeness.

She placed the music on the rack, checking the opening bars, although it was a piece she knew well. Her husband had not taken his hands off her shoulders and the continuous light strokes of his fingers sent ripples of pleasure through her, quite at odds with the serious tone of the music she was about to play.

She wanted this moment to last, cocooned in the beauty of the music and surrounded by his presence. She leaned back slightly, resting her shoulders against his hips and offering him more of her body to touch. She began the familiar music.

He shifted, pressing himself against her. She could feel the solid bulge of his cock against her back. He whispered in her ear, "That's perfect, my little flower. Keep playing. No one can see how I am touching you, but they can hear you and if you make a mistake, it will be obvious, so it is better not to draw their attention."

Clarissa smiled softly, pleased that Lord Anthony still found her irresistible. It was difficult to concentrate on the music while his hands roamed over her back and then slid around to the front. She gave a little start when he cupped her breasts and began to fondle them through the silky softness of her dress.

A laugh caught in the viscount's throat. "That was one missed note. Be careful, you don't want them to add up. There will be consequences."

Clarissa tried to divide her attention between the music and his touch, but the more he caressed her, the more difficult it was to play steadily. She was breathing more quickly and every part of her body was sensitive to the nearness of the viscount. Her breasts were aching and her skin was taut. Shivers rippled over her and every movement of air in the room sent new sensations pulsing through her. Her hands felt clammy and she was light-headed.

Her body was growing warmer and warmer as her blood raced and the heat radiating from her husband increased. She played on, but she knew she was making mistakes, not obvious ones but her timing was off and her fingers slipped on the keys each time Lord Anthony tweaked her nipples or stroked the exposed skin of her décolletage. The fingers of his left hand traced a path up to her throat and settled possessively around the slim column. His right hand continued to play with her breasts.

Faintly, above the music, Clarissa heard his breathing also increase and the soft counting each time she was so distracted that her attention wavered and a note was missed. She looked up at the sheet of music in front of her. Only twelve bars of music remained. She would finish with a flourish, sure that she had won this game with her husband.

Her fingers reached for the last keys. She smiled in triumph, even as Lord Anthony murmured, "Eighteen!"

DONNINGTON ABBEY WAS dark and quiet as Lord Anthony and Clarissa arrived home after dinner. Lucretia was in her own carriage and had left the Bascombes' house sometime before they had. Now, as the night porter opened the door for them and the footmen on duty came to take their coats and gloves, the viscount turned to his wife with a gleam in his eye.

He was very proper and polite in front of the servants, but Clarissa felt a thrill of anticipation wash through her as she turned to go upstairs and he said, "Before you retire for the night, my sweet one, I would like to see you in my dressing room."

Clarissa almost ran up the stairs and as soon as Rose, her lady's maid, had loosened her garments, she dismissed her. She slipped into a soft white lawn nightgown that was almost transparent against the light of the fire that burned in the grate, taking the chill off the late summer evening. Even so, she shivered.

Slowly, she crossed her room and knocked softly on the viscount's dressing room door. He must have been listening for her because his deep, pleasant voice called out immediately, "Come in!"

She opened the door and hesitated. He was standing in the middle of the room beside a sturdy wooden chair. He had removed his coat and cravat and rolled up his sleeves, and Clarissa was reminded of how the muscles of his arms flexed when he had painted her.

Although her attention was focused on her husband, Clarissa was acutely aware of how different his rooms were from the ostentation of her own. His room was comfortable, with cozy chairs, a deep mahogany dressing table and forest green curtains. The brightly burning fire cast a glimmer of welcome over the deep hue of the wood and comforting colors of the cushions. His dinner jacket lay in a rumpled heap on a chair near the armoire and his cravat was draped over the back of the same chair.

Clarissa clasped her hands behind her back and waited. The viscount's eyes raked over her, taking in how her loose hair framed her face and provided a curtain through which her breasts peeked out enticingly. Her white nightgown clung to her limbs and the curve of her buttocks could be seen through the soft material.

"Come closer, my little flower," he instructed, his voice rough with anticipation.

Clarissa took such a deep breath that her breasts rose and fell, and blood surged to the viscount's cock as it eagerly prepared for the coming delights. It continued to throb as Clarissa walked slowly across the room and stood silently before him, her exquisite face turned up to his, her lips slightly parted and her eyes bright and eager.

He sat down on the chair he had placed in the middle of the room. He reached around her waist and drew her closer to him. His legs parted and she was caught between the firm muscles of his thighs. His hands molded her buttocks and his fingers pressed into her soft, inviting flesh. Clarissa was unsteady on her feet as her husband's hands roamed over her.

With a final pinch of her shapely buttock, Lord Anthony, looking more content than he had in a long while, said, "Kneel."

Clarissa was startled by the instruction. She hesitated, lifting uncertain eyes to his face. The viscount quirked an eyebrow and waited for her to obey. Eventually, Clarissa lowered herself before her husband. She looked up at him, taking a deep breath. Strangely, she felt a wave of contentment sweep over her, surrounded as she was by him. All his attention was focused on her.

Lord Anthony traced the outline of her face with his finger and then followed the line down her throat, to the opening of her nightgown. Her breath hitched as he moved his hand beneath the material and found the rise of her breast.

He smiled. "Well done, my little one. We will be able to talk easily now." He ran his finger along the edge of her chin and then cupped her face. When she had taken a few deep breaths to steady herself, he continued, "When you played the piano this evening, I gave you an instruction."

Clarissa bit her lip and nodded, but when her husband's eyebrow shot up, she managed to say, "You did, my lord."

His face was serious but his eyes twinkled. "I also mentioned that there would be consequences for failing to do as I asked."

This time Clarissa's voice caught in her throat and she couldn't verbalize her answer. She shuffled a little closer to the viscount, her eyes still focused on his.

Lord Anthony prompted her with a direct question. "Do you know how many errors there were when you played the Bach sonata?"

Clarissa shook her head and murmured, "I'm not sure, my lord. It was... difficult to keep count. Besides," she defended herself, "playing the piano is not my best accomplishment."

The viscount tilted his head and leaned slightly forward. "I have heard you play that piece perfectly and brilliantly. You're not going to wiggle out of the consequences with such specious arguments."

A thrill of excitement ricocheted through Clarissa. Her voice was husky with arousal. "No, my lord. I wasn't seeking to escape the consequences, only to clarify why I was not as proficient as I should be."

Anthony chuckled. "It is just as well that I was concentrating. I counted eighteen errors."

"Surely not," Clarissa exclaimed, despair tinging her voice. "Oh, how dreadful. I really wanted to make a good impression on people this evening and now they will think I am a silly little girl who does not know her own strengths and weaknesses."

All hint of humor fled from Lord Anthony's face and voice. "My little flower, people enjoyed your fervor, your enthusiasm, and the errors you made were slight, not likely to cause you to be ostracized." He brushed a kiss onto her forehead. "Besides, I enjoyed your performance this evening, and my opinion is more important than all of theirs."

Clarissa gave a low huff of laughter. "Yes, my lord. I enjoy pleasing you."

"That's just as well, because I am going to ask more of you tonight than I have before, and when you yield yourself to me, I will be pleased, and you will be too, eventually."

A frown creased Clarissa's forehead. "Eventually?" she repeated. "Does that mean I won't find it pleasing at first?"

"There are different ways to experience pleasure," was his enigmatic reply.

Clarissa shivered at the look in his eyes and the rough edge of desire in his voice. "What happens now?"

"Now you find out the consequences of being distracted while you played the piano. I need you to place yourself over my lap."

Confusion, dismay and anticipation filled Clarissa's eyes. She stood up slowly and tilted her chin. With her hands clasped in front of her and the flush of arousal brightening her face, she was an appealing mix of innocence and desire. She drew in her breath, wondering what would happen if she resisted her husband's command. "It wasn't my fault that I made mistakes." A small smile hovered on her lips. "I was... distracted."

A glimmer of laughter shone in the viscount's eyes but he kept his voice somber. "Life can be horribly unfair sometimes. Come now, don't dawdle!"

Clarissa moved closer and then stared at Lord Anthony's lap. How was she supposed to arrange herself over those muscular thighs?

Her husband, seeing her uncertainty, placed his hands on her hips and drew her closer but immediately spun her around and bent her over his knees. She squealed but settled into the strange position. Her arms dangled over his left leg and her feet scraped the floor on the other side. Her stomach pressed into his thighs and she blushed when she realized that his cock was hard under her, poking into the softness of her flesh.

Clarissa let her husband tug and pull at her, as limp as a ragdoll, until he grunted in satisfaction. "Now, my sweet one," he spoke conversationally, as if he were about to have a cup of tea with his wife, not spank her over his lap, "I think a smack to your beautiful bottom for each mistake is a fair punishment."

Clarissa twisted quickly, turning her face to look up at him. "Punishment? Smacks? Is that what you meant when you said I might not find it pleasing?"

Lord Anthony's hand was rubbing her buttocks gently but firmly. In spite of her shock at what was about to happen, Clarissa felt the stirrings of desire unfurl in her innermost parts.

"I think you might find it more pleasing than you expect," commented Lord Anthony as he lifted his hand and brought it sharply down on her right buttock. "Remember the last time I spanked you? You found that somewhat enjoyable."

"Ow! Ouch! That stung!" she cried out.

Lord Anthony said nothing, simply rubbed the sore spot tenderly, and Clarissa began to relax as the heat from the sting seeped into her body, warming her. The viscount tugged at the material of her nightgown, pulling it up until her buttocks were bare. "Very pretty," he observed. Then he trailed his finger over the exposed swell of her bottom and slid it into the crack between her legs. Slowly, he traced the path towards her pussy. "Hmm, I think you are going to enjoy the spanking very much indeed. That one smack has already made you wet."

Clarissa squirmed, but she said nothing, just uttered a low moan when Lord Anthony wiped his wet finger on the curve of her bum.

The viscount settled more comfortably in the chair, then placed his left hand on the small of Clarissa's back, while his right hand fondled her bottom cheeks. "We said eighteen smacks, didn't we?"

Clarissa looked back over shoulder at him. "But you've already smacked me once!" she protested.

Lord Anthony chuckled. "That, my little love, was just a warm-up. Now I'm going to begin properly."

Clarissa clenched her cheeks, wondering how much more intense the proper smacks would be than the hard sting of the warm-up, but she said nothing as the viscount continued to speak.

"While I administer this spanking, I want you to stay as still as possible. You must be careful to keep your hands in front of you and not bring them 'round to your bum. I don't want to harm you unintentionally." Clarissa shot another glance over her shoulder, but her husband was still speaking. "If you move, I will have to start again from the beginning. Do you understand?"

Blood was beginning to flow to Clarissa's head and she felt a little light-headed, but she understood what Lord Anthony was asking of her. "Yes, yes, I do," she said with another wriggle, to let him know that she was ready and he should begin.

The viscount took his time, still smoothing his hand over the softness of her arse. Then, as Clarissa went limp on his lap, he quickly raised his hand and brought it down sharply, right in the middle of her left cheek. Clarissa emitted a little cry but soon settled down again, as Lord Anthony smoothed the burning spot, sending the heat right into her body and straight to her most private parts. She could feel the reverberations pulse as the petals of her pussy began to swell.

"Good girl," Anthony soothed and then smacked her right cheek. She was sure she could feel the imprint of his hand and wondered if her skin was turning red. The next landed on the middle of her left cheek, and then he smacked her just below the rise of her right buttock. She was unable to prepare herself for each strike, as she could not guess where it would land. Then, as the viscount increased the pace of the smacks, she lost all ability to think. Her body absorbed the pain and turned it into a burning fire of pleasure that consumed her.

He peppered her backside, precisely and deliberately placing each smack on a different part of her arse until it was burning all over and she was panting hard. The viscount placed the last few smacks over the first ones, and the intensity of the burn scorched her. She was uttering continuous little moans and cries and whimpers and she had not realized that she was gripping his calf with both her hands. Tears dripped down her cheeks.

Her eyes were tightly closed and a red light throbbed behind her eyelids. Never, not even when her husband had claimed her as his wife, had she felt the intensity of pleasure that now over-whelmed her. Her body was tingling all over, every part aching to reach a peak that seemed just out of reach.

Finally, as if from a long way away, through the rush of blood in her ears, she heard the viscount say, "There, that's all done now. You took that very well indeed, my perfect little paragon."

A wry smile quirked her lips. She had never been praised for how well she took a spanking! Then she shivered as Lord Anthony's fingers slipped between her legs and started fingering her folds, which were now soaking wet and slippery.

Lord Anthony gazed down at the beautiful sight of his just-spanked wife and felt that, for a moment at least, all was right with the world. Her pussy was slick and glistening with her body's response to being spanked. He was delighted that she had responded so sensuously to the erotic spanking.

He tugged at the plump, pink outer lips of her pussy, enjoying the surge of wetness that his action induced. Then he ran his finger around the sensitive skin at her entrance and dipped inside, delighted by the tight, wet heat as her core muscles clenched around the intrusion, as if they didn't want to let him go.

With a hard tug, he pulled free and then, using the fingers of his other hand, splayed her petals open so that he could see her more clearly. He felt her tense on his lap, and he slapped her thigh quickly as she tried to close her legs. "No, my love," he admonished, "I want to admire the glories of your body. I am considering which of my paints could reproduce that gorgeous redness of your pussy."

Clarissa raised her head. "No, no, you can't paint my private parts! Just think what a scandal that would be!"

Anthony chuckled as his fingers plunged into her hole and twisted, stretching her tight cunny. "It would make a very pretty miniature that I could keep in my dresser." Then his index finger found the very sensitive knot of nerves in her passage and he began rubbing it with slow, hard strokes. His thumb found her hard nub that was peeping out lewdly from its hood. He pressed her clit as he continued to stimulate her pussy. All resistance dissipated and her head drooped towards the floor. Even her hands had lost their hard grip on his calves.

Her skin was flushed all over, with the redness of where he

had marked her with his slaps growing deeper as blood raced through her body. Her breaths came in short. shallow pants. Her pussy was ripe and ready. He increased the pressure, the pace of his fingers thrusting into her. Her whole body tensed, and then she exploded with a loud cry.

CHAPTER 17

*C*larissa frowned at the dishes displayed on the table in front of her. She had become used to the excellence of meals served at Donnington Abbey, but this array of indifferent dishes fell short of the usual standard. A ragout of beef was so salty that the dish was inedible and a chicken was so overcooked that the meat was dry and hard. The potatoes were not cooked all the way through, and they tasted as if the chef had poured the contents of his salt pot over them.

She glanced down the length of the table to where the viscount was pushing a piece of beef around on his plate with his fork. His face was set in a grim expression, his lips draw into a tight line, and a frown creased his forehead. His disapproving eyes were fixed on his plate. She suppressed a little sigh. It had been two days since the Bascombes' dinner party and its unexpected ending when she had found herself over her husband's lap, but things had returned to their usual pattern the next morning.

She squirmed slightly as she remembered how hard and hot and powerful his hand had felt on her derriere, at how pleasure had so unexpectedly consumed her even as her husband had spanked her. A slight smile replaced her frown as she recalled how, after she had come the first time, he had carried her sated body to his bed and laid her down on the fine linen sheets. There, he had removed her nightgown and caressed every part of her, raining kisses over every inch of her skin. He had even kissed her between her legs, tasting her pussy juices with his skillful tongue that had made her come, again and again. Then he had shucked his clothes and covered her with his naked body, entering her eager pussy with his hard, hot shaft. His long, slow thrusts had sent her arousal to peaks of pleasure. He had plunged into her rhythmically, pulling out each time just far enough to make her cling to him, her legs wrapped around his waist and her fingers digging into his shoulders. She had cried out for more and then when she thought she would sob from desperation, he had increased his pace and thrust hard and fast. He had slid his hand between her legs and flicked her nub with the same rhythm as his thrusts. She had come again so hard that her body had shaken for a long while, even after he had pulled the blankets up around them both and settled her in his arms.

But when she woke up quite late the next morning, he had already left. She had seen very little of him in the intervening two days.

And now, every line of his body conveyed his anger and disgust. He had been working hard out on the farms all day, and it was only right that he should be served a delicious meal, not this sad mess. She watched as he called Fotheringham and spoke quietly to the butler, whose usually implacable face showed signs of intense displeasure. Then the viscount rose, dropping his serviette onto the table, and strode out of the dining room, without even looking at Clarissa. As he left, Lucretia gave him a sympathetic smile and she, too, rose, quickly following the viscount from the room.

Clarissa placed her own fork down onto her plate. She couldn't pretend to eat this travesty of a dinner. It was a wicked waste of food, but it was inedible. It would need to be thrown out.

She was just about to rise from her place at the table when a footman approached her. She was relieved that it was not the supercilious Hubert. "My lady, his lordship requests that you attend him in his bookroom," he announced.

Clarissa thanked him and quickly made her way down the long, wood-paneled corridor in a part of the house she had only been in once before, that dreadful day when the viscount had forbidden her entry to his sanctum. She arrived at the door and stopped, staring up at the dark wood that loomed over her. No footman was on duty outside and she hesitated to knock, recalling the viscount's words on that previous occasion. Did he really want her to enter now? She took a deep breath, reminding herself that he had asked her to see him. She rapped lightly on the door.

The viscount's rich baritone called for her to enter and slowly, she opened the door just wide enough to slip inside. She closed it, and it clicked behind her with a decisive sound. She stood just inside the large, comfortable room, barely aware of the deep brown leather chairs and dark wood shelves that lined the room. Windows let in the evening light, and candles had already been lit in sconces on the walls, giving the room a tranquil, welcoming feel.

But her eyes were riveted on Lord Anthony who was standing in front of a solid, mahogany desk. A tray with a bowl of fruit, some cold ham, cheese and bread, as well as a slice of apple pie had been set on the desk and the viscount was holding a glass of wine while he took a bite of an apple.

His face was still grim and he offered no smile when she entered. Her eyes flickered from his face down to the tray beside him. He, too, glanced at the tray. And then his face softened slightly. "I was looking forward to a good dinner tonight. I have been so busy all day that I have not eaten anything except a slice of bread before seven this morning. I have never before known matters at the Abbey to deteriorate to such an extent that what is served is unpalatable."

Although nothing that the viscount said was directed specifically at Clarissa, she felt each word hammer against her heart like a bruising blow. She had failed in her responsibilities to her husband. It was her duty to ensure that the household ran smoothly. Clarissa dropped her eyes to her hands that she had clenched tightly in front of her. Her voice caught in her throat and she had to swallow to make herself audible. "I am sorry, Anthony, that dinner was not what you expected." She fell silent. She did not want to admit that Mrs. Riggs thought of her as a frivolous young lady more interested in fashion than in taking responsibility for the house.

Lord Anthony gave an annoyed shrug and then scowled. "Why are you hovering there near the door? You look as if you are about to flee."

He had never sounded so brusque when speaking to her and she could not move. Tears blurred her eyes. "I-I'm not sure what you want me to do. I try to please you."

Lord Anthony tossed the apple core into the fireplace and crossed the room in a few quick strides. He stopped in front of her, and his hand cupped her face. "You do please me, little flower. But what has that to do with your reluctance to come in and talk to me now?"

Clarissa's eyes widened until they filled her face. "Just a few days ago you said that I was never, under any circumstances, to enter this room."

For a moment the viscount said nothing, simply examining her. Finally, muttering a rough swear word under his breath, he said, "What makes you think I would refuse you entry to my room?"

Confusion flitted across her face and she swallowed a few times, trying to find the words that would appease her husband.

187

She had not found them when his voice lost the rough edge and his finger stroked her chin. "You are looking very pale and peaked, as well as unusually anxious and uncertain. What has happened to the confident paragon who handled every situation in London society with aplomb?"

She gave a dry, hollow laugh. "I was very good at showing you, along with the rest of the world, the picture of perfection that I had so carefully crafted." She bit back a sob. "I am sorry that the person I really am does not live up to the image I presented, that you married me and not the lady you thought I was."

The hardness in Lord Anthony's eyes softened with sympathy but his expression remained serious. "My little one, I always knew there was much more to you than the perfect society miss. I do not want a puppet or a doll for a wife. I want you, the real you. However, I have become used to your self-assurance, your ability to face difficulties with poise and assurance, and to see it waver as it has since we have been in Dorset concerns me."

All these contradictions sent Clarissa's emotions spinning, as if she were on a merry-go-round. She took a deep breath to steady herself as the viscount wiped away the tears she could not prevent from slipping down her cheek.

He took her hand, saying, "Come, let's go and sit down. It will be easier to talk if we are more comfortable." She followed him to a large leather sofa with deep seats. He sat down and tugged her onto his lap. She sat stiffly at first, still reeling from the chaos in her mind.

Lord Anthony placed his arm around her shoulder, drawing her down towards his chest. He ignored her stiffness and rubbed soothing circles over her back in the way she had come to find so pleasurable. After a minute or so, Clarissa began to relax and let her head drop down onto his shoulder.

"That's better," he said. "Now we can straighten out the

confusion." He glanced around the library and then back at Clarissa. "What makes you think I would not allow you to come into this room, or any room in the house?"

She frowned. Did he not remember what he had said? "When I came to ask you about the invitations we had been receiving, you said that... that I was not under any circumstances to enter this room." Her voice faded as she repeated the words that still cut her each time she thought of them. "I did not mean to disturb you while you were working. I understand that this is your room, where you deal with the estate business and that you do not need a wife interfering with your affairs."

Lord Anthony looked as confused as Clarissa felt. "When was that, my little flower? Perhaps you misunderstood something I said?"

Clarissa shook her head but had little to offer in her defense. "Perhaps," she ventured, "if I understood the rules of being your wife, the preferences that you have, I would be able to follow them in the same way that I implemented the rules of behavior in society."

She was startled by the sudden sound of Lord Anthony's laughter. He suddenly seemed more relaxed, more like the man she had fallen in love with. "There are no rules for being my wife, not in that way. We are two people who love one another and our relationship is not a set of rules. It's about how much we trust one another, and that requires open and honest communication."

Although Clarissa was nestled against Lord Anthony's chest, he could still see her face. She looked a little skeptical as he spoke, and the viscount thought back on the last few weeks. His love for his new bride was steadfast, unwavering, but he hadn't really followed his own guidelines. His beautiful wife had not found him open and available.

He cupped her face with his right hand and smoothed her cheek with his thumb. "You are looking very pale. I had hoped being in the country would suit you, that fresh air and sunshine would refresh you after the noise and rush of London."

She gave a sound somewhere between a dainty snort and a huff. "Fresh air and sunshine do not do very much good when one is confined indoors."

The viscount was puzzled. "Confined? My precious love, I know that being near firing guns frightened you, but the gardens here near the house are perfectly safe." As he spoke, another thought crossed his mind. "Have you taken no exercise at all since we arrived here?"

A flicker of irritation flashed through Clarissa's eyes and her answer was more scornful than she had intended. "I walk in the long gallery for half an hour each morning but I have not ventured into the gardens. My lord, I am not sure if you have always had a problem with your memory, but you gave me orders that I have done my best to comply with and yet now you have no recollection of them at all. And I'm not sure that asking a footman to tell me what you want me to do is the best way to communicate." She finished her grievances with another of the little snorts that Anthony found so endearing.

In spite of the gravity of the points she had raised, the viscount couldn't help grinning as Clarissa showed some of the fire that had been dimmed for a while. "I think you might be right," he placated her. "I don't recall ordering you to take your morning walks in the gallery, or indeed ordering you not to come into this room, and I'm fairly sure I would remember if I had used a footman to convey my wishes to you."

Clarissa sat up and looked at her husband. "You were so angry when you found me wandering in the grove on the day we arrived here, you said I was not to venture outside, and then when you were delayed for the Bascombes' dinner, a footman came and instructed me to leave without you."

Anthony hushed Clarissa after this outburst, running his fingers down her cheeks and finally placing a kiss on her forehead. "Shh, my love. It's all going to be fine. Of course, you can go out into the gardens any time you want. I was angry to arrive home and find my plans to spend time with you thwarted by a multitude of problems. Poachers had set traps near the house, in that grove where you were walking, and I did not want you to come to any harm. I mentioned it at dinner, and then a day or so later, when Trevett assured me that all the traps had been removed, I also explained that the danger was now past."

Clarissa huffed. "The dining room table is hardly conducive to easy conversation. I am placed at one end and you are twenty feet away, at the other."

"You are right, my love. I think we are going to need to make some alterations to things around here." He reached behind him and rang the bell that would summon the butler. While he waited for Fotheringham, he petted Clarissa, kissing her face softly and stroking her arms and back. He cupped her chin and took her mouth in an intense kiss that left her in no doubt as to how much he loved her.

The kiss ended only when Fotheringham knocked on the door and Anthony reluctantly pulled away from Clarissa's sweet lips. She tried to squirm off his lap, but he held her tightly. The butler knew how much he loved his wife, and he was not ashamed to show his affection.

"Milord, you called?" The butler was as implacable as always.

"Fotheringham, I think it is time to make a few changes to the way things happen around here." The viscount ignored the flicker of a smile that shone in the butler's eyes. The man had worked for the Donningtons for many years and had known Anthony when he was just a child.

The butler waited as Lord Anthony explained, "The seating at dinner places my wife too far from me."

The butler nodded, and the smile in his eyes broke out fully on his face. "Indeed, my lord. I had thought that perhaps that should be managed differently. You were too young to remember, but your father did not follow the social conventions when he was married to your mother. At dinner, she sat at his right hand, even when they had guests. It was only when he remarried that he reverted to the more formal seating."

A curious glimmer lit Lord Anthony's eyes, but he just nodded and said, "Then that is what we will do from now on. I also wanted to ask if there are any problems down in the servants' hall that I should know about."

The butler's lips straightened grimly. "I apologize, my lord, for the disaster at dinner."

The viscount's face reflected the same grimness as he said, "It is not just dinner. There have been some other incidents that have come to my attention. For instance, messages and notes seem to go astray and some of the servants are not showing the kind of respect to my wife that she deserves."

The butler glanced at Clarissa and then faced the viscount again. "I understand, my lord. I will look into it." He cleared his throat and when Lord Anthony raised a questioning eyebrow, he added, "I had not wanted to mention something that Mrs. Riggs and I should be able to handle, but there has been some pilfering. Some of the servants are missing little items. So far, nothing has gone missing from the house itself, but it does not do to harbor petty thieves."

Lord Anthony sighed. "Yet more issues that need to be investigated. I am beginning to feel that nothing about what has happened is random, that somehow it all ties together." With a nod and a thank you, he dismissed the butler and focused on Clarissa who was looking at him, her eyes wide with sympathy. His attempted smile brought no light to his eyes. "There was a letter from Theo today. He has been trying to follow up on the shooting in Richmond Park and has found a ranger who might have seen something. But what is most concerning is that he and Charlotte have experienced no further problems, while we seem to be gathering trouble here. Somehow, we need to get to the bottom of it."

Clarissa placed her hands on his face and drew him down for a kiss. "We will; I am sure of it." She kissed him again, and he responded with the intense passion she had come to desire. For a short while, Anthony allowed himself to forget his problems as he enjoyed his wife.

CHAPTER 18

*C*larissa looked up expectantly as the footman, Hubert, entered the morning room. He strode to where she was sitting at the bureau and presented a silver salver on which the morning's post was arrayed. She thanked him and quickly took the pile addressed to her. Before Hubert had left the room, she began to riffle through the pile, and disappointment flooded through her. There were a half dozen or so letters, including one from Lady Amelia at Broadwell and another from Lady Charlotte. The others were invitations to dinners and picnics in the district. But there was no letter from Anthony. Again.

She called out as Hubert was about to close the door. "Is this all the post this morning?"

The footman almost smirked. "Yes, my lady. There is no further post for you."

Clarissa couldn't bring herself to abrade him even though his tone bordered on rude. She had somehow made an enemy of this man and she did not know why. Most of the other servants were pleasant, agreeable, and polite, even kind. But not this one. She watched him leave and then turned back to her letters.

Two weeks ago, after that memorable evening in the library,

Lord Anthony had risen early, and rousing her from her slumber, had explained that urgent business called him to London. He had promised to write every day, but since the first letter that announced his safe arrival, she had heard nothing further from him. She stared at the blank page in front of her. She wrote to him every day, but it was becoming difficult to know what to say when she heard nothing from him.

She derived only small comfort from knowing that Lady Lucretia had not left the Abbey with Lord Anthony. A few days after the viscount's departure, the woman had summoned a carriage, loaded some trunks onto it, and disappeared, after making a vague announcement of being needed in London. In her darker moments, Clarissa couldn't help wondering if the ladies she had heard gossiping at Lady Bascombe's dinner party had been right and that Lucretia was Anthony's mistress. With a tightness in her heart, she wondered if the two were even now enjoying each other's company.

She dipped her pen into the ink and contemplated how to begin today's letter to her husband. Her thoughts were interrupted by another knock on the door, this time heralding Mrs. Riggs. The housekeeper was carrying a tray.

"My lady, I am sorry to disturb you, but I thought you might want a cup of tea and a little something light to eat. Rose tells me that you did not eat much of your breakfast."

Clarissa looked abashed. And then, as the housekeeper placed the tray on a low table next to her, a rush of nausea swelled her throat. The intense, rich aroma of a banana the housekeeper had placed on the little fruit plate that accompanied the tea almost choked Clarissa. She lifted her hand and covered her mouth, swallowing rapidly.

A small frown flashed over the housekeeper's face. "Are you all right, my lady?"

Clarissa managed to nod. "I am well, thank you." But her hand involuntarily covered her stomach.

Mrs. Riggs watched her hand then gave a quick nod as if something had just become clear. "Forgive me, my lady, but can I ask how long you have been experiencing this kind of upset stomach?"

Clarissa swallowed again, and the housekeeper whisked the tray away to a table nearer the door. Clarissa was relieved to be able to breathe again, but the churning in her stomach did not settle.

"It has been a few days now. I will be fine. It is worse in the mornings, but during the day it improves."

Mrs. Riggs, who had appeared so formidable when Clarissa had arrived at Donnington Abbey, now smiled. "My lady, is it possible that you might be with child?"

Clarissa gasped. She had been married for just over a month and had not thought that she would bear a child so soon. She must have conceived on her wedding night. Her face flushed pink as she stared at the housekeeper. She nodded slowly. Just before her wedding, Amelia had told her some of the signs of pregnancy, and she had them all. "Do you think so?" she asked.

Mrs. Riggs nodded briskly. "I am almost certain. I will make you some peppermint tea and bring you some ginger biscuits. They should help to settle you."

Clarissa thanked the housekeeper as she bustled out, overwhelmed by the realization that she was carrying a child. In her heart she knew that Lord Anthony should be the first to hear, but she couldn't tell him this news in a letter. She turned back to the letters on her desk. On top of the pile, was a note from Lady Margaretta. The two ladies had developed a warm friendship and frequently visited one another. Clarissa yearned for the company of the lively young lady.

When the housekeeper returned ten minutes later, carrying a different tray with the tea she had promised, Clarissa asked her to arrange for the open carriage to take her to the Bascombes' house that afternoon. A good chat with her friend would settle her mind.

~

THE OPEN CARRIAGE rumbled through the woods and Clarissa raised her face to the sunshine as it poured through the deep green leaves of the elms and oaks that sheltered the avenue. A delighted laugh fell from her lips as she reveled in the variety and splendor of the woodland. Even though she was concerned about her husband's lack of communication, she felt the thrill of new life growing inside her and could not stop smiling.

The chestnut pair that pulled the carriage trotted with ears up and swishing tails, as if they too shared her exuberance. Clarissa was at peace with the world.

The avenue wound through the trees and the horses quickened their pace as they came 'round a bend and back onto a section of the road that ran straight ahead.

The horses stumbled, whinnying sharply. They reared in panic. The carriage toppled. A loud shot rang out in the woods.

Clarissa tumbled from her seat, hit the ground with a thud and rolled down the embankment to the left. She screamed. Her head bumped along the ground and all went black.

She didn't know how long she lay at the bottom of the ditch, soaked from the two inches of water left by the rain. She awoke to the sound of screeching horses and a man's voice calling, "My lady? My lady?"

Her eyes opened slowly and she looked into the anxious face of Jim, the second coachman. "My lady, are you hurt? Can you stand up?" he asked.

His face was scratched and a bruise was forming beneath his eye. He had lost his hat and twigs and leaves were stuck in his hair. He held his one arm stiffly at his side even as he tried to help Clarissa up.

"I think I am all right." She tried to sound reassuring, even though she could feel sore places all over her body and her head throbbed. Her stomach, too, was cramping painfully. She winced as Jim eased her into a sitting position. He looked at her with concern, but with his help, she was able to move out of the ditch and rest against the strong trunk of an aspen. Cautiously, she looked around her. Just up on the road, the carriage lay on its side. Cushions had been flung from it and now lay tumbled on the ground, torn where they had scraped against rocks and stones. Feathers were scattered along the path.

But the worst was the horses. One lay on its side, his eyes large and rolling with fear and pain. The other was still in its shafts, but the reins were twisted around its neck. Its eyes were also rolling in its head.

Clarissa turned to Jim, even though every little movement was agony. "Please," she begged, "you must help the horses! And where are the footmen?"

Jim rose slowly to his feet, favoring his right side. He winced as he put weight on an ankle that had been twisted. "If you're sure you will be all right here for a bit, my lady, I would like to see to the horses." He glanced at the one that was on the ground. "I think Pandora will be all right, but I fear that Pegasus has broken his leg." Jim stood silently for a moment, looking at the carnage. "I think the viscount will be none too pleased," he murmured almost to himself, and then recalling Clarissa's other question, he added more clearly, "Giles flung himself away from the carriage just as it was falling and he got up with only a few scrapes. He's returned to the house for help. But I think Gerry might also have broken his leg."

Clarissa glanced around wildly. "Where is he? Is there anything I can do to help?"

Jim gave a slight bow. "That's kind of you, my lady, but he's resting easy nearer the road. I gave him a swig of brandy."

The coachman checked to see that Clarissa was as comfortable as she could be, given the circumstances, and handed her a rug which she drew over herself for warmth. She was shivering uncontrollably and her teeth were chattering. Her stomach was hurting worse now and she wanted to retch. She took a deep breath and rested her head against the trunk of the tree. She tried not to think while she watched Jim try to calm the horses.

She dozed off, weary from the pain and anxiety. She did not know how long it was before she heard excited voices that brought her back to full awareness. Several horses and a cart rumbled along the path and Fotheringham's voice was heard above the clatter, barking out orders to the footmen and groomsmen who had come with him. Clarissa was startled to see her lady's maid, Rose, scrambling down the embankment.

"My lady, oh, my lady! Are you all right?" she called out as she knelt beside Clarissa.

Clarissa's head was pounding and cramps continued to tighten her stomach, but she managed a weak smile. "Yes, yes, I think so." The pain that tightened her face and made her voice thin belied her claim.

Rose quickly lifted the rug that Clarissa had pulled over herself and wrapped a shawl around her shoulders. Clarissa began to maneuver herself up, but Rose stopped her. "No, no, my lady, someone will be with you in a moment to help you. We'll get you back to the house and the doctor will see to you. He's been sent for already."

Shortly, Fotheringham himself came and gently carried her to the cart, where blankets and cushions had been placed for her comfort. Rose sat in the back with Clarissa, cradling her head on her lap, while Fotheringham, satisfied that everything else was being sorted out, climbed onto the front seat with the groom who was driving the cart.

Clarissa bit back moans and little cries of pain as the cart made its slow way back to the house. No matter how carefully they went, every little bump jolted Clarissa and sent new shards of pain through her. She was sobbing quietly by the time they reached the front door ten minutes later.

Rose lifted Clarissa's head and then uttered a little cry of horror. Mrs. Riggs had been waiting at the door and she hurried up to the cart. She turned pale and looked around hurriedly. "The doctor, where's the doctor? Is he here yet?"

Clarissa was barely conscious as she was lifted onto a light mattress and carried inside. She was not aware of the blood that soaked her skirts. All she knew was agonizing pain as her body trembled. She cried out and then all went black.

CHAPTER 19

*L*ord Anthony clambered out of his traveling coach as soon as the footman let down the steps. He looked up at the vast grey expanse of Donnington Abbey but felt little of the usual peace he derived from its large, quiet grey walls and silent stones that had endured centuries of turmoil.

A frown creased his forehead as he ran up the steps and pushed open the heavy wooden door. There was no one in the foyer, not even the hall boy who should be at his post all the time. He tugged off his gloves and coat, calling out as he dropped them onto a settle near the door, "Fotheringham? Where is everyone?"

Instead of the butler responding to his call, he was irritated to see Lucretia sweep down the stairs, her arms held out in welcome and a smile gracing her face. "Oh, Tony! How good to see you. I've missed you very much. The Abbey is always quite dull when you are away." She did not mention that she had not been at the Abbey for most of the time he had been in London, returning only two days ago.

The viscount glanced pointedly around the quiet hall. "I can see that. Where are the servants who should be on duty here? Where's Fotheringham?

"I'll make sure that you have everything you need and then you won't be so grumpy," she answered with a light laugh. She had moved closer to him as she spoke and now she placed her hand on his arm, smoothing down the soft material.

Lord Anthony's only answer was a raised eyebrow and a low huff. Quick footsteps coming down the corridor took his attention away from Lucretia. "Finally," he snapped as Fotheringham appeared. "What is happening here? Never before have I come home to such desolation!"

Lucretia gave his arm a light squeeze. "Do calm down, dear. Everything will be fine. I'll soon have everything just the way you like it. Why don't you come and sit down in the drawing room and I will order some refreshments for you?" She gave another light laugh. "Isn't it lucky that cook made some of your favorite lemon biscuits today?"

The viscount felt bile rise in his throat, but he could not be rude to her in front of a servant. With an effort, he spoke politely. "I'm sorry, Fotheringham, but I am agitated." He shrugged in an attempt to remove Lucretia's hold on his arm, but she continued to cling to him.

The butler looked steadily at the viscount's face, ignoring with great deliberation the way in which Lucretia clung to him. "Welcome home, my lord. I trust your journey was pleasant." Then his eyes hardened slightly and his lips narrowed. "We expected you two days ago."

Anthony frowned. "I never gave a specific day for my return." He was aware of a little sigh from Lucretia but his focus was on the butler.

Fotheringham straightened his shoulders even more. "My lord, perhaps I could talk to you in your bookroom?"

With a nod and a growing sense of uneasiness, Anthony

followed the butler as he walked briskly down the corridor, leaving Lucretia alone in the entrance.

By the time the butler opened the office door and stood aside to let the viscount enter, anxiety was churning in Lord Anthony's stomach. He walked over to the side table and poured himself a brandy from the carafe that was always kept there. He turned to the butler as he swallowed a mouthful of the deep amber liquor.

"My lord," Fotheringham began, "I wrote to you as soon as the accident occurred, and I was surprised not to hear back from you, or that you did not return more quickly." His tone was slightly accusatory, and Lord Anthony was taken aback. The butler was always so polite, so placid, that seeing him become emotional knocked the viscount off kilter. He sank down onto the nearest chair.

Cold fear gripped his heart. "What accident?" His voice sounded distant and hoarse in his ears.

The butler's hard demeanor softened slightly. "The Lady Clarissa, my lord. There was an incident with the barouche."

All the blood drained from Anthony's face. "Is she all right?" He started to stand up. He needed to find her.

"She is recovering slowly. Dr. Shaw is confident that she will be fully well very soon."

"Thank God! I must go to her."

The butler cleared his throat. "Before you do, my lord, I think it might be necessary for you to know one or two further things."

Anthony was impatient. "Can't it wait?" Then, as he saw how grim the butler looked, he sank back onto his chair.

"The circumstances of the accident were somewhat peculiar. Jim is a good coachman and he is well able to handle the horses, especially on the roads around the estate. He says a piece of fishing line, or something similar, was drawn across the road and it cut into the horses, startling them and impeding their progress. Almost at the same time, a gun was fired close by." The viscount was sitting bolt upright, his hands clenched tightly around his glass. He said nothing, letting the butler finish outlining the situation.

Fotheringham looked at the viscount with sympathy. "Gerry, the footman, was also quite seriously injured. He will take a while to get better, as his leg was broken. Of course, the carriage is badly damaged and might be beyond repair. The one horse had to be shot."

Lord Anthony winced at this. "Why am I only hearing all of this now?" he demanded. Then he added more softly. "That explains why I haven't heard from Clarissa."

The butler drew in his breath and gave an almost impercepible shake of his head. "I wrote to you, my lord, as soon as the doctor had seen Lady Clarissa." A look of pain crossed his face as he admitted, "There have been some lapses, some unforeseen issues in the management of the household. I had not wanted to concern you with matters that should be under my control, but I did allude to it the day before you left for London. I thought everything would be running smoothly by now, but there are disruptions, disturbances, that I fear might be deliberate. I have my suspicions but I have no proof, as yet."

"One of the servants has been tampering with the mail? Is that what you are suggesting?"

"Among other things, my lord. I would like your permission to investigate my suspicions."

"Of course. Anything that you need, let me know." He hesitated and then added, "I have been working on a few theories of my own. I will share my ideas with you, but first, I really must see Clarissa now."

"Thank you, my lord. But there is one further matter of importance. Although Lady Clarissa is on the mend, the child that she was carrying was lost."

Lord Anthony almost reeled. He clutched at the table next to him to steady himself. He had not even known that he was going to be a father, and now the child was gone.

∼

CLARISSA LAY UNMOVING in her bed, staring at the garish furnishings in the room but hardly noticing anything. Her throat was dry, her eyes burned and her body ached dully. A glass of water had been placed within her reach on a side table, but she could not summon enough energy to reach for it. Her maid, Rose, was in the dressing room and had left the door ajar in case Clarissa needed anything.

She did not move when the bedroom door opened and Lucretia sauntered in. She was carrying a letter, and Clarissa roused herself enough to ask, "Is that for me?"

Lucretia glanced down at it. "This? No, it is from one of my acquaintances in Bath. I thought I would come and entertain you with her descriptions of the scene there." She perched gracefully on the edge of a chair near the bed and perused Clarissa with a faintly derisive smile. "Oh, you were expecting Tony to write to you? I'm sure he has much better things to do. He has many friends in London and now that you have failed in your purpose as a wife—to procure an heir for him—he has lost interest in you. Indeed, you should have realized when he rushed off to London without you so soon after your marriage and didn't bother to write to you that he had grown bored of you. Of course, as usual, Tony has written me many delightful letters, but it would probably be a bit indiscreet for me to share them with you." She smoothed her hand over her skirt and looked archly at Clarissa. "A man like him needs a woman who can fulfill his… needs."

Clarissa did not move, but her eyes flickered towards Lucretia. She was cold and numb. There were no tears to cry. The darkness of despair engulfed her. She had lost her husband and her baby. There was no purpose in life, in living.

Lucretia continued relentlessly, every word wrapping Clarissa in more darkness. Lucretia unfolded the letter she was carrying. "You need not continue to expect any letters from Tony. He has returned to the Abbey."

Clarissa closed her eyes and flinched but said nothing. Lucretia said it for her, her voice tinged with triumph. "Did nobody tell you that he had returned? I suppose he will come to see you when he has time, or inclination." She plucked a piece of non-existent lint off her dress. "I would not be too eager to see him if I were you. He was very angry about your little… incident and the consequences of it. He believes your carelessness led to the death of the baby. It took me quite a while to calm him down."

For the first time, Clarissa moved. Her hand tightened into a fist on top of the blanket and she took a deep breath. Lucretia watched her and then picking up the letter she had brought, began reading.

LUCRETIA HAD TURNED to the last page which contained an account of an assembly in the Lower Rooms. The door of the bedroom opened and the viscount came in, taking in the scene before him. Lucretia looked up and smiled. "I have been doing my best to entertain Clarissa, to lift her spirits with descriptions of the kind of society events that she enjoys so much."

Lord Anthony's eyes were focused on the limp, listless form of Clarissa on her bed. He hardly glanced at Lucretia. "Thank you, but I am here now and I will see to my wife."

Lucretia got up slowly, making a production of folding her letter and placing it in her dress pocket. She brushed against Anthony as she strolled from the room.

The viscount moved to the bed and looked down at his wife.

Her hair lay in a loose braid over her shoulder, and she looked even tinier than usual beneath the heavy blankets. Her face was pale, with faint blue circles under her eyes and a vivid red scratch marking her cheek. He could see big dark purple bruises on her arms. But it was her eyes that disturbed him the most. They were wide open but dull and lifeless, not even a flicker of response in them. He had never seen such sad eyes.

He placed his hand gently over hers, which was balled in a tight fist on top of the blanket. She moved her eyes to his face but still showed no emotion. He took several deep breaths before he could speak. "My little flower, I am sorry, so sorry."

Her only response was a swallowing in her throat and a flicker of uncertainty in her eyes. Even that little response gave Anthony hope that she would break through the heaviness of despair that weighed her down. He leaned forward and brushed a light kiss on her forehead. "I am here now, and I will nurse you until you are better. Everything is going to be well."

Clarissa's head moved in a restless denial on her pillow. "No," she whispered so softly, it was little more than a rush of air. "The baby, I'm sorry."

For the first time since the accident, tears glistened in Clarissa's eyes. Lord Anthony brushed her cheek with his thumb. "I know, I know," he murmured quietly.

Clarissa sniffed, trying to hold back her tears, but Anthony's soft words and gentle touch had breached the dam and the tears began to flow. He lifted her into his arms and cradled her head against his chest. "That's right, my little love. Crying is good."

Sobs wracked Clarissa's body and she clung to the intimate warmth of her husband, drawing comfort from his familiar smell of green woods, sandalwood and bergamot and the slight acridness of paint solvent.

Anthony held her tight against him, stroking her arms and back and nuzzling her hair. His own eyes were glistening with tears. "I should never have left you alone when there was such obvious danger. I was foolish and arrogant enough to believe the attacks had been directed at me. I should have realized they did not begin until I made my love for you known."

As she sobbed, garbled words tumbled from her mouth, painfully wrenched from the depths of her heart. "My baby, my baby," she repeated over and over.

They sat like that for many long minutes, both mourning the loss of the child they had not even had a chance to celebrate. After a while, Clarissa's sobs quietened to sniffles. The viscount pulled his handkerchief out of his pocket, shook it open and began to wipe her face gently. She sniffed, and he held it to her nose so she could blow, then he dropped it onto the side table and tilted her face towards him. He was relieved to see more life in her eyes, but it would take a long while before the sadness would begin to lift.

After a while, Clarissa was able to put some of her tumultuous thoughts into words, although it was still difficult to speak past the lump in her throat. "I'm sorry," she managed to rasp out.

Anthony reached for a glass of water that was on her bedside table and lifted it to her lips. She sipped slowly, glad of the moisture for her lips and throat. When she had had enough, her husband answered her. "There is nothing for you to be sorry for. You just need to concentrate on getting better."

"But... Lucretia said..."

Annoyance flashed in Lord Anthony's eyes and Clarissa stumbled to a halt. She caught her lip between her teeth and closed her eyes, conscious of a distancing between her and her husband, even though he still held her close to his body.

A light knock on the door prevented Anthony from saying anything more. Lucretia was a problem that would need to be sorted out soon, but his focus for the moment was to keep Clarissa free from anxiety so that she could heal her body and her heart.

He placed Clarissa back onto the pillows as Mrs. Riggs

entered with the doctor. The viscount moved aside to let the doctor examine Clarissa. He stood by while Dr. Shaw took her temperature and checked the bruises that marred her smooth skin.

Dr. Shaw pulled the blanket up over Clarissa and turned to the viscount. "Lady Clarissa is healing physically and should be well enough to leave her bed and rest on a couch within two or three days, but she does need to be coaxed to take more nourishment. Good, plain food will go a long way to restore her mind and spirit as well."

Mrs. Riggs, who was plumping up Clarissa's pillows and straightening the blankets, tutted at this. "Renaud has been preparing all kinds of dainties and delicacies, but each day the tray is returned to the kitchen, hardly touched."

"I am here now," declared the viscount, "and I will take responsibility for Clarissa's care." He turned to the housekeeper. "Send up a tray as soon as you can and I will ensure that she has something to eat." He looked around Clarissa's bedroom as if he was seeing it for the first time. "The decorations in this room are not very peaceful. I do not understand how it came to be decorated in such an ostentatious manner, quite unlike the rest of the house or my personal taste. I think it would be best if Clarissa was moved to my bedroom for now."

The doctor looked ready to object, but Lord Anthony preempted him. "I will not interfere with her recovery. If necessary, I will sleep in my dressing room."

Mrs. Riggs had lost her kindly demeanor during this exchange and she now almost bristled with indignation. "I'm sorry, my lord, that you do not like the way the room was redecorated. I did my best to comply with her ladyship's wishes and directions." She did not add, but seemed to imply, that the viscount should have made certain that his wife's taste was more akin to his before rushing into marriage with her.

Clarissa, who had been lying still and half-asleep after the doctor had finished examining her, tossed restlessly, her head moving from side to side. Anthony moved quickly to the bedside and took her hand in his. He huffed as he addressed his house-keeper. "I do not know about any instructions given to you for redecorating this room. We married quite quickly and had not given a thought to changing the furniture to suit Clarissa. I do believe she should have some say in what her room should look like, and I know she does not favor such ostentation."

Clarissa murmured a low agreement and Anthony stroked his thumb over her hand. Mrs. Riggs, however, was both annoyed and indignant. "I have the letters sent by Lady Clarissa before her wedding that catalogued everything she insisted should be done to ensure the room suited her taste." She looked at Clarissa, a slight frown on her face. "But now that I know her, I do find it difficult to believe that she would find this kind of décor appealing."

Lord Anthony was quiet for a few moments. This was just another of the anomalies that had occurred since he had returned to Dorset with his new bride, indeed since he had first begun to court her seriously. Someone was making life very difficult for her, and for him. He would need to discover who was responsible and why. Enough harm had already been done.

He raised an eyebrow and his voice hardened with the authority he was used to wielding. "If you would, Mrs. Riggs, give those letters to me. I would like to see them. Also, Clarissa will be moved into my room, and while she is convalescing, you can consult with her about redoing this room to her liking."

He smiled as he felt some of the tension ease from Clarissa's stiff body. Her comfort was paramount to him. He murmured softly so that only Clarissa could hear, "Although I doubt she will have much need of a separate room. I intend to keep her close to my side always."

CHAPTER 20

*L*ord Anthony looked up from the letter he was reading to reassure himself that Clarissa was comfortable. This morning, for the first time since the accident, she had left her bed and was now resting on a *chaise longue* near the window in the small sitting room. She was dressed in a loose white gown and her hair was in a soft knot at the nape of her neck. She was looking out the window and he could see only the side of her face. The urge to capture her frail beauty consumed him. He whipped out his sketch book, something he had not done for a long while, and a sense of peace settled over him as his pencil flew over the page, recording her delicate lines and perfect profile.

As he drew, he thought about the situation with Clarissa. She was not quite as fragile as she had been five days ago when he had returned home. Some of the bruising was beginning to fade and the anguish in her eyes was not quite as intense as it had been. She had shed many tears in his arms, and that had helped her work through some of the grief and pain, but she had not smiled or laughed, not even when he brought her roses or read her letters from Amelia and Charlotte.

He finished the sketch and held it up to admire. It would be a very special painting. As he put the drawing aside, feeling a little more ready to attempt to solve the problems on the estate that increased day by day, Mrs. Riggs entered the room. She set a tray down near Clarissa and turned to the viscount. "My lord, I have brought some light refreshments for her ladyship. It will be some time before your guests arrive and it is best if Lady Clarissa has something now."

Lord Anthony smiled. "Thank you, that's very kind, Mrs. Riggs." He rose from his seat as the housekeeper moved towards the door. "It seems that Renaud has found his momentum again. For a while, I thought I would need to let him go, but meals are once again of the excellent standard I expect."

The housekeeper stopped, a troubled look on her face. Anthony had never before seen her flustered and he did not know that she could blush. She looked at Clarissa, who was still gazing out the window, and then answered the viscount. "Please accept my apologies. I am not sure what happened in the kitchens but all is under control again. Such a thing has never happened before under my watch, and I will ensure it never does again." She hesitated and then asked, "May I speak frankly, my lord?"

"Of course, Mrs. Riggs. What is it?"

"There are some of the servants who are showing signs of unease. We all know that this is a very good place to work, and yet some are beginning to talk of leaving."

The viscount shuffled the papers that were on the table where he had been working. Was this another way in which he was being sabotaged? "What has caused such dissatisfaction with the servants?" he asked, his voice smooth and controlled, conveying nothing of the tension that he felt at the continuous undermining of everything he had worked hard to achieve since his father's death the previous year.

Mrs. Riggs pursed her mouth. "There are two matters, my

lord. The one is that there has been some pilfering and some of the servants have lost items of personal value from their rooms. Fotheringham and I are looking into it but have not been able to discover who is responsible." She took a breath and her eyes wandered over to where Clarissa had turned from the window and was now following the conversation with interest. "The second issue is that there has been talk of the Abbey being cursed. So many things have gone wrong since... since your father died and you married, my lord. I have heard words like 'uncanny and unnatural' bandied about. Again, Fotheringham and I are doing what we can to quell such nonsense, but one of my best housemaids handed in her notice this morning. I fear that others might follow her lead and we will find it difficult to replace them if these rumors spread."

The viscount listened thoughtfully. "Thank you for bringing this to my attention. I will consider it, along with all the other things that have been happening. Thank you for the work you do to keep this house running smoothly. I could not manage without you and Fotheringham."

Mrs. Riggs left and Anthony crossed the room, drawing up a chair next to the couch on which Clarissa lay.

She raised anxious eyes to him. "Do you think my past is haunting us? That because of my background, I have brought disaster upon you? Am I cursed?" She twisted knots into the fringe of her shawl. "I heard what Mrs. Riggs said. All these troubles began when you married me."

In spite of the stress that churned within him, Lord Anthony managed to laugh. "No, my little flower. You have not brought a curse into my life. I told you that we would find pleasure together, and through that pleasure we will experience all that is good in life. These setbacks are not going to rob us of our joy."

Clarissa looked ready to protest, but Anthony pulled the tray closer to them. "Come, you need to have something to eat."

Clarissa looked at the tray. It was beautifully presented, with a white lace cloth on which a delicate porcelain cup and saucer had been set. A small plate that matched the cup contained dainty fingers of bread and butter and a light sponge cake. A little basket filled with bright green grapes and a rosebud in a slim silver vase brightened the tray, and Clarissa found for the first time in many days, her appetite was returning.

~

THE RUMBLE of carriages drawing up outside the front door of the Abbey echoed through the sitting room. Lord Anthony put down his tea cup and leaned over Clarissa to watch his friends arrive. Clarissa pulled herself up and, leaning against his arm, smiled as Lord Theo handed Charlotte out of the first one while Lord Sherbonne and Baron Loxley dismounted from their horses and handed the reins to waiting grooms. The Duke of Broadwell and Amelia soon followed in their carriage.

About ten minutes later, Fotheringham ushered the guests into the sitting room. Amelia and Charlotte rushed to Clarissa's side and were soon petting and fussing over her, plumping cushions and exclaiming over her troubles like a flock of sparrows protecting their newborn chicks. In a few minutes, they were deeply involved in a lively conversation.

Anthony, satisfied that Clarissa would be well looked after, invited the gentlemen to join him in his bookroom. Soon they were comfortably seated in the deep leather chairs and sipping the viscount's best brandy. But the mood in the room was heavy. This was not just a pleasant jaunt to enjoy the beauties of Dorset and the hunting that the grounds of the Abbey offered.

In a few deftly chosen words, Lord Anthony brought the others up-to-date with all that had happened. When he drew to an end, silence filled the room as the gentlemen pondered the situation.

The Marquess of Raeburne broke the silence. "You cut short

your journey to London and so weren't there when I was able to question the ranger from Richmond Park we had tracked down."

Anthony, who had been leaning against his desk as he spoke, gave an irritated snort. "I had not heard from Clarissa and was worried that something might have happened. And my fears proved valid." He clenched his fists. "If I had been here, I might have been able to prevent the accident."

The duke quirked his eyebrow. "I doubt that your presence would have made much difference. It is clear that whoever has been behind all of this is becoming desperate. But it does not do to dwell on what might have happened and what could have been done. We need to determine who would wish you so much harm that they would damage a horse and endanger your wife." He swirled the brandy in his glass and watched the light glint in its amber depths.

Anthony nodded. "It is difficult to believe that someone is deliberately targeting Clarissa. Why? She is the sweetest, gentlest woman I have ever known."

Adam Loxley patted the cushion of the couch on which he sat. "Do sit down, Tony. You'll be more comfortable and I think we're going to be here for a while."

Lord Anthony gave his friend a quick smile and followed his advice. He had spent enough time pacing the room and not getting anywhere. He leaned his elbows on his knees, took a deep breath to calm his riotous thoughts, and asked Theo, "Did the ranger have anything of interest to say?"

Theo took a long swallow of brandy and shook his head. "Not really. He was not close enough to see anything clearly. However, he did see a man loitering near the gate, and when we were within his range, he took deliberate aim in our direction. By the time the ranger arrived, the man had disappeared."

"So, all we know for certain is that we were actually targeted," mused Lord Anthony. "Was he able to give any description at all?"

"Very nondescript. Apart from saying that he was above average height and his clothes were ordinary, the kind worn by much of the general population... including off-duty servants. His jacket was brown corduroy and he had sandy-colored hair."

The viscount swore under his breath. "That doesn't give us much to go on. It describes about half the male population of London."

"Perhaps not," the Earl of Sherbonne observed from the deep, comfortable chair in which he was sprawled. "But we know some things that can help us. As most of the incidents have occurred here at the Abbey, we should focus on the people here who might also have been in London when you were there. Are there any who fit that general description and who might have a reason to hurt you?"

"I am sure there are quite a few tall men with light brown hair on the estate and we cannot question each one without cause. It would simply increase the uneasy atmosphere that has prevailed lately." Anthony shrugged. "As for who might have a grudge against me, I have no idea. I treat all people with respect and have never given anyone cause to want to harm me."

Sherbonne rose from his usual reclining position. "I do think we're on the wrong tack here. I'm not saying that you have not suffered loss with the fires and floods on the estate, but the real target appears to be Clarissa. You weren't even here when she had the accident."

Tony huffed. "No need to remind me of that. I almost lost her."

Loxley leaned forward. "What do you know about her background? Is there someone from her past who bears her a grudge?"

Sherbonne was once again sprawled on the couch. "Someone has gone to a lot of trouble to try to discredit and harm Clarissa. How many jealous lovers did you leave broken in your wake when you married her?"

The other men all stared at Lawrence for a moment and then turned to Anthony. The viscount shrugged but Loxley gave a little nod. "It doesn't take dozens, only one very jealous lover, but she would have had to have assistance. We know that it was man who fired the gun at the park."

Theo placed his empty glass on a table. "What about that Hemsby fellow? Didn't Clarissa spurn him to marry you?"

Tony's eyebrow shot right up at this. "Hemsby? That fool. I can't believe he would lower himself to dress in servant's clothes or dirty his hands by rigging fishing line across the road on my estate. Besides, he doesn't quite fit the description of a tall man with sandy hair. His is ginger and he is rather short and podgy."

Sherbonne shook his head and poured himself some more brandy. "No, I don't think it is one of her paramours. The actions have all the marks of a lover scorned. I think it is one of Tony's lovers, and someone who had access to the house here."

Lord Anthony swished the brandy in his glass. "You all know that I have been interested in no one except Clarissa for a very long time. I haven't broken any hearts or shattered anyone's hopes. At least not recently."

The duke rose and began to pace the room. "You say that Clarissa never received your letters to her, and that none of the ones sent from the Abbey reached you in London? And there were some odd letters supposedly sent to Mrs. Riggs before the wedding? I suppose you asked Riggs to give them to you?"

Thankful to be doing something practical, Anthony rose quickly and began riffling through the piles of papers that covered his desk. He produced a bundle of three or four tied together with a piece of string. "Here they are. This is not Clarissa's writing, although someone has tried very hard to imitate it. See, the curls under the a's are not like the ones she makes."

The duke took the letters and began reading. "The tone is rather supercilious, giving the impression that Clarissa is arrogant and selfish. And there are a few grammatical errors that someone of Clarissa's education would not make." He turned the letters over. "They have, however, been sent from London."

Theo glanced over his cousin's shoulder at the letters. "Who handles the mail for you?"

Anthony shrugged. "I have no idea. I guess Fotheringham would be in charge, but I suppose one of the footmen actually takes the letters to the post office."

"Let's ask him, then," suggested Sherbonne. Anthony rang the bell to summon his butler and Sherbonne observed languidly, "This kind of hassle is why it's far better to stay single. Getting married has far too many complications, especially if you are foolish enough to fall in love with your wife."

The viscount glared at him, and Theo slapped the earl on his shoulder. "Love is going to hit you hard one of these days, my friend, and then we will all sit back and be vastly amused to watch you running circles around the woman who knocks you off your feet."

The low laughter that greeted this eased the tension in the room. Anthony sat down again. He twirled his brandy glass in his fingers and picked up an earlier thread of the conversation. "I am finding it difficult to imagine that someone feels aggrieved enough by my marriage to Clarissa to want to harm her."

The duke sat up straight, his shoulders back and his face thoughtful. "Congreve was right when he declared that hell has no fury like a woman scorned. I can think of one woman in particular who has been infatuated with you for quite a while, or at least obsessed with your rank, your title, your wealth and perhaps your good looks. I believe she thought you belonged to her, and her position as your wife was settled. She has also had the means and opportunities to carry out these attacks."

Anthony frowned. "You mean Lucretia." He shook his head slowly. "For God's sake, she's my stepmother, and even if she weren't, I have never really liked her, certainly never given her any reason to believe I would marry her." He paused and studied a portrait of his mother that hung behind his desk and which had been one of his earliest works. "Lucretia looks a little like my mother and Papa was so lonely after Mama died that he was desperate to find someone to offer him comfort." He emptied his brandy glass in one gulp. "I believe he regretted his haste in marrying Lucretia. Besides," he returned to more practical considerations, "the handwriting in the letters isn't hers."

The duke was confident that his theory was right. He spoke with conviction. "My intuition tells me that Lucretia is involved. From her very first season, she was on the hunt for a rich husband of rank, and she used her beauty as a lure. She might have married your father, but she has always had her eyes set on you. She doesn't want to lose her position as a countess, and there aren't that many eligible earls and viscounts in society, at least not ones handsome enough to suit her vanity."

"That's all very well," countered Anthony, "but it is a long way from overt flirting to attempted murder." The viscount stood up and paced between his desk and the window. "And even if it is true, she could not have managed without an accomplice, and I would very much like to know who that is. And what is to be done to stop them from causing further harm."

CHAPTER 21

*T*he bookroom was silent as Lord Anthony continued to pace up and down while he waited for Fotheringham. He was sickened by the thought that someone close to him, that Lucretia, who had been raised into the aristocracy on her marriage to his father, could stoop to such sordid acts of jealousy that could destroy all the good work his father had done to improve the lives of the tenants and farmers on his estates. Worse than that, her actions had endangered Clarissa and led to the death of his unborn child.

He was just beginning his third circuit of the room when the butler arrived. The viscount wasted no time in getting to the point. "Fotheringham, have you made any progress in discovering who has been upsetting the servants?"

The butler crooked an eyebrow but was otherwise his usual impassive self. "I have been gathering information, my lord, and what I have discovered is very concerning. I wanted to be certain of my facts before making any accusations, but it seems more and more likely that my conjectures regarding the culprit are correct."

"Yes, yes," Lord Anthony tutted impatiently. "But sharing

what you do know could help us draw the right conclusions. Do you remember which footman it was who took the note I sent to Clarissa the day of the Bascombes' dinner?"

The other gentlemen looked at each other, puzzled by the apparent red herring the viscount was casting, but a gleam of comprehension brightened the butler's eyes. "Perhaps, my lord, it would be best if we brought Hubert in and asked him a few questions."

"Very well, go and call him. Oh, and Fotheringham, I think you should have someone else standing near in case we need some assistance to encourage Hubert to answer our questions— someone you trust implicitly."

"Yes, my lord." The butler left with a quick bow.

Anthony turned to his friends. They were all looking at him with keen interest, even Sherbonne was sitting upright on the sofa now. Lord Anthony gave a dry laugh. "I think we might have identified the accomplice. The trick now is to get him to him to confess and then decide what to do about Lucretia."

Five minutes later, Hubert strode into the library, a smirk on his face and a haughtiness in his gait that suggested he had nothing to fear. Lord Anthony, who was now seated behind his large mahogany desk, raked his eyes over the footman, taking in his height, which was over six foot, and the sandy color of his hair. He was a good-looking man, with broad shoulders and a handsome face. The dark green livery of the Donnington house-hold suited him well. He had the air of someone who knew how to use his looks to his best advantage. Lord Anthony wondered how many of the housemaids had fallen in love with this foot-man. And how many ladies he had seduced with his charm.

"Well, Fotheringham," the viscount began, "is this the footman who handles the mail?"

"Yes, I—" Hubert attempted to speak but was silenced by a quelling looking from the butler.

"My lord, it is one of Hubert's duties to check the letters that arrive and distribute them to the right recipients. He also takes the letters written in the house down to the post office. Any notes delivered to the house are also his responsibility." The butler's usually bland voice held a note of derision. "It is a position of trust, and one not to be taken lightly."

The viscount stared impassively at the footman. "Indeed. How long have you worked for me?"

Hubert tilted his head at a cocky angle. "Just over two years, milord, and four years before that I was at your father's beck and call."

Lord Anthony raised an eyebrow at the open insolence, but he continued asking questions blandly. "And this has been a good position for you?"

A flash of uncertainty crossed the footman's face, but he still sounded sure of himself. "It's been all right, milord."

The viscount nodded. "And you accompany me to London when I open up Donnington House?" His voice was almost conversational now, but an iron inflexibility underscored his words. Hubert shuffled again. "For instance, you were in the London House when I was preparing for my marriage?"

"I was, milord."

"Tell me, Hubert, are you any good with a gun?"

The footman blinked a few times and swallowed at the unexpectedness of the question. "Uhm, why, I s'pose so, milord." A heavy silence filled the library. After a few moments, Hubert's shoulders sagged.

The viscount nodded. "What explanation can you offer for abusing the trust that was placed in you?" His voice was hard and sharp as steel.

The footman flinched, but he quickly recovered his insolent stance. "I'm not sure what you mean. milord."

"Do you recall receiving a note from me addressed to the countess on the day of the Bascombes' dinner party?"

Hubert swallowed and his eyes flickered towards the left.

"No, milord. There are so many messages and notes to deliver. I can't quite recall each specific one."

Lord Anthony's eyes were hard and piercing. He observed the footman in silence for a few moments, considering how to break through his superciliousness.

His thoughts were interrupted by an agitated knocking on the door. Fotheringham quickly crossed the room and opened it. He frowned at the little gathering that crowded the doorway. Mrs. Riggs was grasping the arm of a sobbing kitchen maid, and Lady Clarissa's hand was raised, ready to knock again. Hovering behind them, were both Amelia and Charlotte.

Clarissa gasped out, "We need to see the viscount. Jane has some information to share."

"This is unprecedented." The butler was trying to retain some of the dignity of the household. "Kitchen maids are under the purview of the cook, and their problems should not be brought to the attention of the viscount."

Amelia stepped forward impatiently. "I think the viscount will want to hear what Jane has to say."

The butler glanced back into the room. He was startled to see that Hubert had paled and the arrogant tilt of his head had been replaced by a nervous twitch to his mouth. The butler stepped aside and let the ladies enter. Mrs. Riggs almost dragged the sobbing young kitchen maid into the room.

The housekeeper stopped some distance from where Hubert was standing. The girl's sobs had quietened and now the only sound in the room was her sniffling as she tried to bring her emotions under control.

Lord Anthony addressed the housekeeper, "What has Jane done?"

Mrs. Riggs glanced at Fotheringham before answering the viscount. "My lord, this afternoon we undertook a search of the servants' rooms to see if we could discover who has been pilfering from the others." She glared at Jane. "We found the missing items in Jane's drawer."

The girl resumed her loud sobbing. Fotheringham shrugged impatiently. "Mrs. Riggs, that's all very well, but surely you can handle such a matter. The girl should be sent away without disturbing the viscount about it."

Mrs. Riggs gave Fotheringham a withering look. "That was not all we found." She glanced at Hubert and then produced a little trinket from her pocket. "Lady Clarissa says that this brooch was in her reticule when she was robbed outside the Pantheon Bazaar."

Lord Anthony took the brooch and turned it over thoughtfully. He looked up as the housekeeper continued. "We also discovered this in Hubert's room. It is a ring that belongs to Lady Lucretia."

Hubert was glaring at Jane now, but he had paled and was looking uncertain for the first time since he had been hauled into the library. The duke sat forward, saying, "What is the connection between the two, Mrs. Riggs? Do get to the point."

The housekeeper gave the girl a slight shake. "You need to tell the viscount what you told me. And do try to do so without sniveling so that his lordship can hear you clearly."

Jane was rubbing her sleeve across her face, attempting to get rid of the tears that still poured down her cheeks. "H-he told m-me to hide th-them. I never t-took nothing. I'm a good girl, I am," she protested.

"Who gave them to you?" the viscount's voice was hard and cold.

Jane glanced at Hubert through half-opened eyelids. "Him. Hubert."

Hubert growled. "Don't lie! Why would I give such things to you?" His voice dripped with contempt.

Jane was stung to retort, "You know it's true. And the other things, too. You made me spoil cook's food. You said you loved me and if I helped you, we could get rich enough to set up our own place." A strangled sob ripped at her throat. "You said we would marry."

Hubert snorted sneeringly. "Me, marry the likes of you! I wouldn't want a sniveling little ninny like you. I have a real lady who fancies me!" He turned scornful eyes to Mrs. Riggs. "That there ring you found was given to me. I never took it. You can ask Lucretia herself."

Fotheringham's face was the picture of horror at this outburst. "Watch yourself!" he warned.

"We will be discussing this with *Lady* Lucretia," the viscount assured him, placing emphasis on the word lady. "However, I am, for the moment, more interested in the part you have played in all the troubles that have occurred here and in London."

Hubert straightened his shoulders. "Lady Lucretia has been in love with me for a very long time. We've been carrying on together since even before the last viscount's death." He ignored the shocked gasps from the assembled listeners and proceeded with his boasting. "We needed money so that we could be together. The plan was for her to marry the viscount so we could have access to his accounts and set up another house for us. I would be a gentleman of leisure, same as all of you."

Gales of laughter greeted this announcement. Lord Anthony glanced at his friends. The Earl of Sherbonne was chortling loudly as he sprawled back in his chair. Loxley and the marquess were snorting with laughter. Even the duke was grinning broadly. He shook his head.

It was the earl who pointed out to Hubert what was obvious to all of them. "Lucretia is much too vain and conscious of her position in society to live openly with a footman. She has used you to do her dirty work and would have sent you packing as soon as she had what she wanted."

Hubert was red with pent up fury. "Ask her! She'll tell you she loves me," he spat out.

Lord Anthony stared at the footman. "As I said, we will be talking to Lady Lucretia, but right now I want you to tell us exactly what you have done. Did you shoot at us in Richmond Park?"

"I did, gave you all a good enough fright, that did. And I shot at you when you arrived back here. Lady Lucretia said that if we frightened off the new bride, she would leave and our plan could be back on track."

The viscount shook his head. "If you cannot see how preposterous that plan was, then you are a bigger fool than you look."

"I'm not the one who's a fool. I had you running all over the place, trying to sort out the fires I set on farms and the rivers I dammed up." He sneered at Jane. "It didn't take much to persuade others to help me. A little canoodling and empty promises, and Jane was willing enough to do whatever I asked."

Fotheringham decided that the footman had said enough. "You are clearly unrepentant of all these misdemeanors, even though some of them endangered people's lives." He looked at the viscount, who had crossed to where Clarissa was sitting and had her hand in his. "My lord, I believe that it would be best to keep Hubert under lock and key until I can bring him before the magistrate. He has said enough to indict himself. We do not need to be subject to this nonsense any longer."

"I agree. Take him away and the girl with him. I will write a full account for Sir William this afternoon and ask him to place Hubert under arrest."

The butler placed his hand on Hubert's shoulder and turned to march him out of the library, expecting the housekeeper to follow with Jane.

Clarissa raised pleading eyes to her husband. A great sense of relief had washed over her as she had watched the proceedings, but now she was concerned about the young kitchen maid. "Anthony, can't we show some leniency towards Jane? The girl was fooled by the promises made to her. She is so young and was led astray."

Mrs. Riggs quirked her mouth but said nothing. The young kitchen maid raised her head and looked at Clarissa as if she were an angel come to rescue her.

After a few moments of silence, Lord Donnington answered his wife. "Perhaps she does need a second chance." He turned to the housekeeper. "Mrs. Riggs, I leave her in your hands. Punish her as you see fit, but she must promise to work hard and never to allow herself to get caught up in this kind of behavior again."

"Oh, thank you, milord, milady. I will work ever so hard. Thank you."

The servants left the room, and Lord Anthony sank down onto a chair. "Now to tackle Lucretia."

EPILOGUE

*C*larissa sat at her dressing table, rubbing cream onto her hands. In the mirror she could see the reflection of the room behind her, and she smiled. It was so much more to her liking now that the ostentatious furniture had been replaced with items that she had chosen. The walls were a soft blue, a comfortable cream brocade sofa was nestled in a nook and deeper blue curtains hung at the window. A small porcelain figurine of a lady in a blue dress was displayed on top of her chest of drawers and a small china cupid sat coyly on her dressing table.

Through the open bedroom door, Clarissa could see her bed, inviting, with its soft blue covers and heaps of white fluffy pillows. But she had no desire to climb into its soft comfort. She was not tired, even though it was near midnight.

Almost two months had passed since the accident. There was no longer any hint of her injuries. All her bruises had faded weeks ago and the scratch on her face had healed so well that even she had to peer hard in the mirror to see the faint white scar that remained. There was an underlying sorrow that would always be part of her about the baby that had been lost, but she was only occasionally gripped with anguish and despair. She found herself able to smile and laugh much as she had before the accident. Daily life had resumed its pleasant rhythms and calm pace.

The days after Hubert's confession had been tumultuous, with the magistrate coming frequently to take down accounts of what had happened and the servants packing up Lucretia's belongings while she had alternatively flung herself onto chairs as she wept hysterically or screamed and flung things about in fits of rage.

Not wanting his private affairs to become fodder for public gossip, the viscount had dealt with Lucretia in the seclusion of his own home. It had, however, taken threats of public exposure and imprisonment before Lucretia had accepted the consequences that the viscount had imposed on her. Although she had been given rights to a house in Bath in her husband's will, Anthony had revoked that privilege. She was now incarcerated in a hunting box some miles from Coventry, with only two servants and little access to society. The viscount had threatened to expose her crimes if she did not remain there. Hubert had been convicted and was awaiting transportation to the colony of Australia.

The horrors of those first few weeks of marriage had faded to a distant memory. But Clarissa was not quite as happy as she should be. She replaced the lid on the jar of hand cream and looked at herself in the mirror. Soft candlelight gave a warm glow to her skin and her hair shone from the brushing Rose had given it. She frowned.

Lord Anthony had been solicitous and attentive, declaring his love for her in many different ways every day. He wrote her little notes which she found tucked into pockets of her coats or slipped under her plate on her breakfast tray. He read to her from her favorite books and sat beside her in the evenings, sharing tidbits about his daily activities on the estate. He brought her roses from the garden, but always pink or white ones. Never the red rose of passion like those he had strewn on her bed on the night she had become his wife.

Her eyes wandered to a painting that hung above the fireplace. The viscount had spent many hours with his sketchbook and paints. The portrait he had done of her in London was now in his dressing room, and here, in hers, was one he had completed only a week ago. It showed her reclining on her convalescent couch, the soft light from a window nearby making her seem even more pale and fragile than she remembered being. It was exquisitely executed, but Clarissa almost regretted having it in her room. She did not like the reminder of how vulnerable she had been.

She shook her head as she removed her earrings and placed them in a drawer. Lord Anthony lived with that image of her, frail, listless and sad, in his mind. He did not realize that she had regained her strength, that she was no longer an invalid. She was ready to be a wife in the full sense of the word. His light good-night kisses no longer satisfied her. She wanted more. Her desire for him had increased as she had recovered, but she did not know how to let him know that she wanted him to come to her bed, that she was ready for him.

She got up from the dressing table, fastening the ties of her dressing gown, and approached the closed door that separated her rooms from his. Perhaps, if he did not come to her, she should go to him. She stood before the door, her heart beating so hard that it felt as if it would pound right out of her chest. She folded her hand into a fist but did not knock.

Wives were not supposed to approach their husbands. Good women didn't give in to the kind of passion that raged through their bodies, or if they did, they didn't yield to it. Would the viscount think that she was forward, wanton, if she acted on her desires?

Her momentary qualm faded as she remembered all he had

taught her about embracing pleasure. She took a deep breath and opened the door. The room was empty. Lord Anthony's valet had laid out his night clothes, and candles burned brightly in sconces on the wall, but her husband was not there. Disappointment swamped her.

~

LORD ANTHONY'S brisk pace slowed as he passed Clarissa's door. His cock twinged at the thought of her lying in her bed. He almost opened the door, responding to the urging of his body, but he reprimanded himself and walked on. On many nights, he had woken up, drenched in sweat and his cock hard as iron, but he could not want to risk harming Clarissa with the wildness of his passion.

He opened the door of his bedroom and stopped. Clarissa was standing in the doorway between his room and hers. The light filtering in from her bedroom made her nightgown almost transparent. He groaned as he studied the beautiful lines of her firm young body. Her hair hung loose over her shoulders, gleaming like a halo.

She smiled at him and then her smile faltered when he did not move. She bit her lip and her shoulders sagged. She half-turned as if to go. "I-I'm sorry. I didn't mean to disturb you."

Anthony strode across the room just in time to stop her from closing the door behind herself. He placed his hand on her shoulder. "What is it, my little one? Are you not feeling well?"

Clarissa huffed out a low laugh that sent shivers of expectation to his cock. He tried to ignore it.

She shook her head. "I am feeling very well. Life at the Abbey is so pleasant and I have never been fitter. Just today, I walked five miles to the village to take a basket to old Mrs. Meech."

Her voice was tight and her back stiff. Anthony stroked her

shoulder with his thumb. "Then what is it? Did you need to see me?"

Clarissa dropped her head, but not before Anthony caught a glimpse of tears glittering in the depths of her blue eyes. She shook her head and tried to pull away from him, but he tightened his grasp on her shoulder.

"Perhaps we should talk. But maybe it would be better to discuss what is worrying you in the morning after you have had a good night's sleep."

She bit her lip again. "I am not tired and I do not want to sleep." Anthony had never heard her speak so petulantly. He studied her face for a few moments and then led her to a low, comfortable chair that stood in front of the fireplace.

Once there, he sat down and pulled her onto his lap. She sat stiffly, not at all the comfortable armful of woman he had become used to before the accident. He tugged her closer to his chest and ran the knuckles of his left hand over her cheeks.

She dropped her head onto his shoulder and snuggled closer. "That's better," he soothed. "Now, my little flower, what's troubling you?"

"Am I?" she asked cryptically.

"Are you what, my precious love?"

"Your flower?" she mumbled into his shirt.

"Of course, you are." There was no hesitation in his voice and Clarissa looked up into his eyes. Satisfied with what she saw there, she nodded.

"Why do you ask?" he prompted.

"It's just th-that you no longer seem to want me, a-as your little rose." Blushes of confusion turned her face a deep pink and she stumbled over the words.

He groaned as his hands caressed her, kneading the soft flesh of her breasts. He ground his steel-hard cock into her bum. "Does that feel as if I don't desire you?"

Her blush deepened and she shook her head. He chuckled. "It

seems as if you have forgotten how to speak." Then his voice became more somber. "But why do you think you are no longer special to me?"

Clarissa swallowed and then the words tumbled out. "You no longer come to my bed at night and when you kiss me," she hesitated, searching for the words, "it is almost chaste."

His hands tightened on her. "My little rose, I have not wanted to overwhelm you. You have suffered so much and I do not want to subject you to anything that would cause you further harm."

Clarissa scoffed. "I think it is more harmful when you do not treat me as your wife."

He tweaked her nipple and she uttered a little cry. "If you are sure, then I am more than ready to play with you." And without further ado, he began to show her just how much he loved her.

THE RUSSET and gold of autumn had passed into the grim greyness of November, but the fire burning merrily in the large stone fireplace of Lord Sherbonne's library gave the room a cheerful glow. Clarissa looked around the comfortable room and smiled at Charlotte, who was kneeling on a cushion beside her husband, Lord Theo. Adam Loxley was comfortably ensconced in a deep leather armchair and the earl himself was sprawled on the long couch near the fire.

Clarissa was seated on her husband's lap and his right hand played absently with her breasts as he sipped his brandy, occasionally offering her a taste of the deep amber liquid.

The door of the library opened and the dowager countess, Lady Sherbonne, entered. Her sharp eyes scanned the room and softened when they rested on Charlotte. "How are you, my dear? Quite comfortable?"

"I am, thank you, Lady Lydia," she almost purred as Theo placed his hand possessively on the swell of her abdomen.

"If you need anything, do let me know." She cast a withering glance in the direction of the earl. "After all, it seems unlikely that my son will oblige me with grandchildren to spoil, so I will have to pamper your children instead."

Sherbonne raised his glass in a mock salute. "An excellent plan, Mama. If you have other children to fuss over, you can stop harassing me about getting married." He emptied his glass in one swallow.

Lady Lydia scowled as the others laughed. Then she added, "One day you will finally remember that you need a wife, and I hope it is not too late for you to find love. In the meantime, I just wanted to remind you that the carriage will be ready at nine-thirty tomorrow morning."

Sherbonne groaned and slumped deeper into his chair. "I can think of far better ways to spend my Sunday morning than listening to one of Mr. Calverley's grim sermons. Sometimes the duties of an earl far outweigh the pleasures of my life."

Lady Lydia tutted, and with a pat to Charlotte's head, she swept out of the room.

Charlotte sighed contentedly and leaned against her husband's thigh, but Clarissa, still on Anthony's lap, stiffened.

The viscount pulled her closer to him. He noticed the direction of her eyes and as Adam began talking about the possibility of some shooting the next day, Lord Donnington murmured to Clarissa, "My precious rose, what is it?"

Clarissa pressed into the solid comfort of her husband's arms. "I wonder if I will ever have a child."

Anthony smiled. He slid his hand under the edge of her dress and squeezed her breast. She squealed and glared at him. He chuckled. "Have you noticed, little flower, that your breasts have been rather tender the last week or so?"

Clarissa bit her lip and nodded. When a low rumble sounded in his throat, she said, "Yes, yes, I have. When you touch me, like that, even a slight squeeze hurts."

"I've also noticed that your body heat is higher, and that some foods make you feel slightly nauseous."

Clarissa stared up at him, her eyes wide with dawning comprehension. "You think I might be expecting again?"

Anthony looked as smug as a cat who had just eaten a whole bowl of cream. "I do. I can't wait to see you swollen with my child. You will be the paragon of mothers, just as you are the perfect wife."

WATCH out for the next book in the series: *A Companion for the Earl,* coming soon!

KATHY LEIGH

Kathy Leigh has loved books and writing since she could first follow the stories in her bedtime tales. She began writing stories in old school notebooks when she was eight years old but only recently thought that others might want to read her stories, too.

A romantic at heart, she is inspired by thunderstorms, sunflowers, and the belief that every princess deserves to find her prince. Recently she moved to a small village in France where long walks in the meadows and woods are wonderful inspiration for her writing.

She loves curling up on her couch with a good book, a glass of wine and her cats for company. As a young girl she particularly enjoyed the novels by Georgette Heyer and Jane Austen, and sighed over Mr. Rochester in *Jane Eyre*. She now enjoys historical and contemporary romance with an edge. She also enjoys fantasy, especially if it has a touch of romance.

Visit her website here:
https://kathyleighauthor.wordpress.com

Don't miss these exciting titles by Kathy Leigh and Blushing Books!

Lords of Voluptas Series
A Wife for the Duke
An Heiress for the Marquess
A Paragon for the Viscount

BLUSHING BOOKS

Blushing Books is the oldest eBook publisher on the web. We've been running websites that publish steamy romance and erotica since 1999, and we have been selling eBooks since 2003. We have free and promotional offerings that change weekly, so please do visit us at http://www.blushingbooks.com/free.

Made in the USA
Las Vegas, NV
28 August 2021